"**I loved *Queer as a Five Dollar Bill*!** The twists and turns of Wyatt's experiences, both of pondering his own sexuality and of attempting to bring questions about Lincoln's experiences to light, make this an exciting story. . . .**Will keep any reader turning the pages. Highly recommended!**"

—Elisabeth Abarbanel, school librarian for grades 7-12

"This novel shines with quirky brilliance! As a fan of YA fiction I found Wind's ability to intertwine historical facts through a relatable story of a teenager trying to make his way refreshing and addictive. ***Queer as a Five-Dollar Bill* is engaging, heartfelt, and superb. You won't want to put it down.**"

—Cindy Maloney

"*Queer as a Five-Dollar Bill* **is the perfect way for our LGBTQ youth to know about their history.** We hope they all enjoy this novel as much as we did!"

—Kayla & Jessica Weissbuch, Co-Founders of Camp Brave Trails

"Lincoln, gay? I'm 94-years old and it had never occurred to me. But as I read along with Wyatt, I had a flash of instant recognition of the truth . . . Lincoln's unhappy marriage, unhappy wife, his constraint. **Hopefully young people who struggle with their own truth will no longer need to struggle. The truth is the truth, and Lee's book will help them find it.**"

—Godeane Eagle

"**Jack calls Abraham Lincoln a power gay on #WillAndGrace, but I think @leewind did it first.** Check out Wind's blog & #QueerAsAFiveDollarBill."

—Rhonda, on Twitter

"**Ok, I am seriously hooked here! Love the writing: characters, immediacy, high school life for anyone who's different. Plot is emotionally gripping** without being overdone. I know there is debate (actual evidence-based debate, as opposed to dismissive prejudice) about whether or not Lincoln was gay, and I love how the author unfolds the evidence just the way any smart high school student who is passionate about his thesis would."

—Coryl, on I'm Here. I'm Queer. What The Hell Do I Read?

"**The world will never be the same ❤**"

—Rita, on Facebook

Queer as a Five-Dollar Bill

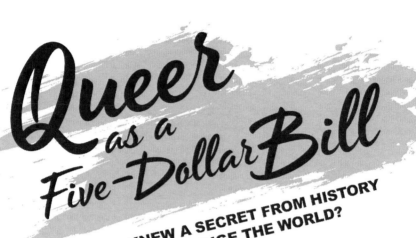

Queer as a Five-Dollar Bill

WHAT IF YOU KNEW A SECRET FROM HISTORY
THAT COULD CHANGE THE WORLD?

LEE WIND

Publisher's Cataloging-in-Publication Data

Names: Wind, Lee, author.
Title: Queer as a five-dollar bill / Lee Wind.
Description: Los Angeles : I'm Here, I'm Queer, What The Hell Do I Read?, 2018. | Summary: Wyatt, a bullied and closeted teen, triggers a backlash when he reveals evidence Abraham Lincoln was gay.
Identifiers: LCCN 2018905030 | ISBN 978-1-7322281-0-8 (hardcover) | ISBN 978-1-7322281-1-5 (pbk.) | ISBN 978-1-7322281-2-2 (ebook)
Subjects: LCSH: Gay teenagers--Juvenile fiction. | CYAC: Gay teenagers--Fiction. | Coming out (Sexual orientation)--Fiction. | Bullying--Fiction. | Lincoln, Abraham, 1809-1865--Fiction. | Young adult fiction. | BISAC: YOUNG ADULT FICTION / LGBT. | YOUNG ADULT FICTION / Coming of Age. | YOUNG ADULT FICTION / Boys & Men. | GSAFD: Bildungsromans.
Classification: LCC PZ7.1.W5837 Qu 2018 (print) | LCC PZ7.1.W5837 (ebook) | DDC [Fic]--dc23.

Book design by Laurie L. Young. Cover design by Watch This!
Images used under license from Shutterstock.com: Pages 127, 133-134, 147, 173, 178, 180, 195, 224, 347-348, Thomas Pajot/Shutterstock.com. Page 218, PannaKotta/Shutterstock.com. Page 219, Travel_maker/Shutterstock.com

Printed in the United States of America.
2 4 6 8 10 9 7 5 3 1

Published by I'm Here. I'm Queer. What The Hell Do I Read?
Los Angeles, CA

For my husband, Mark, whose love gives me wings;

for our daughter, who fills our days with joy and gratitude;

and for you, reader.

This book is for us all.

Chapter 1
Monday, January 5

IT'S FUNNY THAT they called the Civil War *civil*, because there's not much polite about trying to kill the people you don't like. Following that same logic, Wyatt figured he should call Lincolnville High School *Civil* High—because ninth grade was a war, too. Every day.

But he wasn't due back in battle for a few hours—it was still a reassuring black outside. And he told himself, for the millionth time, that he wasn't going to give Jonathon the power to ruin stuff outside school, when he wasn't even around. It didn't really work.

A thin stream of cold coffee pooled onto his sock, and Wyatt jerked the sodden paper back over the plastic bin. He swore under his breath, working the wet sock off with one hand and tossing it onto the needs-to-get-washed pile by his desk.

He studied the dripping paper. It was ready. He grabbed the red long-reach lighter from the living room fireplace to singe an edge of this sixteenth Emancipation Proclamation. The wet paper took a few seconds to catch. Once it was on fire, he quick-snuffed it out in the coffee so it didn't burn too far.

Two more sides had gotten crisped when the pocket of the thrift-store, fake-leather motorcycle jacket he was wearing vibrated. Wyatt fumbled for the phone. Having a new cell (even his mom's four-year-old hand-me-down) so he could get a call without waking up the whole bed-and-breakfast rocked.

"Hey, handsome. Good morning!" *Mackenzie.*

Plugging in the headphone jack, he fit the plastic bud in his ear. "I'm so glad it's you." As soon as the words were out of his mouth, he realized how ridiculous he sounded—they both knew no one else would be calling him. He pushed the thought away as he burned the final edge. "Can you get online? I uploaded the new video last night."

"Just two more emails to delete," Mackenzie said. "How's it going?"

"Sucks. I'm not even going to get my run in because of this stupid antiquing." The last bit of flame sizzled out in the coffee, and Wyatt swapped the wet sheet for the dry one in the microwave on his bedroom floor. Forty-eight seconds. Start. The laser-printed, coffee-aged, fire-singed paper rotated on the plate inside. Predictably, the cracked-glass ceiling light dimmed as the microwave hogged the power on that circuit. It would dim in the third-floor bathroom, too, but Wyatt hadn't heard any guests up yet. Just his dad, in the attic above the part of Wyatt's room that wasn't the tower. He'd gotten Wyatt up at 4:30 a.m. to do this stupid antiquing job while he headed up to reseal the dormers for the storm on its way.

Even with the people-height windows open, the smell of burned paper and coffee hung in the cold air between all the furniture that didn't match their B&B's 1830s–1860s thing. The good news was that Wyatt's 2000s black wood bed, no-style pressboard wardrobe, and 1940s gunmetal navy-surplus desk were such a period mash-up that his dad wouldn't let any guests see it, so Wyatt didn't need to keep it neat.

But even when the windows were closed, guests used to complain that sleeping in the Tower Room was like sleeping outside. New windows cost too much, so Wyatt got one of the nicest rooms in their

Queen Anne Victorian. He just had to wear a lot of layers, camping-style. He liked camping.

He pulled on a dry sock, reasoning that all white sweat socks matched—even if one was cleaner than the other—and headed over to the clunky laptop that wouldn't work unless it was plugged in. He'd already cued up the video, waiting for her call. Mackenzie was clicking at the keys of the pretty-much-new laptop that she took notes on in class. He pictured her sitting at the kitchen counter in her dad's condo, Monday-morning oatmeal in a bowl beside her.

The dingy white microwave beeped, but Wyatt ignored it and the lights surging back to full strength. There was plenty of time to finish them before school—Mackenzie had finally called, and he was bursting to share.

"Okay," Mackenzie said. "I'm there."

Wyatt gave her the countdown so they could watch it simultaneously. "Three, two, one . . . play!"

**_Crazy History_, Episode 3:
"_Do Svidaniya_, Lincoln!"**

Wyatt has tousled hair and wears jeans and a green waffle-knit shirt. He waves as he talks to the camera.

WYATT
Hey, everyone. Wyatt here at the Lincoln Slept Here B&B with another episode of _Crazy History!_ Check out a five-dollar bill.

The face of the bill fills the screen.

|◀ ▶ ▶|

WYATT
See that eagle with the ribbon in its beak
there? That's the seal of the United States. The
ribbon says *E Pluribus Unum,* which is Latin or
something for *out of many, one.* And next to
that eagle is President Abraham Lincoln.

The bill moves away, and Wyatt stuffs it in his back
pocket. He's standing in a converted sitting room that
now exhibits Civil War artifacts.

WYATT
After George Washington, Abe's like the most
famous president we've ever had, right? So
what would you say if you found out that at
one point he thought about moving to *Russia?*

His eyes glint, all *this is a good one.*

WYATT
Check out what he wrote in a letter five years
before he became president:

Wyatt flips open a leather-bound book to a marked
passage.

WYATT
**"As a nation, we began by declaring that *all men
are created equal.* We now practically read it
all men are created equal, except Negroes.
When the Know-Nothings get control . . ."**

◀ ▶ ▶|

He glances up to explain.

> WYATT
> The Know-Nothings were a political party
> back then—and yeah, they actually called
> themselves that!

With a shake of his head at how wackadoodle that was,
he resumes reading.

> WYATT
> **"When the Know-Nothings get control, it will
> read, *all men are created equal, except
> Negroes and foreigners and Catholics.* When
> it comes to this, I shall prefer emigrating to
> some country where they make no pretense
> of loving liberty—to Russia, for instance . . ."**

Wyatt stops there, shutting the book with an amazed look.

> WYATT
> Imagine if Abe hadn't become president and
> instead moved to Russia! *Do svidaniya,
> Lincoln!*—That's Russian for "see you later."

Wyatt grabs the tripod and keeps talking. The image is
jerky as he shoots himself walking through the displays,
past a Fort Sumter cannonball on a pedestal, and
toward a green velvet curtain.

WYATT

If Abe had gone to Russia, what would America look like today? What would Russia look like? How about the cover of the *Sports Illustrated Swimsuit Issue?*

He starts to blush, but we cut to a photo of a bikini-clad model with huge breasts, standing on a glacier, with penguins behind her. She doesn't seem cold. We hear him say,

WYATT (voice-over)

Okay, *that* probably wouldn't change.

We cut back to Wyatt—not blushing anymore—as he rounds the curtain to reveal a life-size Abraham Lincoln wax figure, complete with a seven-inch-tall black stovepipe hat. Wax Lincoln's right arm reaches out, like he's about to shake your hand. Wyatt stands next to him.

WYATT

Crazy to think how much this one guy did. Became president. Freed the slaves. And saved the Union. Keeping us *out of many, one.*

Wyatt puts his hand up on Wax Lincoln's shoulder.

WYATT

Glad you stayed in the USA, Abe. More cool— and crazy—history next time. On . . .

The words flash on the screen as Wyatt says them, his voice echoing over action-movie music.

|◀   ▶   ▶|

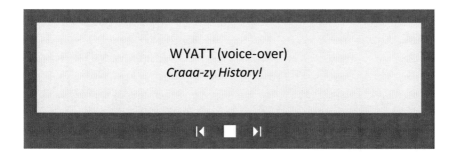

WYATT (voice-over)
Craaa-zy History!

"The swimsuit issue? Really?" Mackenzie sounded pissed, and the theme music hadn't even stopped playing yet.

Wyatt hated that she didn't like it, and almost wished he hadn't put that part in. But Jonathon had been giving him such a hard time all December about being a "history fairy," he had to do *something*. He heard himself get defensive. "You wouldn't understand. *Guys* like that." He hoped he sounded gruff enough.

"I understand that it's objectifying. And insulting. And ridiculous! Don't *guys* know about hypothermia?"

Wyatt knew she was right, but he couldn't say it. It was up for debate which were faker: the model's breasts or the Antarctica she was supposed to be standing in. He'd just wanted Mackenzie to tell him the video was great. Of the probably only ten people who'd see it, she was the only one he wasn't related to.

"I'm sorry," she said, and he figured she knew him well enough to know his silence wasn't happy. "I just . . . think it would be better without the testosterone-caveman moment. I'm not saying you're not allowed to like it, but you don't need to be *that* kind of guy."

Or maybe, Wyatt remembered with a pang, his best friend—okay, his *only* friend—didn't know him at all. He decided to cut his losses. "Let's just go back to the list." Closing his laptop, he returned to the makeshift assembly line laid out on the skinny wood floor planks. He grabbed the seventeenth copy of the Emancipation Proclamation and slid it into the tub of yesterday's cold coffee.

"Fine. . . ." At least she didn't sound quite so annoyed with him anymore. Mackenzie had found this old slang website, and at her insistence they'd been working through it over the past few days. She was hoping to find more of her own "touches" to add to Wyatt's family's tours of their exhibit rooms. Wyatt's tours, if they were after school. Another one of his mom's *your father's working around the clock, and I'm killing myself for the mayor, so the least you can do is pitch in* chores.

"See if you can guess this one." Mackenzie giggled, like she already knew how many clowns were about to come out of the circus car. *"Queer as a three-dollar bill!"*

Wyatt's whole face flushed hot as he lifted the paper and let the coffee pour off, back into the bin. "I don't know!" His voice sounded all pinched, and he told himself to calm down. At school he'd have to worry about Jonathon seeing him turn bright red and shouting something like, *Look! It's the blushing bride!* just to get everyone to laugh at him, but it wasn't like Mackenzie could see him.

And he told himself *Queer* must have meant something else back then.

He blew out a steadying breath, willing the color to seep back inside so he could fade from pomegranate red back to pale Wyatt in January. It was like his skin was some boy litmus test for embarrassment, and he failed every time.

She rolled the words on her tongue—"Queer as a three-dollar bill"—like she was seeing how it would sound on one of their tours. She'd never get *him* to say it. "Give up, studly?"

Studly? That was Mackenzie, trying to build him up. She knew how much he didn't want to go to school today, the first day after winter break. They'd be getting their first-semester History finals back. For two weeks in December, Jonathon had kept threatening that he'd kill him if Wyatt ruined the curve for him and the other guys on the freshman basketball team. Half of them were on the edge of academic disqualification—though how hard was it to know the US presidents in order when they were the street names in your town, all the way through the second Bush? And after all they'd done to make his life miserable, Wyatt was supposed to care? To spite Jonathon, Wyatt had aced the test.

What was he thinking?

They weren't getting their grades until third period, but Wyatt would still have to deal with Jonathon in PE before that. Everyone else thought PE was short for *physical education,* but Jonathon seemed to be working on the theory that it stood for *popular embarrassment,* as in, the more he embarrassed Wyatt, the more popular Jonathon got.

Wyatt grimaced. He was so dead. "Okay, trivia goddess. What's the . . . three-dollar-bill thing mean?"

Mackenzie swallowed some oatmeal. "It says, *older term to describe something extremely unexpected, odd, or rare.*"

Like me in Lincolnville, he thought.

Mackenzie finished, "That's because they never made a three-dollar bill."

Nope, Wyatt mused, as he clicked the lighter to burn the first edge. *Not even here in crazy Oregon.*

"Hmm. Can't see where we can use that one," Mackenzie said, like she was crossing *Queer as a three-dollar bill* off a mental list. "Your dad wants everything to be just what you'd expect if you visited Lincoln by time machine. No surprises. Everything 'authentic.'"

Wyatt knew she was making air quotes, and he knew they were aimed at what he was doing. But people *liked* fake. They'd much rather buy a Gettysburg Address, or an Emancipation Proclamation, or even a President Abraham Lincoln Timeline that *looked* real and old, even if they knew it wasn't, than a boring copy they could just print themselves off the internet.

"Yup." He agreed fast, to change the subject. "What's the next one that grabs you?" Swapping the papers in the microwave, he hit START and ran downstairs to get the envelopes.

"Oh my gosh—*fart-catcher!*" Mackenzie laughed, and this time, Wyatt let himself laugh, too. He whipped around the second-floor landing post and remembered to be quiet on the stairs down to the entryway. His parents' room was right off the kitchen, and he wanted this antiquing chore done before his mom got a chance to lecture him about time management skills—and how he didn't have any.

"Got a guess?" Mackenzie asked. He heard her rinsing her bowl and putting it in their actual dishwasher. Wyatt's dad was all concerned with "anachronisms" and keeping the illusion that they were offering a "real Civil War–era experience." He'd drawn the modern line right after a refrigerator and Wyatt's mom's beloved coffee machine. But if they could do those, along with indoor plumbing and electric fake-gas lights, Wyatt didn't see why they couldn't have a dishwasher. But he wasn't in charge. Clearly.

He took a stab at *fart-catcher* as he headed over to Reception. "What they called those old hoop skirts?"

Mackenzie gave a fake-offended gasp before trying on an even faker Southern accent. "Dear sir, that is *not* the answer. I'll have you know, real ladies do not expel gas in the coarse manner you suggest."

Wyatt laid on the accent himself, feeling his face finally cooling down. "I'm sure they don't, ma'am. . . . But how would anyone know, when you're wearing all them skirts?"

They both snorted a laugh as Wyatt pulled out the clear plastic bin of office supplies, searching for the pale green envelopes.

"*Fart-catcher,*" Mackenzie read. "*A valet or footman, from walking so close behind their mistress or master.*"

"That's ridiculous," Wyatt said. "*And* funny."

"I wonder where we can use it on the tour."

"Not sure," Wyatt mumbled, rifling through the box. Mackenzie would rewrite the whole tour if he let her. She'd probably grow up to tell the president what to say—be the presidential speechwriter. Forget that—she'd probably be president herself.

Not Wyatt. Maybe he'd be a park ranger, or a wildlife photographer, and finally get to spend every day outside. Trees, animals, birds. Rivers like Jenson's Stream. He could do all these videos of wildlife, and maybe add in some cool or crazy history angle . . . Who was he kidding? He knew he'd have to end up in some big city, somewhere far away from all that. But anywhere sounded better than the shark-infested waters of *Civil* High.

Outside, the night was softening to a Union blue. Too soon! Wyatt forced himself to focus: envelopes.

"I'd love to, but I don't see how we can use *fart-catcher,*" Mackenzie said. "Let's move on."

There they were. Wyatt counted out twenty Genuine Reproduction Antiqued Emancipation Proclamation! envelopes and shoved the box back into its spot under the sideboard.

Mackenzie's voice was light. "Okay, I'm covering the definition column, and I'm going to try to guess this one, too: *Can't see a hole in a ladder . . .*"

She started tossing out possibilities. Wyatt stood to head back upstairs when he saw his soldier—smiling out at him from this poster-size Civil War photo, behind their collection of Confederate and Union firearms in the six-foot glass display case.

Wyatt stopped.

His soldier was standing in a group of eleven Civil War soldiers. Everyone else was holding a rifle, bayonet, or sword, but his hands were empty. Some of the guys seemed proud, others excited, a few grim. But *his* soldier just looked sweet. Like he wanted to say, *Hey, Wyatt. Good to see you. Always good to see you.*

What if his soldier came to life and were right in front of him? Standing here? He couldn't just lock eyes with the guy forever. . . .

What could he say back? What *would* he say?

Hey . . . I've been wondering. Wyatt could feel his cheeks heat up again. *What's your name?*

"Wyatt!" Mackenzie's raised voice through the earbud snapped him back to reality. She'd been talking, but he hadn't heard any of it. *"Can't see a hole in a ladder?"*

What was he doing? He needed to focus. He couldn't slip up and maybe say something that would blow up his whole life! Not with Mackenzie. Not here. Not anywhere in Lincolnville, Oregon, population: 5,817 closed minds. Plus one Wyatt Yarrow.

"Sorry, no idea. What's it mean?" He jogged back up the stairs as Mackenzie read that *can't see a hole in a ladder* was what they used to call drunk people. There was an awkward silence, which Wyatt figured was because of that whole thing with Mackenzie's dad three years ago. But her dad didn't drink anymore, something he told them three times a week when he dropped Mackenzie off for Tuesday and Thursday dinners and Sunday afternoon "homework club," as Wyatt's mom put it, while he drove the forty-five minutes into Corvallis for his AA meetings.

Wyatt wasn't sure what to say, so he stayed quiet. He passed their Lincoln Room and was halfway to the third floor when Mackenzie asked, "Don't we need to get going?"

He pulled his phone out of his jacket pocket to check the time: 6:52? Homeroom started in *eighteen* minutes, and PE was right after that! He still had to make his own lunch . . .

"I gotta run," Wyatt told her, as he hustled into his room.

"You nervous?" she asked.

Her question slowed him down, like he was suddenly underwater. Was it that obvious?

"*I* know how great you are," Mackenzie said. "Just be yourself, and other people will start to see it, too."

Sure . . . except being yourself worked only if you were like everyone else to start with. Wyatt fought his way back to the surface and started folding finished Emancipation Proclamations in thirds, stuffing envelopes fast. They looked perfect. After four years of doing them, he'd finally gotten the recipe down. But seventeen would have to be enough.

Mackenzie said, "I should go. My dad wants to drive me, to remind 'all those hormonal teenage boys'—his words, not mine—that he's 'with the police force.'" Wyatt could almost hear her eye roll. Her dad was their town's parking enforcement officer. "Can you believe that?"

Wyatt wasn't sure what he wasn't supposed to believe. There were worse things than not having any chores and getting driven to school.

The sky was lighter now, nearly a Confederate gray—he was racing daybreak and the first bell. *Move,* he told himself, as he kept folding and stuffing. A gust of air brought the smell of outdoors. Fresh, green. He'd be out in it soon.

After a moment, Mackenzie said, "I'll see you in History. Good luck with PE."

"See you. And . . . thanks." Wyatt hung up. He needed the luck. Because his life was *so* Queer as a three-dollar bill.

Lincolnville, Oregon, streetlamp banner:

Celebrate February 14!
Abe and Mary: a Great Love
Parade 9:00 a.m. @ Union Square

Chapter 2
Monday, January 5

EXACTLY FOUR MINUTES after everyone should have already been out in the gym, Wyatt raced into the locker room. He stopped in his tracks. The freshman basketball team guys were still there, gathered around Jonathon, who stood next to a stack of twelve shoeboxes. They were all already in their Fighting Soldiers PE uniform T-shirts and black shorts. And anyone else who might have been a buffer between him and these guys was already in the gym, playing badminton.

His stalling had backfired. Big-time.

Wyatt stood there, trying to figure out how not to be seen. He'd have to go through them to change. . . . Maybe he could just go back to the gym, say he'd forgotten his PE uniform at home, and take the two-point grade hit. Except . . . he was holding the drawstring bag with his change of clothes. That wouldn't work.

"You've got to be kidding me!"

"These suck."

"I'm not wearing them."

Hold on. Wyatt realized what he was hearing—Jonathon's own pack of sharks was attacking him! This was maybe too good to miss.

"Pink?" Charlie razzed Jonathon.

"Will you all just shut up?"

Wyatt could have sworn there was a hint of panic in Jonathon's voice.

What was going on?

Jonathon was holding one of the shoes—purple, gold, and white. And then Wyatt saw it: the entire sole of the sneaker was neon pink. "It . . . just means we'll be crushing the sissies with every step!"

Jonathon looked over and saw Wyatt. He kind of smiled, and Wyatt wasn't sure what that was about. Was Jonathon maybe getting how sucky it was to be on the receiving end of all that crap? Should he smile back?

Suddenly, Jonathon lunged over the bench, knocked Wyatt's feet out from under him, and pinned him flat out on his back. Pain shot through Wyatt's butt and shoulder and the back of his head when he smacked the floor, lightning smashing together inside him, every nerve overloading, the whole system threatening blackout. He was staring at the fluorescent tube lights and, like a fish on land, couldn't seem to get his lungs to work. His eyes prickled with tears, but he wouldn't allow the rain. He couldn't. *No, dammit. Hail, maybe. But no rain. Not in front of them.*

Shoe in his hand, Jonathon squished the pink rubber into Wyatt's cheek, forcing his face down into the floor. "Like I'm crushing Little Miss Yarrow here!"

They laughed. Every one of them. And Wyatt saw something else. From Miguel Abelardo—who they called Lardo, even though he was skinnier than Wyatt—to Jonathon's right-hand shark, Charlie, they were all really glad they weren't him.

He wished he wasn't himself, too.

Under the grit and dirt his nose was shoved into, Wyatt figured whatever they cleaned the floor with must be pretty toxic, because his eyes started to fog up.

"Come on, ladies. Let's go!" Coach Rails wandered into the locker room at just that moment. He gaped at them.

Wyatt managed to swallow the storm cloud in his throat. It was over, at least.

Jonathon quickly got up off Wyatt, saying, "No homo, man," so his dad wouldn't dare think he was on top of Wyatt because he *liked* him.

Wyatt sat up, his ears so hot he guessed they were the color of the sneaker soles. Staring at the small rip in his own sneaker, he waited in the silence for Coach Rails to say something. But no one said anything.

Finally, Jonathon shouted to the other guys, "All right, bitches. Team spirit! Everyone wears them!" and started tossing out sneaker boxes.

"What are you waiting for, you bunch of fags?" Coach Rails barked. "Get your shoes on and get out there! I want five laps around the track. All of you. For being late."

Groans.

"You want me to make it ten?" Coach Rails threatened.

That quieted them down.

Wyatt almost smiled. At least Jonathon was getting punished, even if it was hidden inside the whole team's getting penalized. And if he kept still, maybe no one would notice him there on the floor. He'd wait for them to clear out and then change in peace.

"That means you, too, Yarrow!" Coach Rails snapped at him.

What? Wyatt looked at him in disbelief. Coach Rails scratched at the beard he was growing out to be Lincoln in their town's Lincoln's birthday–Valentine's Day parade in just over a month. Like last year, he'd be a too-short, country-western-singing Abe, next to his wife, the mayor's too-thin-and-tall, real estate–selling Mary— but it was like no one in their town cared about the terrible casting. As Wyatt's mom kept saying, it was the mayor's parade and everyone else was just invited to it.

"Get changed. Get out there. And give me five laps." Coach Rails lowered his eyebrows at him. "No one with four healthy limbs gets a pass in life—or my PE class."

Freshman History First-Term Final—Selected Grades

Miguel Abelardo:	C	Jonathon Rails:	D
Charlie Anderson:	D	Jennie Woo:	B
Mackenzie Miller:	A+	Wyatt Yarrow:	A

Sharks ahead. By the lockers.

Wyatt stopped walking, pretending he'd just gotten a text. His arms felt raw from his first-ever lunchtime workout, which he'd snuck in instead of eating, but he was so over being Jonathon meat that he was going to deal with it. And he'd needed some plan, because from the moment that substitute had read their History final grades out loud, Jonathon and his sharks had been out for blood.

At least they hadn't seen him yet.

Sneakers and macho body sprays blurred by his chipped phone casing as he strategized for the second time that day how to get past them. He'd escaped after History—one advantage of going to the weight room off the gym was that it had been the last place Jonathon would have expected him to go—but now Wyatt had only three minutes until the bell. There was no time to go around the whole building before Algebra. And there was a sandwich waiting for him twenty feet down that hall to the corner, and eight feet to the right.

Jonathon tossed a textbook to the floor of his locker. *Bam!* "You're such a girl, Anderson."

Charlie was right behind Jonathon and made a sarcastic kissy sound back.

Fart-catcher! Charlie was Jonathon's fart-catcher! Wyatt couldn't wait to tell Mackenzie he'd found a place to use it. That was, if he survived the next three minutes.

He placed each foot carefully forward to move with the crowd. To seem busy and blend in even more, he was tapping out the longest fake text message ever. If Mackenzie's dad let her have her phone on at school, Wyatt would be texting: GET ME OUT OF HERE! and he'd fill the screen with a million exclamation points. As it was, his thumbs were flying at random.

"You're so Gay." Jonathon hurled the words at Charlie.

"Takes one to know one!" Charlie shoved Tai to agree. "Right?"

Tai's laugh died like a hiccup when he saw Jonathon's *watch who you're making fun of* glare.

He was almost past them . . .

"Yo! Fruitcake!" Jonathon shouted at him.

Wyatt didn't stop.

"Don't walk away from me, I'm talking to you!"

The entire hallway stared.

Every capillary on Wyatt's face and ears popped with red heat, betraying him.

No . . . !

He pocketed the phone before anyone could notice he wasn't actually texting anybody and make fun of him for that, too. He tried to push through the get-to-your-locker-before-fifth-period surge, but it was like every kid in their whole town was in that hallway and Wyatt was the only one going upstream.

All of a sudden, Jonathon was blocking his path. "How dumb are you?"

Wyatt considered explaining that including David Rice Atchison as president number 11.5 (in between James Polk and Zachary Taylor) wasn't really a mistake, and that he'd wanted to talk to Mrs. Elliot about the "President for a Day" article he'd read—since she'd marked it wrong—but then she was gone on maternity leave and he wasn't sure about that substitute, Mr. Guzman. . . . But then he noticed that Jonathon's biceps were bigger than his own calves and kept his mouth shut.

Jonathon's Abercrombie & Fitch–model face got all snarly. "We talked about this. What were you thinking, pulling a ninety-eight percent?"

Wyatt jerked back as spittle landed on his dark blue T-shirt. He imagined it burning through like acid and wished he were one of those superheroes with armor.

Jonathon was up in Wyatt's face. "You killed the curve. So now"— Wyatt didn't want to flinch, but he also didn't want to get punched by that fist—"I'm either going to have to kick your a—"

"*There* you are!" With a flash of her Harvard sweatshirt, Mackenzie grabbed Wyatt like a lifeguard saving a drowner. Before he could say anything, she'd squished her lips into his.

Wyatt clamped his mouth shut and fell back, pinned between his best friend's lips and the cold wall of lockers. Through his green canvas bag, books cut into his stomach and the scent of fake strawberries overpowered his nose.

It was genius. Jonathon stood there like a squirrel in the road, not sure what to do.

Ha!

Wyatt didn't want to get caught looking at Jonathon, so he shifted his eyes to Mackenzie. Up close, he noticed her eyebrows were brown and didn't really match her waist-long, copper-red hair. *Huh.*

Kids hooted at them. Wyatt hadn't even made it through the first day of the spring semester, but between Jonathon's second shark attack and Mackenzie's lip lock, he was the big show at *Civil* High.

"Check out the lovebirds!" someone yelled.

"Big deal." Another girl sounded bored and slammed her locker shut.

One-one thousand. Two-one thousand. How long was Mackenzie going to make this last? The sharks were whispering to each other.

Someone else said, real loud, "Is he keeping his eyes open? Freak." Wyatt shut them.

But then all he could feel was Mackenzie's lip gloss sticking to his lips like half-dry, half-wet Elmer's glue. His first kiss . . .

It doesn't count.

It doesn't.

This is what it must be like to kiss your sister.

Mackenzie let out a sigh, little notes falling. Like she was part of some big finale, with birds and chipmunks and little people. . . . Wyatt tried not to snort in her face, but she was going for the Oscar.

He kicked himself mentally—if the sharks were watching, he needed to play along! He'd been standing stock-still, like Wax Lincoln downstairs in the B&B. He lifted his free hand to Mackenzie's shoulder. *Ow.* The back of his arm burned. Muscle targeted: triceps.

What next? Should he move his hand to her back? Touch her braid? He wasn't sure, but he had to do *something*. Cautiously, he cupped his hand around her neck. It was warm.

Mackenzie noticed. She leaned into him a little and then, after another moment, broke away. Wyatt took a breath.

She whispered down to him, "They still watching?"

Wyatt checked. The pink-soled sharks had moved ten feet along the hallway, and only one of them was still staring: Jonathon. His eyes were narrowed slits, but his mouth was . . . closed. Without thinking, Wyatt had the back of his hand up to wipe the kiss off his lips—but he caught himself and scratched his jaw instead. Wondering if he had just climbed up the food chain a bit, he gave Mackenzie a tiny dip of his head.

Mackenzie said, loudly enough for their audience to hear, "Come on, boyfriend!" She squeezed Wyatt's arm, and he winced but fast-turned it into a toothy smile. Holding hands, they headed up the hallway and turned the corner.

All clear.

They pressed flat against the wall, side by side. Mouth open wide, Wyatt laughed silently.

"You were amazing!" he whispered to her.

"I was, wasn't I?" Mackenzie's eyes sparkled.

Wyatt nodded. "Like Mother Teresa, saving the day with plan B!"

"If plan A was getting punched, that's not much of a plan."

Wyatt counted down five lockers and dropped the dead weight of his backpack. He rubbed the ache in his shoulder. "My plan A sucked. But plan B rocked. Did you see his face?"

Mackenzie stayed close as Wyatt spun his combination lock. He was so excited, he was babbling. "It's like we have ESP or something. I mean, I was fake-texting you, and then . . . *pow!* There you were!" He got it open. The swimsuit model floating on the inside of his locker door hovered in the specially modified Air Force plane. Wyatt reminded himself not to laugh at how ridiculous she looked in the photo, bikini top not up to the zero-gravity challenge of her breasts. He starting dumping stuff out of his backpack. They needed to design a zero-gravity backpack.

"I knew something was wrong when you were missing at lunch."

Wyatt thought, with a flash of envy, that Mackenzie blushed like a regular person, just the slightest pink behind her sprinkle of freckles.

"You were awesome, too," she told him.

Wyatt shrugged. It was really all her.

"Wyatt . . . you know, plan *B* has sort of been on my mind for a long time. And how to make it our plan *A*." She leaned in as Wyatt grabbed his turkey sandwich out of its bag. He was starving.

"Huh?" He turned, and her lips were on his again. Mackenzie's face pressed in. This kiss was different. Softer. Not for anyone else to see.

Wyatt froze.

The pretend one didn't count, but he didn't want *this* to be his first kiss, either.

Not a girl. And not *Mackenzie!*

One-one thousand. Two—

She pulled back, her face all dreamy satisfaction. "I guess we'll just have to thank Jonathon for the push."

Thank Jonathon?

She saw his confused look. "I wasn't sure how to change tracks from friends to . . . *more*. But I knew we'd be great together."

Mackenzie put her hand on Wyatt's chest. His heart was pounding. "It's nice, kissing you. Don't you think?"

"Uh . . ." He glanced around. Nearly everyone was already in class. The bell was going to ring any second—he hoped. The swimsuit model hovered next to him, all flirty, with nail-polished fingers by her lipstick-shellacked mouth. *You're what got me into this mess,* he thought at her.

Mackenzie's eyes followed Wyatt's to the floating swimsuit model, then flicked down to her own oversize Harvard sweatshirt and four-leaf-clover leggings. She pulled her braid around to the front and smoothed it. She nodded, like he'd made a great point. "It'll probably be better without an audience."

"Yeah!" Wyatt heard himself say, juggling his Algebra book and sandwich. "That'll . . . definitely help." What was he saying? He stuffed a bite of sandwich in his mouth to shut himself up.

"Three is supposed to be a magic number. . . ." Mackenzie looked at him, all smiles. "We'll save our third kiss for when it's just you and me. Sound like a plan?"

He forced the dry bread and meat down his throat so he could talk. "It's . . . a plan," he managed, and palmed his locker shut.

He hadn't meant to agree to it, but the echo of his words sure sounded like he had. What he'd meant was that it was *a* plan, but not *his* plan.

Oh my gosh. It's her *plan.*

"See you, boyfriend." With a wink, Mackenzie two-stepped away, like the hall speakers were playing dance music only she could hear.

The start-of-class bell rang.

Wyatt bonked his forehead against his locker. Resting there, he told himself, *Mental note: never be alone with Mackenzie, ever again.*

Chapter 3
Monday, January 5

THAT'S WHAT I get for never telling her. And now I can't. She'll hate me.

School was out, and Wyatt was running, taking the back way to avoid Mackenzie. And Jonathon. Well, everyone.

He turned at the far side of the gym and raced past their school rock, its foot-high purple and gold letters shouting,

GO FIGHTING SOLDIERS!

Sprinting along the edge of the field, he passed the faculty parking lot to get to the chain-link fence. There was a gap at the bottom, blocked by an old log, but there was enough room for Wyatt—and the occasional soccer ball—to scoot through. He'd been sent to get enough of them during PE.

Nearly empty backpack in his hand, he slid through the gap. He shouldered the bag and noticed, on the ridge across from him, a family of tourists posing in front of the log cabin that was supposed to be like the one Lincoln had been born in. They were so happy to be in Lincolnville. Everyone was. Everyone but him.

He dashed down the ravine to the trail along the stream, and ran.

Where Jenson's Stream widened out to the ford, he jumped across the flat concrete stones that made a path, and kept going on the other side. It was just him and the rushing water, his heartbeat, his lungs, and the rhythm of his feet pushing him away from school as fast as they could go.

Twenty minutes later, his side cramped and Wyatt stumbled to a sweaty stop. He dropped his backpack and let the cold afternoon water run through his fingers, on its way to Corvallis. And Portland. And then the ocean, and maybe . . . San Francisco. Or LA.

But me? I'm stuck here.

He wiped his hands on his jeans, got out his phone, and pulled up the photo of his soldier. Wyatt imagined him saying, *Hey there again, Wyatt. Fancy meeting you in a place like this.* He knew it was corny. Stupid. But it made him feel better anyway.

Not for the first time, Wyatt wished his soldier were real. That he could tell him about Mackenzie, those weird kisses, and what a disaster everything was.

The day came crashing in on him—early wake-up, getting ambushed, sore muscles, clueless Mr. Guzman announcing his A and Jonathon's D, and because of that, Jonathon almost pounding him, and then that kiss—both kisses. . . . *Ugh!*

He kicked a fist-size rock into the current, and it splashed water back onto him. Great. Now he was wet, too.

Everything ached as he lay out on a boulder that edged the stream. His shoulders protested as he lifted his phone—which hardly weighed anything—above him, but Wyatt didn't care. He focused on his soldier.

The guy was staring right at the camera, kind of smiling, like he and whoever had taken the picture shared some secret. His coat was way too big, and the forage cap on his head—the same kind they sold in the B and B and that looked so awkward on their plastic military mannequin, whether it was dressed in Union blues or Confederate butternut-gray—looked pretty cool on him. There was another young guy behind him, holding a sword, all *check this out,* and Wyatt wondered if they were friends.

He figured his soldier was only a little older than he was—you could tell he wasn't shaving yet. Well, okay, Wyatt knew he was a lot older—the Civil War was, like, 150 years ago. Who was he? Who was he staring at like that? What was his secret?

All Wyatt could do was look at him, across time, and imagine he was just dressed up for the reenactments. That he was some teenager from another town and was going to lie back right here next to Wyatt. And they'd get to listen to the stream together. And talk, about the stuff Wyatt couldn't tell anybody. And Wyatt imagined, in that tightly locked secret place in his heart, that maybe that smile— like some guy version of the *Mona Lisa*—might be the way he'd get looked at someday.

Somewhere in the trees above them, a bird wheezed like it had just swallowed a kazoo. *Cooper's hawk,* Wyatt guessed. He closed his eyes and breathed in the mossy wet, letting it fill up every part of him.

His soldier was crazy cute. Wyatt could imagine wanting to kiss *him.* The corners of his mouth tugged up at the idea.

But Mackenzie? A tremor went through him, and it had nothing to do with his clammy T-shirt or the clouds stealing the last warmth of daylight.

Wyatt lurched up to sitting, the muscle knot under his ribs clenching tight.

It was all impossible. He *wanted* to want to kiss her. But he didn't want to.

He couldn't be himself, either—not till he was hundreds of miles away at some college. He'd go to a random big city where no one knew him and no one cared about what he did or who he was . . . or who he wanted to kiss.

Until then, he just had to survive. Fit in, somehow.

Bulk up? He imagined working out every day at lunch and feeling this sore all the time. How would he ever get as strong or as big as Jonathon, who was a high school Hulk? It would take him forever to even try. And he needed a way to get through tomorrow.

Maybe, if it helped him not bleed into the water like shark food, maybe . . . plan B? He *could* have a girlfriend, instantly. He kind of already did.

Wyatt struggled to stand, rubbing at the cramp just now easing in his side. *But not telling Mackenzie . . .*

She was going to hate him sooner or later, no matter what he did. He had three and a half more years in Lincolnville before he was free. He'd rather she hated him later.

I have a girlfriend.

He tried saying it out loud, but it came out as a question. "I have a girlfriend?"

Tuesday, January 6

"So, this is just like the room where Lincoln lived in Springfield, Illinois, from 1837 to 1841, when he was twenty-eight to thirty-two years old." It was the finale of Wyatt's tour, and the Lincoln Room at the top of the stairs was crowded with second-graders. He pointed out the furniture: the low antique dresser; the rocking chair that was just like the one that had ended up at the White House; the oval mirror with candlesticks and a little shelf for shaving things at the right height for Abe's face; the could-have-been-there china water pitcher and basin.

"And this is Lincoln's cherry-pine-rope bed." Wyatt walked over to the bed-and-breakfast's shrine, the actual bed Abraham Lincoln had slept in. The kids crowded closer, red velvet ropes on brass posts holding them back. The bed was just a little bigger than his own twin bed one more flight up, but Abe's had polished wood balls at the corners and an old green-and-blue quilt at the foot and was made up with Wyatt's great-grandmother's linens from Italy. Once a month, Wyatt put a dent in the pillow with a spaghetti squash to make it seem like maybe Abe himself had just gotten up. Over winter break, he'd even yanked a couple of hairs from Wax Lincoln's head and put them on the pillow. Mackenzie had given him a hard time about how it was starting to feel like lying, but he told her museums were kind of like theater and he was just helping set the stage.

He couldn't tell whether any of the kids noticed the hairs on the pillow or not, but they were in awe in the presence of a real piece of history. Wyatt's dad had bought the Lincoln bed at auction years ago, and that was how they'd ended up in Lincolnville, right before third grade. His folks had taken over the Lincolnville Civil War Bed & Breakfast and renamed it the Lincoln Slept Here Bed & Breakfast. He'd been assigned a desk next to Mackenzie. They'd bonded over her never teasing him for being new, and *him* never teasing *her* for having a mom who was sometimes around, but most of the time not. They'd studied together and listened to each other, and been friends ever since.

Behind the field-trip teachers in the doorway, Mackenzie waved to get his attention.

And now she's my girlfriend. . . .

Shaking it off, he jumped back into the tour, lifting the mattress edge so everyone could see the ropes underneath. "Even though it's never used, every six months we have to tighten the rope grid so it doesn't get saggy. Tight ropes made the bed more comfortable, which, we used to tell people, is where they got the expression *sleep tight*."

"Ohs!" traveled the room like applause.

"But, turns out, that's not really true." Wyatt glanced at Mackenzie—correcting their mistake had been her first addition to the tour. "People didn't start saying *sleep tight* until a generation later, when rope beds weren't even that popular anymore. *The Oxford English Dictionary* says *tight* used to mean *soundly* or *well*. *Sleep well—sleep tight.* History can surprise you, sometimes."

Mackenzie winked at him, then spun her pointer fingers around each other: *Wrap it up.*

But once the tour was gone, they'd be alone.

"Can we touch it?" a girl asked.

He took the chance to stall. "Just the wood parts." Avoiding eye contact with Mackenzie, he unhooked the velvet rope closest to the bed and stepped aside. Forty-three pairs of hands darted out to rub the wood smooth, like the bed of the most admired president in history was somehow good luck.

"Excuse me. Sorry . . ." Mackenzie got past the teachers and tiptoed to Wyatt's side. He tried to drift away, but she took his hand. Clearing her throat, she announced, "This way to the souvenir shop and the end of the tour!" And, pulling Wyatt with her, she teetered out of the room.

Wyatt checked to see if she'd hurt her foot. *Since when does she wear high heels?*

"*Pishhu!*"

"*Pa-pa-pa-pow!*"

"*Pishhu!*"

The sound effects for the rifle pens were more sci-fi than Civil War, but they were the last two kids. Their teacher checked the time on her cell. "If you're going to buy those, you need to do it now."

Wyatt knew better than to waste a bag or receipt that he'd just have to pick up from the parking lot gravel later, and handed the first kid his change. As he paid for his, the second boy asked, "Were there *really* eight-year old soldiers?"

"They were mostly drummers, but yeah." Wyatt had told them about Edward Black, 21st Indiana Volunteer Infantry Regiment. There was a portrait of him in what used to be the dining room, part of this new display on child soldiers his dad had been working on forever.

"Lucky!" the first boy said, and the second nodded like one of their bobblehead plastic Lincolns.

Lucky? Wyatt didn't think so. Edward Black died at eighteen. Of soldier's heart, what they called post-traumatic stress disorder back then. Who wanted to fight a war and be so freaked out by it all that it killed you, before you even got to live your life? And that was *if* you survived in the first place. "I'd hate to be a soldier," Wyatt told them.

"Pffft!" The second kid spit-took air, like that was the stupidest thing he'd ever heard.

The first kid targeted Wyatt with his new gun. *"Pishhu! Pishhu!"*

Baby sharks.

"All right, you two. That's enough. Everyone's waiting." Their teacher steered them outside.

"Thanks for visiting!" Mackenzie waved from the front porch as the stragglers joined the rest of their class on the bus. Next, they'd go to Jennie's family's put-on-a–Civil War–costume-and-have-your-old-time-photo-taken store.

Mackenzie closed the front door and headed back to where Wyatt stood in their Lincoln and Civil War Memorabilia Alcove. They were alone.

Yikes.

"Hey . . ."

Wyatt got very busy at the register. She stood right next to him, waiting.

"You're really good with kids," Mackenzie said, balancing a stuffed bear on one of the little speakers by the reception computer.

Wyatt shrugged, spotting the mess of rifle pens. Typical. They had to examine every one before deciding. He scooped them up and started sorting, Richmond carbines in the JEFFERSON DAVIS: PRESIDENT OF THE CONFERACY mug, Springfield rifles in the ABRAHAM LINCOLN: PRESIDENT OF THE UNION one.

Mackenzie pulled her matching pink argyle wallet from her backpack and grabbed a ten-dollar bill. She put it on the glass counter in front of him.

"What's that for?" Wyatt risked a quick glance at her.

She snuggled two grapefruit-size, give-a-Lincoln-get-a-Lincoln, $4.99 teddy bears under her chin. "I can't decide between the blue one or the gray one, so I'm going to get both."

Wyatt was out of pens to sort. "You don't have to pay for those." He bent down to straighten the line of infantry soldiers on the Civil War chess set.

"It's your family business. I'm not going to steal them!"

"You're my girlfriend, aren't you? Just take 'em."

Wyatt stood, and it took everything he had not to look at his soldier in the display case against the sitting-room wall. Before he could figure out something else to do, Mackenzie wrapped her arms around him. "Honeybear!"

"Honeybear?"

Her shirt was silky, and he searched for an excuse to slip away.

She nodded. "Sometimes you're like a growly bear on the outside, but in there"—she touched his chest through his T-shirt—"you are so sweet." She tilted her lips down to his, going for kiss number three.

Oddly purple-red lips closing in, Wyatt thought fast. He grabbed a loose bear and, with a lip-smack sound effect, pressed its nose to Mackenzie's cheek instead. He broke free and acted like he was being all funny and playful.

Something cracked inside Mackenzie's face, and her hand flew up to cover her mouth. "Are my braces that horrible?"

"No! It's not . . ." Wyatt stopped. He had no idea what to say. "Mom!"

Wyatt's mom, still in work clothes, walked in from the kitchen corridor holding a folding plastic RAILS REALTY sign. It was broken. "I finally got Kelly to let your father make one of these out of wood, so they'll last. If she likes it, it will be some extra money. . . ."

Mackenzie whispered, like she was trying to believe it, "You knew she was coming home now?"

Wyatt took the excuse. "I thought, maybe . . ."

His mom stashed the sign behind the reception counter and focused on them. "Mackenzie, you're looking beautiful!"

"Hi, Liz," Mackenzie said.

Wyatt's mom came over and hugged her. Then, instead of letting go, she held Mackenzie out at arm's length, staring at her like Mackenzie hadn't spent the last seven years hanging out there practically every day. His mom repeated the compliment: "Just . . . beautiful."

That got Mackenzie blushing, which always showed off her freckles, which she hated. *Actually, where are her freckles?*

"Don't you think so?" Wyatt's mom turned to him, and Wyatt startled. He didn't want Mackenzie to catch him staring at her. That would send the wrong . . . *Oh, man.* He didn't even know anymore.

"Yeah, sure." He rubbed at a spot of ink on his hand.

"Sweetie." Wyatt's mom gave him a quick kiss on the head. "I still have a few calls to make for the parade, and your dad's too busy cooking. . . . I noticed the breakfast buffet never got put away. How about you pitch in, and then you two can set the table for dinner?"

More chores. Great. But, to avoid the lecture, Wyatt just said, "Sure." And gave Mackenzie a *you in?* look.

Lipstick. And no freckles.

"I'd love to." Mackenzie tossed a flowy, big-hair curl over her shoulder, all game. Wyatt pushed down this queasy feeling that he wasn't going to listen to. He just had to make sure they didn't spend any more time alone together.

"Honestly, Mr. Yarrow, I would never have guessed it's rabbit!" Mackenzie gushed about the meal Wyatt's dad was trying out, since there were no guests eating with them at the big table in the kitchen tonight. Weekly

Civil War–era meals were the next "big thing" supposed to get money finally "pouring in."

Wyatt eyed the dandelion greens and pieces of slimy-looking meat on his plate. His mom was going to need to keep her job for the mayor. Another thing for Jonathon to lord over him, like, because Wyatt's mom worked for his mom, it made them Jonathon's family's servants or something.

The bottle in his hand made a plastic farting sound as he coated his rabbit salad and heap of turnip-potato pie in an oozing blanket of red.

"Ketchup? Really?" Wyatt's dad bookmarked the nineteenth-century cookbook he'd been reading and decided to pay attention to actual living people.

"Gregory . . . ," Wyatt's mom started.

"He hasn't even tried it!" Wyatt's dad shook his head. "It's supposed to be *period* food."

Wyatt held out the family-size bottle, label facing his dad. He pointed to the small red print below HEINZ and read it out loud. "Established 1869."

"Really?" It was like Mackenzie was interested in everything today. She reached for the ketchup bottle with matching red fingernails. *Nail polish, too?*

Wyatt's mom patted his dad's hand. "It's delicious." She turned to Wyatt. "So, how was your day?"

"Fine." Wyatt poked in vain for something else on his plate.

"Anything new to share?" his mom asked.

"Nope." Wyatt answered, wondering whether, if he just cut it up and moved it around on his plate and then volunteered to do dishes, he could get away without eating it.

"That's funny," his mom said nonchalantly, "because when I was updating the mayor's status earlier, I noticed Mackenzie's profile says she's now *in a relationship.*"

Wyatt kept his eyes on his plate. *Don't tell them. Don't tell them.* He tried to send the thought to Mackenzie—maybe they did have some kind of ESP.

"You didn't tell them?" she asked Wyatt, totally telling them.

Wyatt's mom shrieked and leaped out of her chair to squeeze them both into a giant hug. "Why didn't you tell us? Mackenzie Miller! Oh my gosh—what's your middle name? I don't know your middle name!"

"Liz," his dad said, and Wyatt's mom released her death grip on them.

"Okay, okay! But you can't blame a mother for being excited about her little boy growing up and finding *love.*"

Wyatt could feel the hole he was in getting deeper and deeper. He managed to lift his lips apart and show his teeth, just like a real smile.

His dad picked up his wineglass in a toast. "That makes this your first official meal as Wyatt's girlfriend!"

"Guys!" Wyatt squirmed. *Do all parents do this?*

"And now that you're dating, we need to make sure you're respecting each other. I won't be a grandfather before I'm fifty."

"Gregory!" Wyatt's mom sounded shocked. "They're only in ninth grade."

"I remember being a teenager. And we have a double responsibility here." Wyatt's dad pointed at him and Mackenzie. "No more alone time in either of your bedrooms. Understood?"

Wyatt felt like he'd just been handed a late Christmas present.

He nodded quickly.

Wyatt's dad sipped his wine. "Mackenzie, now that you're even more a member of our family . . ."

Mackenzie made a little squeaking noise. Wyatt didn't look at her, because he didn't want to embarrass her. But anytime Wyatt complained, Mackenzie told him how great his family was and how he needed to appreciate his parents more. How "you don't know how important it is until you lose it." And he never knew what to say. And now she was thinking his dad and mom could be like her dad and mom, too, so she'd have three parents, instead of just one. And it was all built on a lie. He felt like pond scum, if pond scum could feel bad about itself.

His dad continued, looking at Mackenzie in a way that felt parental, "Why don't *you* choose our Sunday movie this week?"

Wyatt couldn't believe his dad was giving it to Mackenzie. "It was my turn!"

"Sweetie," his mom scolded. "It's a lovely idea of your father's. Be gracious."

"Sorry," Wyatt said, but he wasn't. Even pond scum had stuff it looked forward to. "I've . . . just been waiting to see the new Bond movie since Thanksgiving, and it's finally out on DVD, and it's my week!"

His mom ignored him. "Tell us, Mackenzie. What movie would you like us all to watch?"

Wyatt slumped back and stared at the floor under the table. Pink leopard-print high heels kicked off, Mackenzie's bare feet were crossed at the ankles. What was going on?

"I've always tried to get Wyatt to watch *Little House on the Prairie* with me. Maybe this would be a good chance?"

"Uuugh!" Wyatt rolled his head and eyes all the way back. Something kicked his leg. "Ow!" Bending forward to rub his shin, he was pretty sure he heard Mackenzie smother a laugh.

He glared at his dad, who shifted into lecture mode. "Being in a relationship means some give-and-take. *Little House on the Prairie* sounds perfect, Mackenzie. And we can all watch the new double-o-six movie next week. Agreed?"

"It's double-o-seven." Wyatt pouted. Like his dad even cared. If it wasn't about the Civil War, he was just going to sit there and read an auction catalog no matter what they watched.

His mom leaned toward his dad. "We're supposed to let them sort it out."

His dad shrugged. "Why, when it's so simple?"

"Young love is never simple," Wyatt's mom said. "Remember?"

His parents got all mushy, and Wyatt paid attention to the food he wasn't eating.

Mackenzie chimed in, "How about we watch Wyatt's movie this week, and next week we can watch *Little House?*"

Wyatt looked at her. *Thanks,* he mouthed silently.

Mackenzie locked eyes with him, all intense, all *I'll sacrifice my happiness for yours,* and suddenly Wyatt got it. The makeup. The big hair. The heels. It was all for him!

And he didn't want it. Any of it.

He looked away.

"See? They worked it out." Wyatt's mom said, kissing his dad's hand.

It's like I'm being tortured.

Wyatt survived the rest of dinner, and even managed a couple of bites of cinnamon-apple-and-raisin dessert, until his dad launched into one of his footnote monologues. It was the kind of thing guests found charming for a weekend stay, but they didn't have to live with it full-time. It was all about how he was sorry it was Braeburn apples, instead of the York Imperial or Ben Davis varieties they would have made it with back in 1863 in Gettysburg, Pennsylvania, since this was Gettysburg fruitcake.

And all Wyatt could think about was Jonathon hearing that and telling everyone *Wyatt* was the Gettysburg fruitcake. But he wouldn't, now that Wyatt had a girlfriend. Right?

He dropped his spoon to the plate, appetite gone.

Wyatt's mom brought up junior prom—two years away—and how now she would volunteer to chaperone. *How am I going to keep this up for that long?*

Then they were talking outfits, and how Mackenzie didn't even have one for the Purple and Gold Pep Rally in two weeks.

"What I'm really not sure about are the shoes," Mackenzie said. "These gave me blisters, and I nearly twisted my ankle, twice."

"You need to start with kitten heels," Wyatt's mom told her.

"Maybe I have something . . . I'm a size eight. What size are you?"

"But, *I* wear a size eight!" Mackenzie's words came out in a giggle. Before Wyatt knew it, with his mom in the lead, Mackenzie was pulling him along to his parents' bedroom. "Come on, Honeybear!"

Wyatt stalled out in the doorway, watching his mom throw open her shoe wardrobe. Mackenzie acted like a starving person at a buffet, touching and oohing and aahing over each shoe. She didn't have a mom to do this with, since hers was . . . well, no one knew where her mom was, so Wyatt figured it was a big deal.

"Here, try this one!" Wyatt's mom held out a pair of low heels, whose shifting purple-blue colors reminded Wyatt of iridescent butter-fly wings.

Carefully, Mackenzie slipped on the left shoe. "It fits!" she said, all Cinderella.

Wyatt's mom came up behind Mackenzie and studied her reflection in the IKEA standing mirror. "Beautiful. And you don't have to wait for the pep rally." Wyatt's mom was all fairy godmother. "You can borrow any pair you want, anytime."

Mackenzie gulped air, and Wyatt could barely make out her whispered "Gaia. My mom gave me a totally embarrassing hippie middle name."

Wyatt's mom moved to face Mackenzie. "She doesn't know what she's missing." She tucked a loose strand of hair gently behind Mackenzie's ear. "Mackenzie Gaia Miller, you are a lovely young woman. I couldn't be happier . . . for all of us."

Wyatt was out of there. He couldn't be the prince in this fairy tale. He just couldn't.

WHILE MR. GUZMAN droned on about how they had to stop thinking of him as a substitute and that he was a real teacher and was going to
hold them to real expectations, Wyatt stared at one of the five new motivational posters surrounding them. Redecorating the room pretty much
cemented the fact that Mrs. Elliot wasn't coming back until her new baby
was stuck in high school, too. This poster had a fortune cookie saying
ONE PERSON CAN CHANGE THE WORLD over a circle of ripples spreading from the center of an otherwise still body of water. The photo made it
seem like the ripples would go on forever. Something about it felt wrong.

"Annual President Lincoln book reports." Mr. Guzman had
changed topics, and Wyatt shook his head as he tuned back in.

"This year, you'll do those reports as a series of blog posts on your
very own blogs!" He said it like it was something they should be excited
about. "The student with the most traffic to their blog by February
twelfth not only will get an automatic A, but, as the ninth-grade Lincoln
book report winner, also will have a place of honor in the upcoming
parade, as ninth-grade grand marshal!"

It was a cool prize—like being a celebrity for a day—but no one in the room was willing to admit they wanted it.

Even though his mom had organized the parade for the past two years, Wyatt didn't get to be in it. Jonathon and his sister rode along with their parents, since their mom had been voted mayor back in sixth grade, but the rest of them hadn't been in their town's Lincoln's birthday/Valentine's Day parade since they were little kids riding with Tykes on Bikes.

Wyatt did notice Mackenzie had sat up straighter. He figured she was thinking *ninth-grade grand marshal* would sound good on her college applications. She was all dressed up again, this time in some lichen-green shirt with a bow on it, like a lawyer on one of those TV shows. He missed the big Ivy League sweatshirts. He missed them just being friends.

Mr. Guzman peered sideways at them. "Did I mention the hundred-dollar cash prize, donated by Rails Realty?" The room exploded in excitement.

Wyatt thought that could buy a pretty nice pair of sneakers. New ones, not from the thrift store.

When he could talk loudly enough to be heard again, Mr. Guzman continued. "For your first blog post—which must be online by six a.m. Monday, when I'll read them—you'll each share your first impression of President Lincoln from your book. Over the course of the subsequent weeks and posts, you'll dig deeper into your primary source material, develop a thesis, and go about proving it. To accomplish this, of course, each of you will need a book on Lincoln." Mr. Guzman stood up. "And, to that end, we're off to the library."

"Now?" The word was out of Wyatt's mouth before he could edit himself. The only time they went to the library was for their once-a-month field trip, when no one really checked anything out anyway. They'd never gone in the middle of a class before.

"You're such a dweeb, Yarrow!" Jonathon imitated a little girl's voice: "Oh no! I'm going to miss some precious learning!" He cracked up, like he was a comedian with his own TV talk show. Everyone laughed along with him.

Wyatt felt his face blazing with heat. He squeezed his pencil between his thumb and fingers so hard, he imagined crushing the space between the molecules of wood and lead and turning the whole thing into a diamond. *A diamond pencil would be pretty cool. I could sell it and go to some private boarding school in a city somewhere. And never have to see these idiots again.*

Frowning, Mr. Guzman tried to quiet the class with a wave. "Now."

Jonathon shouted his question: "Can we drive, if we have awesome rides?" He backhanded Charlie on the shoulder. His fart-catcher smirked, full of their superiority—Jonathon was the only freshman in their whole school old enough to drive.

"No, Mr. Rails. *In loco parentis* means we're walking. All of us. One big, happy family."

Chairs scraped the floor as everyone got up for the sudden walking-into-town field trip, and it hit Wyatt—the problem with the poster. Life wasn't some still body of water, where you could make a ripple that changed everything. It was more like a whitewater river. With sharks. You were so busy swimming for your life, any ripples didn't have a chance.

After his latest humiliation, Wyatt didn't feel like talking. And once Mackenzie informed him, making it sound like Mr. Guzman had made a mistake, that *in loco parentis* actually meant *in the place of a parent,* she was silent, too. They walked together, though.

Keeping his eyes on the trees that lined both sides of Route 37, Wyatt could almost remember what it felt like when they were just best friends. But now, everything was different. The class trailed behind them as they followed Jennie and Mr. Guzman on the sidewalk. Mackenzie wore her backpack, but Wyatt carried his in both hands. It wasn't that heavy, but this way he didn't need to deal with figuring out what to do if Mackenzie tried to hold his hand.

Jennie answered their new teacher's question about the best donuts in town (Sandee's Liquor and Candy Mart, hands down), and they crossed under the covered bridge with its sign:

WELCOME TO LINCOLNVILLE—REAL AMERICA

Ten minutes later, the age-old riddle "What do you get when you take thirty-five ninth-graders to a public library in the middle of the school day?" was answered: chaos.

"Please have your library card ready!" Mr. Guzman tried to control things, but he sounded like he was about to lose his voice. "Once you get your Lincoln book, head out to the steps, and you can start reading before we all head back!"

Wyatt straggled behind the team guys, not wanting to get called out for being too into it. One advantage of having a last name starting with *y* was that no one ever complained if he was at the end of the line.

"So, whaddaya think? Mud flaps?" Jonathon was four guys ahead of him.

"The kind with the naked-girl silhouettes with the pointy tits?" Charlie snickered. "Becca would kill you!"

Jonathon shook his head. "The only reason I'm not going to punch you for saying something as girly as *silhouettes* is because you used it in a sentence with *tits.*"

"That's big of you," Wyatt said to himself.

"I'm bigger than you!" Jonathon shot back.

He heard that? Oh, man.

Wyatt looked away. Where was Mackenzie?

Jonathon said to Charlie, loudly enough for the whole library to hear, "Does that guy even have any balls?"

Wyatt spotted her. Mackenzie already had her book, but something had pissed her off—she was all waving arms at Mr. Guzman. She clomped over to Wyatt in his mom's knee-high black boots. His mom and his girlfriend sharing shoes was something that was going to take some getting used to.

"They're not even letting us choose!" She showed Wyatt proof of the injustice: her book had an oval cover photo of Lincoln and his son reading together, under the title, *Lincoln at Home: Two Glimpses of Abraham Lincoln's Family Life*. She made a face. "I wanted something important. Not a bunch of 'how are the children?' love letters!"

Wyatt wanted to commiserate, but was hyperaware Jonathon was tracking every word. "How many pages is it?"

Mackenzie rolled her eyes. "That's such a guy question."

Wyatt shrugged. "I'm a guy. Sue me."

She flipped to the end. "One hundred and twenty-four. And the type is huge!" With a growl that made Wyatt grin—there was the old Mackenzie!—she shoved the book in her backpack.

"Hey, Mackenzie," Jonathon said, all smooth. They must have switched places with Tai and Miguel, because now he and Charlie were right in front of Wyatt. It put Wyatt even more on edge. And was Jonathon checking Mackenzie out?

"Once again!" Mr. Guzman called out. "If you have received your book, you should be outside, reading!"

"Hi," she answered Jonathon, then focused back on Wyatt. "Here." She pressed a square of folded paper into Wyatt's hand. "I better go. . . . See you out there."

"Sure." Wyatt wove his fingers through hers, holding her a moment. He was pretty sure she wouldn't try to kiss him with all the people around, and he wanted to make sure Jonathon saw them connect.

She smiled down at the library's worn shag carpet. All the makeup meant Wyatt couldn't even tell if she was blushing. With a squeeze of his hand, Mackenzie headed out, all glowy.

Wyatt unfolded the note. She had drawn their initials across lined paper. *M and W* in a 3-D cartoon heart. Wyatt's throat tightened. *I'm such a jerk.*

"Whatcha got there, freak?" Jonathon was trying to see over Wyatt's shoulder, so Wyatt shifted back to acting mode and showed him. He gave Jonathon a *Got that? She's mine* look.

Jonathon turned to Charlie. "I feel sorry for her. Dating a guy with mosquito balls."

They burst out laughing and, once they started, couldn't seem to stop.

"Mosquito balls!" Charlie howled.

Wyatt pretended he didn't notice, but he could feel his face get hot, like a sunburn. Welts and boils. Pus oozing down his cheeks. Fourth-degree, life-threatening sunburn. He made like the books on the shelves were suddenly interesting. Really interesting.

Everything would be so much easier if I really did love Mackenzie that way.

The line crept forward. Twenty-five kids left. They passed the teen shelves, the handful of books Wyatt was never going to check out. Nobody ever checked them out.

Boy Meets Boy.

Rainbow Boys.

Absolutely, Positively Not.

Over Thanksgiving break, Wyatt had tried to grab *Absolutely . . .* He'd hidden it inside this giant soccer bio *The Great Dens* and tried to read it in the far back by the parking lot window. He'd even shelved it in between some ancient issues of *Ladies' Home Journal*, whatever the heck that was, so he could grab it the next time, to keep reading about Steven and his secret—he square-danced with his mother—and his other secret. . . . To cover his tracks, Wyatt had even checked out Pete Schmeichel's bio. But when he'd come back to read more, *Absolutely . . .* wasn't there.

He hadn't worked up the nerve to try again.

Wyatt tried not to stare at the books, but he was jumpy, like they might throw themselves out at him and ruin everything. Jonathon and Charlie were right next to him. *Real guys don't ache to read stuff like that. So I won't.*

Fifteen kids left ahead of him. Six.

Mr. Guzman came up to them. "We needed to start back two minutes ago. Get your books and hustle up to join us. Can I trust you gentlemen?" They all bobbed their heads yes. Mr. Guzman looked at each of them in turn. He gave a nod and then took long strides out the door.

Wyatt heard Mr. Guzman call, "Okay, just a few more students to go, so let's start heading back. Miss Miller, lead the way!"

When they were the last three in line, Jonathon asked the librarian, "You got anything short?"

Mr. Clifton, who was Wyatt's dad's age but dressed like an old man even when the two of them went bowling, jerked his head up in surprise. Jonathon gave him his teeth-whitening-brochure grin, all *Recognize me? I'm the mayor's son, and you owe me.* After all, there used to be six librarians in their town, but last summer Mayor Rails closed all the school libraries as a cost-saving measure and all the books came here. So now there was just Mr. Clifton.

Their town librarian reached for the smaller of the two books left. *Of course.* He knew who Jonathon was, all right.

Jonathon squinted at the title. "You've got to be kidding me. *The Lincoln-Douglas Debates?* Boooring!"

"I have some encyclopedia-length sets I was saving for the upper-classmen, if you would prefer . . ."

Jonathon put up a muscle-veined hand and grumbled, "I'll make this work." On his way out, he lowered his voice so just Wyatt could hear. "You better make sure my grade's better than yours on this . . . if you know what's good for you, Mosquito Balls."

Wyatt didn't say anything. You don't provoke a shark.

Charlie got his book next. Jogging over to where Jonathon was waiting by the door, he tossed it up in the air while he spun around, and almost dropped it.

"Nice move, Twinkle Toes," Jonathon teased.

Charlie shot back, "Bitch, shut up!"

Mr. Clifton scolded them, "Please respect library property!"

They ignored him.

Charlie clapped Jonathon on the shoulder. "Let's blow this dump."

They headed out, pausing in the patch of sun on the stone landing. Jonathon nudged Charlie. "Hey, let's stop at Sandee's. Guzman practically gave us a late pass!"

Hooting, they ran down the steps.

Mr. Clifton and Wyatt both let out a sigh. The librarian chuckled, and Wyatt turned back to him.

"You the last one, Wyatt?" He glanced around for stragglers. There weren't any.

"Looks like it." Wyatt handed him his library card.

"That was my last ninth-grade book." Mr. Clifton gestured to the counter. The pile he'd been pulling from was gone.

"You mean I get out of this?"

"Hardly." He sounded amused as he ran the scanner's red light over Wyatt's card. "But there is a title I thought you might enjoy." From somewhere under the counter, he fished out a book. It was thin, with a worn brown cover. It seemed old, like something Wyatt's dad would read to fix the hot-water faucet in the third-floor bathroom, which was still dripping after he'd "fixed" it the first two times.

Mr. Clifton scanned the book's bar code and handed it and Wyatt's card over.

Wyatt read the title. "*Joshua Fry Speed?*" He looked up at the librarian. "That doesn't make any sense. It isn't even about Lincoln."

The skin around Mr. Clifton's eyes crinkled, like he knew something Wyatt didn't. "You never know where a book might take you."

"You keep talking about the payment deadlines we missed, but shouldn't we get some credit for sending in January's early? If you count that, we made ten out of the last twelve!" The panic in his dad's voice stopped Wyatt just before the kitchen doorway. His dad was on the phone, and while Wyatt wasn't an eavesdropper, he was hungry. Maybe he'd just wait.

"The Richardson wedding really helped—and they said they had friends who were planning an April wedding that might . . . Okay—I'm listening." A few seconds later, his dad blurted out, "Benny, you know we're good for it! Liz works for the mayor, for God's sake, and that's a solid income!" His dad's voice dropped. "Business will pick up, I know it."

Wyatt was thinking maybe he should go up to his room after all, but he didn't move.

"I know I've been saying that for years. Come on . . ."

Wyatt and his dad were both silent for nearly a whole minute.

"I hear you. Last chance, I promise. Thanks." His dad hung up, and Wyatt counted to ten before heading in.

Making sure to keep his voice light, like he hadn't heard any of it, Wyatt said, "Hey, Dad."

Reading glasses on top of his head, his dad jerked away, but not before Wyatt could see that his eyes were all red. Wyatt took his time staring at the bulk-case yogurt packs in the fridge.

"How'd your day go?" his dad asked, voice still raw.

Wyatt kept his back turned, but he could see his dad in his mind: He was forty-eight years old, ran a failing business, was always stressed about money, and spent most of his time lost in history. He would never understand. So all Wyatt said was, "Fine."

"Good."

Wyatt grabbed a mango yogurt, peeled off the top, and snagged a spoon.

"Don't ruin your dinner," his dad said, sounding nearly back to normal.

Mouth full, Wyatt grunted that he heard him. He headed to the stairs, but his dad pushed out the chair next to him. "We need to talk."

All the muscles in Wyatt's shoulders tensed up. Not much good ever followed those words. He swiveled slowly. His dad pointed to the spot next to him at the American pine and poplar farm table, 1820s, Kentucky.

Wyatt sat down, wary, staring at the upside-down pile of bank documents in front of them. He didn't want to hear about his dad's argument with the guy at the bank. Were they going to lose the B and B? Where would they move? Wyatt squished down his questions and waited, the yogurt all of a suddenly violently sweet on his tongue.

"So," his dad said, "are you being careful? You know, with Mackenzie?"

With her feelings? Wyatt resisted the wave of guilt that threatened to swamp him.

"I mean, you're using . . . protection, right?"

"Dad!"

"Your first girlfriend, you must be in a rush to try everything, but—"

"*Dad!*"

"But you need to be smart."

"I don't want to be having this conversation!"

"I don't want to be changing your kid's diaper while you're still a freshman in high school!"

Wyatt couldn't help but smile. "Babies take nine months. I'd be a sophomore."

His dad brandished his reading glasses. "Don't get funny with me! This is serious!"

Wyatt met his dad's eye—on this, he could be totally honest. "Dad, I promise. You have nothing to worry about."

"Why? How far did she let you get?"

"I'm not having this conversation!" Wyatt leaped up and ran to the stairs.

"Wyatt!" His dad called after him. "We haven't even talked about STDs!"

Chapter 5
Sunday, January 11

IT WAS SEVEN o'clock, the exhibits were shut for the day, and Wyatt was just about to pick up a second kitchen chair to carry to the exhibition screen in the old dining room, when Mackenzie walked in from the hallway. "Hi, Honeybear!" She was back from dinner with her dad, joining them for the first time for their family movie night.

"Oh." She had been waving a packet of microwave popcorn, but Mackenzie's face fell as she smelled the rich wafts of steam and heard the *puhp-p-p-p-p-p-p!* coming from the covered cast-iron pot by Wyatt's dad.

Wyatt nodded hi from behind the chair back he was still holding.

His dad shouted over the popping, "This is going to be way more delicious than from a microwave! Just like in old times!"

"Thank you, Mackenzie. That's very thoughtful." Wyatt's mom took the package from Mackenzie's hand and gave her a big hug. "We'll save this for next time." She shot her husband a look, then turned to Wyatt. "Sweetie, why don't you offer your girlfriend something to drink?"

Wyatt felt bad that he hadn't warned Mackenzie about his dad's latest circa-1860s kitchen toy. *But how was I supposed to know she was going to bring anything? She never brings anything.* Then he remembered. This wasn't just her coming over while her dad was at an AA meeting, like this afternoon, when she'd hung out and done homework while Wyatt antiqued a bunch of President Abraham Lincoln Timelines. This was more like a date. *Oh, man.* How was he going to survive a date?

His mom prodded him with her eyes. Wyatt let go of the chair and played his part. "We've got some sparkling apple juice. . . ."

"That sounds great." Mackenzie joined him at the counter to help with the glasses.

Wyatt's mom peered down the empty hallway. "Your dad couldn't join us after all?"

Mackenzie shook her head. "He wanted to study. There's another police officer test coming up."

Banished to the converted dining room to set things up so his mom and Mackenzie could have "a little girl time" before the movie, Wyatt set the fourth chair in front of the only TV in their B and B. He hit EJECT and put the *Civil War in Four Minutes* DVD in its case. His dad was already reading the latest *Kovels' Antiques & Collectibles,* all ready for the Bond movie, since it wasn't some boring documentary on nineteenth-century field hospitals.

Wyatt loaded the DVD. At least he could watch the previews.

Wyatt looked up as Mackenzie and his mom finally came in, each with a large bowl of popcorn—one for his parents to share, the other for Mackenzie and Wyatt.

He would have been happier with his own.

This preview was more soda commercial than spy thriller anyway. "Ready for the movie?" Wyatt aimed the remote to go back to the main menu, but his mom took it from him and hit MUTE instead.

"Let's visit a little first."

Wyatt knew it was because she was in no rush to see the inevitable action movie he always chose.

Mackenzie scooted her chair right up against Wyatt's, explaining, "We can share better this way."

Wyatt grabbed a handful of popcorn and stuffed his mouth.

Wyatt's mom gestured to the TV screen, her voice light, like it was just a casual suggestion. "Maybe we could do one of our own. A commercial, for the B and B." She glanced at Wyatt's dad, who was frowning.

His dad wasn't hearing any of it. "Word of mouth is the best advertising, and it's free."

"But Wyatt has his new camera, and we could put it online. It doesn't need to cost any—"

"Liz!" His dad cut her off. "I'll thank you to let me handle things my way."

In the silence, Wyatt could almost hear his mom thinking that his dad's way wasn't working so well. That was what the bank guy thought, too—but his mom would never say it.

To Wyatt's surprise, his mom tried once more: "How could it hurt to let more people know about us?"

"New topic." His dad bristled, giving her a *move on* look.

Wyatt leaned over and whispered to Mackenzie, "You're really family, if they're fighting in front of you."

Mackenzie stifled a giggle.

"Okay," Wyatt's mom said, putting up a hand in surrender. "And we're not fighting. It was just a suggestion. . . ."

If you avoid making waves, your boat never capsizes. His mom had told him that fortune cookie–worthy motto enough times. But it occurred to Wyatt that a boat that didn't make waves was a boat that didn't move.

"So . . ." His mom included them all in the conversation's new direction. "Mackenzie was telling me that the Lincolns had séances in the White House!"

Séances? Wyatt gave Mackenzie a quick glance. *Why didn't she mention that earlier?*

"Eight of them, at least." Mackenzie sparkled at the attention. "Trying to communicate with their dead son."

"Which one?" Wyatt's dad asked over his glasses.

"Willie, who died a year into the Civil War. He was twelve." Mackenzie answered, and then glanced at Wyatt's mom. "At least they knew he was dead."

No one said anything, and Wyatt wondered if Mackenzie was talking about her own mom, off on some journey to "find herself." It had been something like three years since Mackenzie had heard anything from her.

Mackenzie spoke first. "It turns out my book's a lot more interesting than I thought it would be."

Wyatt's dad said, "Ah, *don't judge a book by its cover.*" Trust his dad to pull out the most time-worn cliché possible, dust it off, and put it out there like it was new wisdom.

His mom eyed the Bond movie menu screen that had come up after the final preview, and he knew she was wishing it were some HGTV house-staging marathon instead. She stalled with one more question, this time for him. "How about your book, sweetie? What's it about?"

His book. Still in his backpack, untouched. Because really, what was he supposed to do? He had to do a good job, or his parents would kill him, but not *too* good a job, or Jonathon would really kill him. So he just . . . hadn't done anything.

Wyatt tried to say it like it was no big deal. "I still have a little reading to do." But as soon as the words left his mouth, he knew he was sunk. There was plenty of time, but his mom fixated on how he hadn't even cracked the book. And then Mackenzie chimed in that their "first impression" blog posts had to be online by 6:00 a.m., and hers had taken a lot longer than she'd expected, because of all the footnotes.

Not helpful.

So, no cool cars or gadgets or supervillains for 007—or Wyatt. Just his mom's relieved scolding, as she put the disc away for next Sunday.

Just his own pathetic apology to Mackenzie: "Sorry this pushes your movie back a week." Just her saying, "It was still one of the nicest family nights I've had in a long time. You don't know how lucky you all are." Just him not feeling lucky at all.

Just an awkward hug where Mackenzie tried to kiss Wyatt good night—on the lips—and at the last millisecond he turned his head so she kissed his cheek instead, and then he pretended he didn't notice anything weird.

Just a look askance from his dad as he got up to drive Mackenzie home. "You know better than this, young man."

Just Wyatt standing in the kitchen, filling sandwich bags with popcorn—snacks for him to take to school for the whole week ahead, though they'd be stale by Tuesday.

Just . . . Lincoln.

Wyatt thought about watching something online but didn't think he could get away with it. Instead, he killed time designing his own Bond car—one that could drive like a race car but also maneuver like a hummingbird in the air and like an otter through the water . . . and still shoot out lasers to stop the bad guys in their tracks. He drew his soldier's face. Then drew himself in next to him. Wyatt imagined going for a drive, a Bond guy and him. He added them holding hands and doodled the beginning of a heart—*Stop!*

He crossed it out. All of it. Again and again, soaking the paper with blue ink. Then he cut the paper into thin strips, first one way, then the other, hand-shredding it like confetti. He threw a third of it in his trash can and another third in the bathroom trash can and tossed the rest in the toilet. *Flusshhh!* No one would be able to put that back together.

At ten o'clock, when he figured the movie would have been over anyway, Wyatt pulled the top comforter up over his feet and grabbed the stupid Lincoln book.

It was thin, seventy pages. He loved Mr. Clifton. Not like that. Just, cool. At least it wouldn't take all night.

He opened the cover. It was a bit crumbly at the spine. How old was this thing?

The full title read:

Joshua Fry Speed:
Lincoln's Most Intimate Friend
by Robert L. Kincaid

The copyright page said 1943. Wyatt figured back then *intimate* just meant close. Best friends. Maybe today it would be

Joshua Fry Speed: Lincoln's BFF

Maybe that's what he'd call his blog.

He opened the book at random. Page 55. It was a letter, signed

Yours Forever,
Lincoln.

Sounded like a love letter. Like it should be in Mackenzie's book, love letters between Abe and Mary. With séances thrown in to keep it interesting. It was weird that Abe had signed it "Lincoln." Wyatt scanned back to the top of page 54, where the letter began.

Springfield, October 5, 1842
Dear Speed:

It was a letter to Joshua Fry Speed. Did everyone write like this back then? Why was Abe calling him by his last name? It was like they were in PE together or something.

Wyatt started to read the letter. Joshua had been married eight months. Sounded like Abe had to talk him into it. And then Abe asked,

> **"But I want to ask a closer question,**
> **"Are you now in *feeling* as well as *judgment***
> **glad that you are married as you are?"**
> **From anybody but me this would be an**
> **impudent question, not to be tolerated;**
> **but I know you will pardon it in me.**
> **Please answer it quickly,**
> **as I feel impatient to know."**

Wyatt reasoned it through: So, Joshua got married because he judged he should, not because he felt it. And Abe wanted to know if the feeling came later.

When was this? He fished a piece of paper out of his jeans pocket and uncrumpled it to mark the page. It was Mackenzie's note, the *M* and *W* for their names inside a heart.

He ran downstairs to grab a fresh President Abraham Lincoln Timeline. Back in his room, the stiff, coffee-stained paper crackled as he unfolded it, and he searched for the year.

1842:   Reconciles with Mary Todd.
        Marries her on November 4.

This letter was before that wedding. Just a month before.

**"Please answer it quickly,
as I feel impatient to know."**

Abe was asking his BFF,

**"Are you now in *feeling* as well as *judgment*,
glad that you are married as you are?"**

Maybe Abe wasn't sure if he should get married, either. Joshua hadn't been.

Wyatt stared at the heart note from Mackenzie. Goose bumps broke out along his upper back and arms. *Whoa.* He and Mackenzie weren't married, but that was how he felt! He *judged*—it kind of made sense to be her boyfriend. But he didn't *feel* it. Not the way he was supposed to.

But . . .

The goose bumps traveled all the way along his spine, down his legs. The hair on his scalp stood up.

Was *their* reason for not feeling it the same as his?

It wasn't possible. Was it?

He turned the pages backward. This section was all letters, almost all of them from Abe to Joshua. He checked out how they ended:

**Ever Yours,
As Ever,
Yours Forever,
As Ever, Your Friend
Yours Forever,**

Who was this guy Joshua? Wyatt flipped to the beginning. He ran a store.

A tall, angular young man with lean, wrinkled cheeks and sad, gray eyes, walked into a general store in Springfield, Illinois, more than a century ago, and laid on the counter a pair of saddle bags which he carried in the crook of his long arm. He asked the young proprietor of the store the price of a mattress, blankets, sheets, coverlid, and a pillow for a single bed. The items came to seventeen dollars.

"It is perhaps cheap enough," the young man with the saddle bags said, **"but small as it is, I am unable to pay it. If you will credit me until Christmas, I will pay you then, if I do well; but if I do not, I may never be able to pay you."**

The proprietor looked up into the face of his prospective customer and was moved by the forlorn expression in his eyes. He said: *"You seem to be so much pained at contracting so small a debt, I think I can suggest a plan by which you can avoid the debt and at the same time attain your end. I have a large room with a double bed which you are welcome to share with me."*

"Where is your room?"

"Upstairs," the proprietor replied, pointing to a pair of winding stairs which led from the store to the room.

The tall young man picked up his saddle bags, went upstairs, set them down on the floor, returned below with a beaming countenance and exclaimed jovially:

"Well, Speed, I'm moved!"

That sounded weird. They didn't know each other, but Joshua offered to share his bed with him? That *was* pretty intimate.

> This episode is familiar to all students of the life
> of Abraham Lincoln. The date of its occurrence,
> April 15, 1837, marked the transition of Lincoln
> into a career which led to immortality."

Wyatt kept reading. Turned out Abe was really successful in Springfield. But long after he could afford his own bed, he still shared that bed with Joshua. They shared it for four years.

The bed!

Quickly, Wyatt thumbed back through the pages, scanning for the facts.

"1837"

"Springfield, Illinois"

"a double bed"

He raced out of his room to the stairs, nearly colliding with his dad, who was coming out of the laundry room with a basket of folded kitchen towels and napkins. His dad put a finger to his lips, signaling there were guests in Room 6. "Where are you going?" he whispered.

"Homework." Wyatt held up the book.

"Seems like there's more to it than you thought. Good thing we didn't watch the movie."

"Yeah. I guess you and Mom were right." Wyatt kept his head down. There was no way they could know he'd just started.

"Well, do your best. And don't stay up too late."

Wyatt nodded to get away and hustled one flight down, trying not to be too loud. Or too excited.

He opened the door to their Lincoln Room and hit the switch on the electric-posing-as-oil lamp. Orange-yellow light flickered across the rocking chair, the dresser, the sheets.

Suddenly, in his mind Wyatt saw a second pillow by the first. He blinked it away. Abe hadn't bought one, so maybe they shared the pillow, too?

He knew the dates but had to check anyway. The small bronze plaque on its wooden stand in front of the bed announced,

LINCOLN SLEPT HERE

1837–1841

It was theirs. The bed Abe and Joshua shared. It was *their* bed!

In *judgment* but not in *feeling*.

Was it code?

Could Abe and Joshua have been . . .

Gay?

Wyatt's legs gave way, and then he was sitting on the floor, heart pounding. He opened the book and read like his life depended on it.

It was past midnight when, back in his room, Wyatt went online. He'd read *Joshua Fry Speed: Lincoln's Most Intimate Friend* cover to cover, but now he hesitated, cursor in the search box. This was something he couldn't take back. His mom had disabled "clear history" and checked his browser once a week, part of their family Internet compromise: *If you'd be embarrassed for your mother to know you've been there, you shouldn't be there in the first place.* If it were up to his dad, they wouldn't have Internet at all.

But Wyatt had to know, and he could figure out how to cover his tracks later. He typed, *was lincoln gay?* and hit RETURN.

Fifty million results.

One of the hits on the first page was a review of some book, *The Intimate World of Abraham Lincoln*. There was that word again. *Intimate*. Wyatt toggled and did a book search instead. It was the only book that popped up for *abraham lincoln gay*.

But for *abraham lincoln*, 38,355 books came up. If the Gay thing came up in only one of them, how could it be true?

Wyatt's book didn't come out and say he was Gay, but those letters . . .

And Lincoln was a hero. Lots of people wouldn't want him to be in love with another guy. But what if he was?

Wyatt smoothed out the President Abraham Lincoln Timeline on his desk.

> 1837:   Moves to Springfield (new capital) and
> begins practicing as a trial lawyer.

Nothing about where he lived, or sharing a bed, or maybe falling in love with Joshua Fry Speed. The only stuff about Lincoln's personal life was

> 1840:   Becomes engaged to Mary Todd.
> 1841:   Breaks engagement to Mary Todd and
> plunges into deep depression. This is one
> of many bouts of depression that Lincoln
> suffered throughout his life.
> 1842:   Reconciles with Mary Todd.
> Marries her on November 4.

The Fatal First of January 1841 was supposed to be the trigger of Lincoln's giant depression. It was when he broke his engagement to Mary the first time around.

But in *Joshua Fry Speed: Lincoln's Most Intimate Friend*, January 1, 1841, was also when Joshua told Abe he was moving back to Kentucky.

Away from Abe. Marking the end of their four years of living together. The end of their sharing that bed one floor down from where Wyatt was sitting right now.

Nobody really had a reason why Abe broke things off with Mary the first time and got so depressed. But . . . what if Abe's depression wasn't about Mary, but about being freaked out about being in love with Joshua? About Joshua kind of breaking up with him, moving away, and eventually marrying that woman Fanny?

And then eight months after Joshua got married, Abe went ahead and married Mary because he *judged* it the right thing to do. The politically smart thing to do. Even if his heart, and Joshua's heart—their *feelings*—were elsewhere . . .

In judgment but not in feeling.

But no one's ever said anything about it!

Wyatt remembered that one book that came up in the search. *Or maybe when they did say it, no one listened.* He got back on the computer.

was president lincoln gay?

A lot of the sites that popped up were angry: "the very question insults the memory of our greatest president"—stuff like that.

One site argued that no one could be a "homosexual" before this Austrian guy invented the word for it in 1869, four years after John Wilkes Booth gunned down Lincoln in that theater. *What a load of crap. Guys falling in love with other guys didn't all of a sudden start when they came up with a word for it.*

I didn't need any words to know.

Wyatt found a video clip: *Was Lincoln Gay?* And hit PLAY.

Was Lincoln Gay?

A professor in a suit stands at a podium in a small conference room. Words on the screen read "Family Values in Christ Coalition Summit." He speaks with an I-know-better-than-you attitude.

PROFESSOR

Rumors of President Lincoln having a deviant "alternative lifestyle" are simply that—wild expressions of a shrill homosexual agenda that no serious historian takes seriously. And what proof do they have?

The professor holds up a copy of *The Intimate World of Abraham Lincoln* and sneers.

PROFESSOR

Conjecture and fantasy, by an activist with a pro-homosexual agenda. Pure trash.

He uses his foot to open the lid of a conveniently placed trash can and drops the book in with a clang.

PROFESSOR

Can you imagine lipstick and pink eye shadow on Lincoln's face on Mount Rushmore?

The video cuts to a cartoon image of that very thing, with a pink feather boa around Lincoln's made-up face on the mountainside. An unseen audience bursts out laughing.

Wyatt hit STOP.

He didn't want to dress up like a girl, or be a girl. And he didn't know if Lincoln did or didn't, but that had nothing to do with whether or not Lincoln was Gay. Or Bi. Or whatever you'd call it if Abe's *feeling* was for Joshua, instead of Mary. . . .

Next to the frozen image of Lincoln's Mt. Rushmore face in drag, the website suggested:

Other videos you might like:
Marcia Gay Harden Visits Mt. Rushmore
Dead Presidents Punk and Rock Washington, DC
George Washington's Gay Inspector General

What was that one about?
Cautiously, Wyatt hit PLAY.

George Washington's Gay Inspector General

A handsome teen guy sits in front of an outdoor-size Gay Pride Rainbow flag pinned to the wall behind him. He wears a rainbow bracelet and is strumming a fast intro on a blue acoustic guitar. The tune is "Yankee Doodle Dandy."

An inset picture of an oil painting pops into the frame next to him. It's of an old military guy in one of those white wigs from Revolutionary War time, in a gold vest with lots of medals pinned to his jacket.

Words scroll on the bottom of the screen:

Music: George M. Cohan
New Lyrics: Martin Sykes

|◄ ▶ ►|

The teen, Martin, smiles, teeth brilliant white against his darker skin. His fingers fly, building the song to the familiar chorus.

> MARTIN (sings)
> *Von Steuben's a Yankee Doodle Dandy!*
> *A Yankee Doodle who liked guys . . .*
> *Friedrich Wilhelm von Steu-eu-ben,*
> *Without him there'd be no Fourth of July!*

The inset image changes as Martin continues singing, showing other old paintings of:

Fireworks
Ben Franklin
Washington at Valley Forge, inspecting troops
And, finally, the famous painting *George Washington Crossing the Delaware,* the new flag of the United States of America unfurling behind him.

> MARTIN (sings)
> *Ben Franklin knew that our army, need-ed help*
> *General Washington, he knew it, too.*
> *Fried-rich. Went. To. Valley. Forge. Just. To.*
> *Train.   Our. Sol-diers.*
> *He's why America's here for you!*

Martin finishes the song with a flourish of strumming. For the first time, he looks directly at the camera.

> MARTIN
> And that's all true.

The video ended, and Wyatt stared at the guy on the screen, letting it sink in. He was so out. And proud. Probably lived in New York City, with some model boyfriend. And that song—a Gay general who helped America win the Revolutionary War against the British?

So cool.

The video player suggested another video, *Also from Martin Sykes:*

Legal Advocates of Oregon: Rhonda Sykes on Two Years of Speaking Truth to Power

Not so interesting. And he was getting distracted.

Back to Lincoln and those letters. What if this Kincaid guy who wrote *Joshua Fry Speed: Lincoln's Most Intimate Friend* was making it all up? What if the letters weren't even real?

Wyatt picked up the book and checked the boring stuff in the beginning. On the title page, above the year, it read, "Department of Lincolnalia, Lincoln Memorial University, Harrogate, Tennessee." The author couldn't have made up the letters and still gotten it published by a university named after Lincoln! They had to be real.

Still, Wyatt had never even heard of Joshua Fry Speed before. And if they were an item, wouldn't he have?

Maybe not. Maybe historians were trying to keep this a secret.

He'd never heard of von Steuben—and his being Gay—either, until a minute ago.

But since everyone loved Lincoln, if the world knew Abe was Gay—that he loved another guy—maybe they'd start to feel differently about Gay people. Maybe, if Abe was out, everybody Gay would be able to come out.

Wyatt had a first impression about Abraham Lincoln, that was for sure. But if he was going to pull off this blog post, he had a lot to do.

It was past 4:00 A.M. when Wyatt finished and his post was live on the school blog host. He unplugged his laptop and fast-carried it to the bathroom sink before the two-minute battery charge gave out. Careful not to electrocute himself, he leaned the laptop on its side under the faucet and turned the water on. It poured into the side slot, drenching the keyboard. Something inside whirred and shorted out. The screen went blank.

A dead computer tells no tales.

He carried it back to his desk wrapped in a towel, and spilled a glass of water on the wood floor right below the table edge. He let it soak in, making sure his story would make sense.

Tracks covered.

Wyatt fell into bed, head swimming. He thought about brushing his teeth, but just pulled up the three comforters, overwhelmed and desperately tired. As he lay there, waiting to slip into sleep, one thought surfaced.

Lincoln freed the slaves. Maybe now, he can free the Gays.

Maybe, he can free me.

Chapter 6

Book: *Joshua Fry Speed: Lincoln's Most Intimate Friend,*
by Robert Kincaid

QUEER AS A FIVE-DOLLAR BILL

First Impression Blog Post: Monday, January 12, 3:56 a.m.

President Abraham Lincoln Was Gay!

FACT: When Abraham Lincoln was 28 years old, he was a brand-new lawyer and moved to Springfield, Illinois. He went into Joshua Fry Speed's store to buy the stuff for a bed so he'd have somewhere to sleep.

FACT: Abe was so poor, he didn't even have $17 to pay for the stuff he'd need for his own bed.

FACT: Joshua told Abe he could share *his* bed.

FACT: Abe was a success as a lawyer and had the money, but still shared the bed with Joshua for four years!

FACT: The bed was a double bed, 53 inches wide (less than 4.5 feet) and not even 6 feet long.

FACT: Abe was 6 feet, 4 inches tall. Lying down, even like a soldier at attention, he'd cover 29 inches across from shoulder to shoulder.

FACT: If Joshua was average height (and the Internet says that in the mid-1800s, that was around 5 feet, 7 inches tall), his shoulders would have been at least 24 inches across.

FACT: 29 + 24 = 53. Not an inch to spare.

The facts add up: There's no way they could have shared that bed and not been touching practically the whole time. Here, I'll prove it.

Abraham Lincoln Was Gay: BEDMATES!

A hand moves away, and Wyatt backs up from the lens. He's in the Lincoln Room, black-suited Wax Lincoln by his side. Wyatt looks right at the camera.

WYATT
Okay . . . Hi. I'm Wyatt, and this is my video proof that President Abraham Lincoln was Gay. Or, at least, had a thing with Joshua Fry Speed. Like, a love thing.

I◀ ▶ ▶I

This . . . is a life-size wax figure of our sixteenth
president, six feet, four inches tall. And that . . .

Wyatt points over his shoulder to the bed, where the
old military mannequin, changed into his mismatched
Union dark blue wool coat, light blue pants, and
brown boots, lies on his back.

> WYATT
> Is a guy pretty much the size of Joshua Fry
> Speed.

Wyatt struggles to carry Wax Lincoln over
to the bed. The sculpture tips backward, and Wyatt
catches the right arm that's out to shake just before it
smacks into the sideboard and breaks. Cradling the
arm and leveraging Wax Lincoln onto the bed, Wyatt
talks to the camera.

> WYATT
> Lincoln was tall. He would have had to scrunch
> up in any bed, even one today, and this wax
> figure's knees don't bend.

The video jump-cuts, and Wyatt approaches to take
the camera off its tripod.

> WYATT
> Here . . .

The camera aims back at the bed. Wax Lincoln is on his
left side and at an angle, size 14 shoes sticking past the
footboard. His right arm rests across the other
mannequin's chest.

|◄ ▶ ►|

From the end of the bed, the camera pans left to right.
The two figures are pressed against each other, with
no extra room.

WYATT
See?

The camera flips around to show Wyatt's face, Lincoln
and the soldier on the bed behind him.

WYATT
They didn't need to share it. They chose to.
For four years! Do the math: Lincoln was Gay.

MR. GUZMAN FAKED a yawn as he examined Jennie's blog on his handheld tablet. "So, Lincoln established Thanksgiving as our national holiday. . . . Why should we care? Where's your first impression?" Their *I'm not a substitute teacher* walked the front of the room like it was his own personal kingdom. He'd been telling everyone what was wrong with their blog posts and why he'd given them some version of a C. Eight minutes of class left, and there were only four still standing: Jennie—who was under the ax—Mackenzie, Wyatt, and Jonathon.

Jennie giggled nervously.

Mr. Guzman continued his video game–worthy massacre. "You're in high school now, Miss Woo, and you need to dig deeper. C-minus, but I'm being generous."

Jennie giggled again, which Wyatt thought was just weird.

"And now, to use the technical term, the *batshit-crazy* book reports." That made the class titter. He swiped the screen to call up the next blog. "Miss Miller!"

Mackenzie stopped playing with the end of her fancy French braid and poised her fingers over her laptop keyboard, ready to take down every word Mr. Guzman said.

"Calling Lincoln an occultist and arguing that his belief that the living could communicate with the dead inspired his Gettysburg Address, among other speeches, is quite the first impression."

Mackenzie broke in, "I said it *influenced* him. Not inspired." She was the first one of them to protest at all. Wyatt gave her props for that. "It's possible Lincoln was just so in love with Mary that he went along with it, but he went to a séance! Surrounded with all the deaths in the Civil War, his own two sons dying, and the guilt . . . I think he at least wanted to believe that you could talk to dead people."

Mr. Guzman made a snapping sound with his mouth. "I'm not sure how you're going to prove that, but, either way, annotating *one* speech would have been sufficient. No one has time to read what would print out to be eighteen pages of material on a blog. Consider the math of it: I have four classes. "C-minus *again*."

The color drained from Mackenzie's face. Wyatt knew it was the lowest grade she'd ever gotten, and it could ruin her perfect GPA.

"Speaking of math, Mr. Yarrow . . ." Mr. Guzman put down the tablet on his desk, entwined his fingers, and stretched them out, like this particular grading murder was going to be extra work.

Wyatt tried to keep his face blank. He told himself he wouldn't react, no matter what happened.

"What a load of crap you posted."

Jonathon led the room's explosion of laughter.

Mr. Guzman waited for them to settle. "For someone whose family lives and breathes the history of Abraham Lincoln, I must say I was roundly disappointed. While I applaud your use of video, I found it hard to believe your book *came out*—forgive the pun—and said that Abraham Lincoln was Gay."

Whispers of disbelief swirled around him. Wyatt guessed no one had read his post.

Mr. Guzman continued, "In fact, when I spoke with Mr. Clifton at the library an hour ago, he assured me that was *not* in your book. Thus, what you've presented to the world is *lies,* or, if I'm continuing to be generous, I might call it *offensive conjecture.* A book report is not where we make things up. F. The one failing mark for the entire ninth grade."

But . . . I didn't make it up!

With Jonathon snickering and nasty stares boring into him from all sides, Wyatt felt Thai chili pepper–level heat engulf him. He sank down in his chair.

Jonathon stage-whispered to Charlie, "What a fag!"

Charlie answered, in the same *let everyone hear but pretend it's just between us voice,* "Yeah, Mosquito Ball fag!"

They cracked up.

"Gentlemen, that's enough." A scowling Mr. Guzman picked up his tablet again. "And finally, Mr. Rails . . ."

Jonathon swung around from smirking at Wyatt. He'd been giving him that *I'm so happy to watch you crash and burn* attitude all first-period PE, too, but Wyatt couldn't figure out how Jonathon had known in advance Mr. Guzman had failed him.

"I saved your critique for last, because, frankly, even though you clocked in with only one minute to spare"—here, Mr. Guzman's voice changed, sounding pleasantly surprised—"you used your time relatively well."

Jonathon grinned, letting every one of his dentist brochure–white teeth show.

Mr. Guzman continued, "Mr. Rails's book contains transcripts of the famous Lincoln-Douglas Debates. In an elegant display of how 'the medium is the message,' his entire blog post took the form of a debate rebuttal to Mr. Yarrow's blogged piece of . . . well, we've established what it was."

Waves of laugher smashed into Wyatt. He slipped down even lower, wishing he could disappear.

"Also, Mr. Rails used a quote from his book, citing the source material. And his post was . . . let's be real, people, I had to read one hundred and forty-two of these, blessedly short. Nicely done, Mr. Rails. You would have received a B-plus. But bullying, in any form, is not acceptable in my classroom, and your blogs are an extension of that domain. Accordingly, I've dropped you down to a B-minus."

"Dude! Still the highest grade in the class!" Jonathon bragged, and high-fived Charlie. Then he turned and aimed his finger like a gun at Mackenzie, all, *I got you this time.*

Mr. Guzman raised his voice to be heard. "Note that you will need to delete the personal attack as soon as humanly possible."

Personal attack? Wyatt couldn't see the screen in Mr. Guzman's hand.

Mr. Guzman clicked his tongue and set down his handheld computer. "That's everyone. Remember, as we move forward, to state your thesis, and then back it up with evidence from your primary source materials." He walked over and circled *Thesis* on the white board. "Keep in mind that the more you blog, the more traffic you'll get. I expect you to address the concerns we discussed . . ."

Wyatt stopped listening. He'd ask Mackenzie to borrow her phone right after class—and turn it on—so he could get online and see what Jonathon had said about him.

He wanted to know. He needed to know. But his stomach clenched at the thought of what he'd discover.

Jonathon Rails's Book Report Blog
for Mr. Guzman's 9th Grade History Class
Lincolnville High School

Book: *The Lincoln-Douglas Debates,*
by Abraham Lincoln and Stephen A. Douglas

REAL MEN. REAL AMERICA.

First Impression Blog Post: Monday, January 12, 5:59 a.m.

Lincoln was not gay.

Our greatest president ever, Abraham Lincoln, the founder of the Republican Party, was arguing with his advisors and said to them:

"If you call a sheep's tail a leg, how many legs does a sheep have?"

"Five," the advisors agreed.

"No," replied Lincoln. **"A sheep only has four legs."**
Then Lincoln added, **"Calling a tail a leg doesn't make it so"** (page 4).

Abraham Lincoln was one of the greatest debaters ever. Calling him gay doesn't make him gay.

And calling him gay, like Wyatt Yarrow did in his blog? You'd have to be some kind of gay idiot to do that.

"I want you to delete your post." It was the first thing Mr. Guzman said in their "chat" after school. "Your whole blog, in fact. Start over."

"I don't want to start over!" Reading Jonathon's blog post had made Wyatt want to prove this even more.

Mr. Guzman made a clicking sound and sighed. "Mr. Yarrow, I failed you because you were making things up—"

"I didn't!"

"And a failing grade requires me to notify your parents."

"That's not fair! I worked hard on it, and it's true!" Wyatt realized he was shouting and fought to get himself back under control.

Mr. Guzman swiveled in his desk chair. "You really believe your book, this"—he scanned a spreadsheet he'd printed out—"*Joshua Fry Speed*, proves Abraham Lincoln was Gay?"

"Yes."

"It's the first I've heard of it."

"I thought we were supposed to dig deep."

Wyatt's teacher chuckled at that. "Not so far that you lose touch with reality. There is a core to the earth, after all. Molten lava, I believe."

"You're letting Mackenzie do séances. . . ." Wyatt got an inspiration. "And if I pull it, what's Jonathon going to debate?"

Mr. Guzman seemed on the fence.

"Come on . . . I read the whole book, I did the assignment. I've got a thesis! Let me prove it."

Mr. Guzman considered. "David Rice Atchison, president eleven point five, huh?" He was quiet for a moment more. Wyatt waited, not sure which way it would go. Finally, his teacher decided. "How about I let you do a make-up post? And when I say *make-up*, you need to show me you're *not* making it up. I want to see sound reasoning, and citations." He stood and started packing his satchel. "I'll give you till midnight Friday to post something to back up your thesis, such as it is, so I can see where this is going. And if you can't convince me, then on Monday I'm afraid you'll have to start over."

Wyatt was relieved he was getting a chance.

"I'm curious." Mr. Guzman paused and looked over at Wyatt. "You don't have any new material on Lincoln—your book is older than I am. So, if you're working from the same body of evidence as the rest of the world, why are you suddenly able to see that Lincoln was Gay, when no one else has?"

Wyatt felt the trap there, and he blustered, "Well, it's not like I'm Gay or anything! I'm dating Mackenzie!"

Mr. Guzman gave a nod. "She seems like a girl who knows what she wants."

The fact that he didn't just slam Gay people was a silence that shouted in Wyatt's mind. He needed to test the waters a little more. How would Jonathon put it? "I don't know any fags myself, but if Lincoln was one, that's important, isn't it?"

Mr. Guzman studied Wyatt for a long moment. "Mr. Yarrow. I don't want to hear that word in my classroom again."

"Sorry," Wyatt shrugged, elated but trying to keep his emotions in check. "What about you telling my folks?"

After a tongue click, Mr. Guzman said, "I'll hold off on contacting your parents. For now. Do we have an understanding?"

Fine. He'd show that jerk Jonathon and Mr. Guzman that he was right. That Abe was Gay. But all he said was, "Yeah," and got the heck out of there before Mr. Guzman could change his mind.

Wyatt was in the living room, on the red-and-yellow Turkish rug by the fireplace. If asked, he could tell guests these kinds of rugs were popular in the 1800s. But this one was from Costco.

He had a bunch of volumes of *The Complete Works of Abraham Lincoln* out of the glass bookcase, and he was going through the huge index (all of Volume 12) when the doorbell rang. Which was odd, because they were kind of like a hotel—during the day, people just walked in. The clouds were already showing off pink and gold sunset colors, and it was just after 5:00 p.m.

Wyatt heard his mom open the front door. "Ira? Where did the time go—is it seven already? Let me get Gregory. . . ."

"Um, no. Actually, Mrs. Yarrow, no bowling for me tonight. I'm here on official library business."

Wyatt put Volume 12 on top of *Joshua Fry Speed* to hold his spot in both, curious. What was Mr. Clifton talking about?

"Really, Ira. You can call me Liz. 'Mrs. Yarrow' makes me sound like my mother-in-law."

"I just feel we should keep things official. Me being here on business and all."

Wyatt inched to the doorway, careful to keep out of sight.

"Oh!" His mom chuckled. "You make it sound like you work for the FBI!"

"I wish I could find some humor in this as well, Mrs. Yarrow. Unfortunately, there's a matter about which I might lose my job, and I need your help. Specifically, I need Wyatt's help."

Mine?

His mom's voice got quieter. "Come in. Wyatt's doing homework in the living room. This Lincoln blog project has him all fired up."

"Ira!" Wyatt's dad's voice. "You're early!"

There was a pause. Wyatt guessed they were shaking hands.

"He has something he needs to discuss with Wyatt?" His mom tried to explain, but she sounded baffled. Wyatt was, too.

Adult steps came down the hall. Wyatt scrambled back to his pile of books, pretending to study. As they walked in, he was underlining *Mrs. Abraham Lincoln, letters* to in his notebook.

"Wyatt?" his dad said.

To seem busy, Wyatt added an exclamation point. He glanced up, feigning surprise.

"Sorry to interrupt you. Your mom and I love that you're studying; it's just that Mr. Clifton stopped by, and he's saying he needs our help."

Their town librarian was sweating, and it was January. What was going on?

Mr. Clifton stammered out the words: "Wyatt. Th-th-the book about President Lincoln I gave you . . ."

Wyatt made a huge effort not to let his eyes move to it, under Volume 12, right in front of him. One brown corner was poking out. "Yeah?"

"I . . . I made a mistake in allowing it to be checked out. You see, it's really a reference book, and I've violated a rather important guideline of library science by allowing it to enter circulation."

Wyatt thought about the crumbly spine and how he'd been careful with it. But right now, it *was* being squished. "I didn't hurt it or anything!"

"I just . . . I need to get it back."

"But I need it for my report! I'm supposed to have it for six weeks!"

"I'm sure we can find you another book. That one needs to come back to the library. Tonight."

Wyatt couldn't hold the words in. "But you gave it to me! *You never know where a book can take you,* remember?"

Mr. Clifton flushed and puffed out his cheeks. "I have no idea what you're talking about. Every Lincoln book was assigned randomly, and your getting a reference book was simply a mistake."

He's lying!

"The bottom line is, I need that book back, now." Mr. Clifton took a step toward Wyatt, but Wyatt's dad got between them.

"Ira . . . I don't know how appropriate this is. Wyatt didn't do anything wrong."

"I'm not saying he did. It's just that I could lose my job over this!"

"That's ridiculous." Wyatt's mom rolled her eyes. "No one's going to fire you for checking out a reference book."

Mr. Clifton sniffed. "Some of us serve at the whim of the mayor. You should understand that."

Wyatt's dad shifted to the tone of voice he used when someone complained about running out of hot water, or the rooms being too drafty, and he tried to convince them that what they got was actually what they had wanted in the first place—a real Civil War–era experience. "What's the harm in letting the boy have the book for now? I've used the Historical Reference section. It's not like there are hordes of people lined up for those books. He'll return it safe and sound when it's due."

Mr. Clifton gaped at the three of them. "You don't understand!"

"We'll make sure he returns it not a day late. But until then, Wyatt has homework." With an iron grip on his arm, Wyatt's dad guided Mr. Clifton out of the room. It felt really good, his dad standing up for him and everything.

His mom gave Wyatt a worried look, then followed them.

He listened to the adults argue in the entry hall. Mr. Clifton's voice was shrill. "I told her no one's going to believe a high school kid's book report, but the mayor wants this dealt with. Have you seen his blog post?"

There was a pause, like they were calling it up on the reception computer.

Moving quietly, Wyatt took *Joshua Fry Speed: Lincoln's Most Intimate Friend,* turned it so the plain back cover faced out, and sandwiched it in the glass bookcase behind Volumes 11 and 12 of *The Complete Works of Abraham Lincoln.* Then he pulled out Volumes 1 through 10 so they were all even.

Completely hidden.

He could hear his video playing on the tinny desk speakers. With a twist of the old-fashioned skeleton key, he locked the bookcase and slid the key into his jeans pocket. Slipping out to the stairs, he stayed silent as a Civil War ghost. He stopped on the second-floor landing, listening.

Mr. Clifton cleared his throat. "It's like Pandora's box."

Who?

"All hell is going to break loose because of this," Mr. Clifton continued. "I'm just trying to close it again."

But he gave me the book on purpose! Does he know about me? Wyatt tried to figure it out. Maybe Mr. Clifton had seen him hide *Absolutely* . . . But if he did know, and that was why he had given Wyatt *Joshua Fry Speed,* wasn't it because he wanted Wyatt to find out about Lincoln?

He couldn't hear what his parents said, but Mr. Clifton's words hit him in the gut. "Did Wyatt tell you he got an F on this report?"

That bastard.

Wyatt snuck the rest of the way up to the third floor. He had to get ready for the inquisition.

A thought stopped him at the hallway bookcase by Room 8. His laptop was dead—at breakfast, his mom had given him a twenty-minute lecture about responsibility, and how he wouldn't get a new computer until he could buy one with his own money. Given that he barely had twenty dollars saved up and made only twenty-nine cents for every coffee-aged document they sold downstairs, that was going to take a while.

The reception computer was off-limits, except for homework. His parents and Mr. Clifton were on that now, anyway . . . but they did have this old set of encyclopedias. Wyatt had never really thought of the cream-blue-and-red-striped, leather-bound set as anything more than period wallpaper, but maybe it had something on Pandora. After all, Wyatt figured, that was what people did before the Internet, right?

He grabbed Volume 18, ORN-PHT, and headed to his room.

Turned out Pandora was this girl who got a box from the king of the gods. Only she wasn't allowed to open it. Of course, she did open it, and from inside all the different kinds of evil escaped into the world.

Why would the truth about Abe loving another guy be evil?

As the evils were escaping, Pandora panicked and slammed the lid shut. But that left only one thing trapped inside: *hope.*

Wyatt wondered if she ever let that out.

He wished he hadn't ruined his laptop after all. Maybe in computer lab he could add his blog as an external link to the Wikipedia article on Lincoln.

The world needed to know, and he wanted to tell everybody. It was time to let hope out.

But first he'd have to deal with his dad and mom and make sure they didn't know about *him*.

Chapter 8
Monday, January 12

TWENTY QUESTIONS

Wyatt's mom's turn:

1. "What were you thinking?"
2. "Why would you say Lincoln was Gay?"
3. "Does this book come right out and say he was Gay?"
4. "Well, if it doesn't, why would you make something like that up?"
5. "So you, without even a ninth-grade education, are suddenly a Lincoln scholar?"
6. "You know more than all those PhDs and experts combined?"
7. "Were you going to tell us about the F?
8. "Do you just want to fail out of school now?"
9. "It's like a tidal wave about to smash our boat! Did you ever stop and think what effect this could have?"
10. "What about your father—and all of this, his dream?"
11. "How are we going to keep our business?"

12. "How are you ever going to get a job?"
13. "You don't think HR departments check on things like this?"
14. "Colleges?"
15. "You could be sued! It's called *libel*. Heard of it?"
16. "Can we erase it from the Internet?"
17. "We were right when we said you weren't mature enough yet to be on social media, weren't we?"
18. "Why didn't you just give the book back to him?"
19. "What are people going to say?"

Wyatt's dad's turn:
20. "Are you Gay?"

"I have a girlfriend—I'm not Gay!" Wyatt managed to work up some outrage with his lie. "But Lincoln was!"

He wasn't ready, and they were too freaked out. What if they hated him when they found out—stopped loving him? If they knew the truth, would anyone love him, ever again?

He'd thought this would be a way to break the news gently. *I mean, if Abe was Gay, and great, it shouldn't be that big a deal, right?*

Wrong. Look how upset they are about Lincoln. And he's not their only son.

"Lincoln was not Gay!" The pressure-cooker vein in Wyatt's dad's forehead stood out. "Just saying it, and on somewhere as public as the Internet, is like inviting disaster—the word of mouth on this will kill us!"

Gay = disaster. Gee, thanks, Dad.

"Why? Why is it so bad if he was?" Wyatt was getting mad, and it was safer to move the focus and defend someone else's right to be Gay—someone long dead, far from him. "If you read the letters, if you look at the facts, it's really obvious that Abe was in love with Joshua—and that makes them Gay, or Bi, or whatever you want to call it, but two guys in love with each other? That's pretty Gay! Which means that history is just a bunch of lies we're being fed. And we're feeding them!" He turned on his mom. "And the parade, all about Abe and Mary's romance? It's like this conspiracy to make a famous Gay person straight. I mean, who else was Gay that the people in charge of history aren't telling us about? Alexander the Great? Shakespeare? Gandhi?"

His mom frowned at him. "Sweetie . . . you can't start imagining that everyone is Gay."

Wyatt's whole face felt scrunched up. "Well, why is it okay to imagine that everyone in history is straight, when we know that can't possibly be true, either?"

His dad measured every word. "Lincoln. Was. Not. Gay."

"Yeah, Dad. I hear you. But you're wrong. And I'm going to prove it."

BEFORE HE EVEN got to the History classroom door, Mackenzie pulled Wyatt aside. She sounded angry. "Did you see this?" She handed him her phone. Wyatt took it and read.

**Jonathon Rails's Book Report Blog
for Mr. Guzman's 9th Grade History Class**
Lincolnville High School

Book: *The Lincoln-Douglas Debates,*
by Abraham Lincoln and Stephen A. Douglas

REAL MEN. REAL AMERICA. NO QUEERS.

Blog Post: Monday, January 13, 4:42 p.m.

Wyatt is a big queer.

That's why he's saying one of the greatest presidents in our nation's history was gay.

By choosing a hero from our history to make *pretend* gay, Wyatt is trying to make himself feel better about his own sick lifestyle choice.

It's like Lincoln said in his first public debate with Douglas (page 32):

**"With public sentiment, nothing can fail.
Without it, nothing can succeed."**

So Wyatt can try to rewrite history by inventing all this stuff about Lincoln being gay, but as long as no one believes him, he won't succeed.

Keep reading this blog, because I'm here to save history. And all Wyatt's doing is letting everyone know that he's a big homo.

Wyatt looked up at Mackenzie, feeling shell-shocked.

"You've got to stop saying this stuff about Lincoln," she told him. "It's becoming a problem for us."

"Us?" Wyatt said. "He's trash-talking me, thank you very much."

"I'm your girlfriend." Mackenzie pulled her black skirt straighter. "This affects me, too! It's like you're on some vendetta to ruin Lincoln's reputation."

Wyatt could feel the anger building inside him. "Why does it diminish who he was or what he did if he loved another guy?"

"You can't seriously be asking me that. That's, like, the gayest question I've ever heard. Lincoln was married!"

"That's what Gay people did back then. They hid how they really felt—"

Mackenzie cut him off. "They had four children, two of whom died—Eddie at four, Willie when he was twelve. Lincoln suffered huge depressions about it, and Mary? She was a wreck, even with the séances. How can you have so little respect for her legacy? For their whole family?"

Strolling to their classroom, Jonathon lobbed, "Hey, homo!" at Wyatt, then paused to check Mackenzie out. "Heyyy, Mackenzie."

Homo? He'd show Jonathon. Fighting past the awkwardness, Wyatt leaned forward and pursed his lips to kiss his girlfriend. Mackenzie stepped back, away from him. He knew she was feeling used. And he was using her—or he'd just *tried* to. He could feel the shame rising up his neck to his ears. The start-of-class bell rang.

Mackenzie sounded bitter as she eyed Wyatt coldly. "You have a decision to make. Lincoln and Mary had this beautiful, traditional family—and there's power in that. Maybe because you have it, you don't appreciate just how precious it is. But if we're going to stay together, you need to stop saying that Lincoln was Gay. You need to start believing in the beauty of family. Otherwise, I can't keep doing this." She stomped into the classroom.

Jonathon hung back, smirking. "It must be hard for a Queer to keep a girl happy. Especially one as hot as Mackenzie."

Wyatt's hands balled into fists, but he didn't dare say any of the million comebacks swirling in his mind, all of which started with *Shut up!*

Instead, Wyatt stared at the linoleum and started planning the stuff he could say about Jonathon online—how'd he get to be so muscle-bound at sixteen, anyway? If they drug-tested for the Olympics, why not for high school athletes? Under his breath, Wyatt said, "Just wait till you read *my* blog. . . ."

There was a tongue click, and then Mr. Guzman said, "There's a saying about how getting something off the Internet is like getting pee out of a swimming pool." When he spoke, both Wyatt and Jonathon realized their teacher was standing in the doorway, listening. "You can try to cover it up, but it's always going to be there. Why don't you gentlemen join us? We need to have a class discussion about flame wars, and how yours stops now."

"HELLO, WYATT?" THE woman had called his cell in the middle of his algebra homework.

"Yeah?" he answered cautiously. He didn't recognize her voice.

"This is Roz, from Q Satellite Radio. I'd like to interview you about your blog."

"Uh, wow." Wyatt got up and closed the door to his bedroom. She sounded friendly.

"We're always interested in local LGBTQ news with national interest."

National interest? "That . . . sounds cool. But I'm not . . ." He couldn't say the word.

"We won't even talk about you," Roz assured him. "Just the blog and Lincoln. Okay?"

"Okay."

"And before I start recording, you're eighteen, so I don't need parental permission, right?"

"Actually," Wyatt started, but Roz cut him off.

"I'm going to stop you right there, before I hear anything I can't unhear."

There was a moment of quiet that made Wyatt nervous.

"Let me ask you this," Roz said. "Do you think your parents listen to *Q Satellite Radio: News for the Lesbian, Gay, Bi, Trans, Questioning, and Queer Community?*"

Wyatt snorted a laugh. "That's a no."

"Well, then. I'll ask again. And this time, I'm recording. Hi, Wyatt. Just confirming: You're eighteen, so you don't need parental permission?"

Wyatt swallowed hard. Who knew? Maybe getting on this radio program and talking about his blog would even help him win the who-can-get-the-most-visits contest, and then he could get those new running shoes. Get an A in history. Be one of the grand marshals in the parade. And more people would know the truth about Lincoln.

But his dad and mom . . . Well, like she said. They wouldn't even know.

"Yeah, I'm eighteen," he heard himself say. "We don't need it."

Q SATELLITE RADIO: News for the Lesbian, Gay, Bi, Trans, Questioning and Queer Community

Transcript of Thursday, January 15, Broadcast
7:07 – 7:09 p.m., Pacific Time

ROZ: Next, we have a local news story that will warm your Gay little hearts. When you were in high school, what did you want to do? Get over your acne? Get the girl? Get the boy? Get both? Oregon high-schooler Wyatt has set his sights quite a bit higher—he wants to change the world.

WYATT: I just think, if people knew the truth, things would be different.

ROZ: And that truth?

WYATT: Lincoln was Gay.

ROZ: That's Abraham Lincoln he's speaking of. And Wyatt should know. He's something of a Lincoln expert.

WYATT: So, Lincoln wrote all these letters to this guy, Joshua Fry Speed, and they're in this book . . .

ROZ: Wyatt says that the 175-year-old letters reveal something no one would have expected.

WYATT: I think he loved Speed. But they didn't have Gay marriage back then. They didn't have any chance . . .

ROZ: Not like today. But even today, there are still places in our world where it's illegal to be Gay. Illegal to follow your heart. Illegal to just be yourself. And Wyatt wants to change that, with his blog on President Lincoln's love life, *Queer as a Five-Dollar Bill.* What do you hope happens with your blog?

WYATT: I hope people look at it and really think about it. If Lincoln loved another guy, it says something about who he was. About who anybody can be. It can change how everyone sees Gay people. It can change . . . the world!

ROZ: Pretty inspiring. Thanks for talking with us, Wyatt, and good luck with changing the world. It needs teenagers like you.

WYATT: Thanks, Roz.

ROZ: That was Wyatt, who attends high school, and whose family owns the Lincoln Slept Here B and B, in Lincolnville, Oregon.

"It turned out to be a great piece," Roz said. She'd emailed Wyatt the audio file, and he'd snuck down to the Reception computer to listen to it.

It had been pretty cool to hear himself, even if it was satellite radio and nobody he knew would ever hear it. "Hey, Roz?" he asked when he called her afterward. A question nagged at him. "How did you find out about my blog?"

"Our tip line, actually." Roz explained. "We're always looking for stories, but this one came to us. The caller didn't give a name but left your website and phone number. They said it was a story that could be a big deal."

Mackenzie? Wyatt wondered. "Was it a girl?"

"No, sounded like a boy," Roz said. "I remember because he called it 'Death Star big,' which was a rather unique way of putting it."

Death Star big? Who the heck?

He had no idea.

"Oh well. Thanks, Roz."

"Sure."

Chapter 11

Friday, January 16

"THE RAID ON the arsenal at Harper's Ferry happened more than a year before Lincoln was elected president!" Mr. Guzman was in the middle of telling them about this White abolitionist, John Brown, and how he had tried to start an armed slave revolt, when the class phone rang and Wyatt was summoned to the principal's office. Everyone went, "Ooooh!" like he was in trouble.

He had a sinking feeling that he was.

Leering at him, Jonathon had dragged a finger across his own neck, international sign language for *you're so dead.*

So now Wyatt was fidgeting in the chair where the school secretary had told him to wait, with no idea what he'd done. Principal Jackson's door opened, and Coach Rails paused on his way out. Scratching at his half-grown-in Lincoln beard, he called back over his shoulder, "Andrew! Your next victim is here."

Victim?

"Send Mr. Yarrow in."

Wyatt kept his eyes on his feet, to avoid looking at Coach Rails or

Principal Jackson, and sat in the chair opposite the principal's desk—somewhere he'd never been before. The words crashed into him like a stormy sea. "Wildly irresponsible." "Reputations are fragile things." "The risk of retraction is that it would allow the conversation to continue!"

Was this about the radio interview? Principal Jackson didn't seem like the kind of guy who listened to Q Satellite Radio.

"God forbid the press gets ahold of this," Principal Jackson was saying.

So he didn't know about it. Wyatt let out a long breath, trying to calm down. It didn't work.

"Son! Look at me."

Wyatt clamped his teeth together to keep from showing anything on his face and looked up.

"This, unfortunately, will become a distraction for your fellow students. And I am sorely tempted to suspend you until we are past that distraction." Principal Jackson used a wooden fork to rake the sand in his desktop Zen garden, carefully lifting each stone to make his raked lines perfect and then setting it back down. "And if you are suspended, beyond failing History, if you miss too many days in all your subjects, we will be required to hold you back and have you repeat ninth grade."

Oh, man. Dad and Mom would freak!

Principal Jackson went on and on and on about how what Wyatt had done was a reflection not just on Lincolnville High School but on their whole town. Wyatt's eyes wandered to a framed picture of Principal Jackson shaking hands with Mayor Rails at the library consolidation ceremony, American stars and stripes and Oregon's blue-and-gold state flag behind them. Principal Jackson and the mayor were tight.

The next photo over was of the principal's family trout fishing with Jonathon's. It was an old picture, from back when Wyatt, Jonathon, and Mackenzie had been in third grade. The three of them had actually been friends. Or at least friendly. Becca, Jonathon's sister who was one grade under them, was there next to her brother, her at-the-time candy cane–striped prosthetic leg unmistakable. Jonathon had his arm around her and a big smile on his face. And a *Star Wars* T-shirt! Wyatt studied it to make sure. Yeah, Luke holding a lightsaber. Jonathon had been so into *Star Wars* back then.

Death Star big . . . What the heck?

Why would Jonathon help get the word out about Lincoln being Gay, when he was such an ass about it in real life and on his blog? That didn't make any sense.

His leg was jittery, but under his hand, Wyatt could feel the outline of the skeleton key in his pocket. Those letters were his proof. He wanted to tell Principal Jackson that Mr. Guzman had given him another chance. That he was working on another blog post that would really prove Abe loved Joshua. But would that get Mr. Guzman in trouble, too?

"Do you have *anything* to say for yourself?" Principal Jackson asked, and then waited for . . . what? A teary apology?

Wyatt tried to keep his voice reasonable. "But . . . I just did the assignment!"

"Entirely too many people have found out about this."

Wyatt hadn't thought to check his visitor stats on the reception computer last night, when he'd added his blog as an external link on the Lincoln Wikipedia entry. It had *sort of* been homework. . . . Was that link already working? Had listeners from the radio show checked it out? "How many people?"

Principal Jackson's hand jerked, ruining his neat rows. "Too many." He exhaled like some asthmatic dinosaur and this time pulled out all five rocks, lining them up one by one on the side of the Zen garden's wood frame.

If it's enough to bother him, that's pretty cool.

Carefully dragging the rake the other way through the grains of sand, Principal Jackson said, "We need you to delete your blog and stop all this nonsense about Lincoln being . . . well, you know what you're saying."

It's not nonsense.

Wait . . . *we?*

Principal Jackson. The mayor. Mr. Clifton. None of them cared whether it was true or not. They just didn't want people thinking Lincoln was Queer. Somehow, it was like that would make them look bad. They wanted to squash it.

"Son, am I getting through to you?" Principal Jackson raised his voice like he was shouting across the cafeteria, not four feet away on the other side of his desk, holding a doll-size yard tool. "It's your choice: the path forward can be pleasant, or difficult." He set down the fourth stone and started raking a circle around it. "It's a lot like firing a gun. The bullet goes forward, but the gun kicks back. Every action has its reaction." Final stone in his hand, he frowned at the arrangement like it was a chess game and he was losing.

Wyatt took his chance to escape. "I hear you. Can I leave now?"

"Fine." Principal Jackson waved him away. "But this gets resolved ASAP, or you will start to experience serious consequences. Consequences that will start with three weeks of detention if this isn't gone from the Internet by the end of the day!"

Wyatt couldn't get out of there fast enough.

Wyatt logged on to the reception computer the second he got home. There was a statistical counter Mr. Guzman had set up, so they could know how many people were reading their blogs, and from where. So they could see that it was "truly a global enterprise." He found the link and clicked on it.

It took him a moment to figure it out. It was a graph chart, with green vertical lines. Actually, just one vertical line on the far right, which he guessed was the scale, to show how high you could go. The rest were super-short green rectangles. At the bottom were some names.

The first was C. Anderson—four visits. That was one from Mr. Guzman, and maybe Charlie's parents and an unlucky uncle. Wyatt scanned across, pausing at a bigger rectangle. M. Miller—sixty-eight visits. *Ouch.* Usually people liked to check out Mackenzie's work so they knew what to do to get an A. This time, it was like they'd been giddy to see her first C. Another rectangle, bigger than the others. J. Rails—ninety-two visits. How many of them had read the post where he'd called Wyatt a Queer homo? Mr. Guzman had made him take it down, but it had been online for almost a whole day.

Had he done better than Jonathon? It was possible, wasn't it, if Principal Jackson was so bent out of shape about it. . . .

He found his name, last, as usual. W. Yarrow. Wyatt squinted, then toggled the screen bigger. It wasn't a scale. The tall green vertical line was his blog hits: 1,742.

One thousand seven hundred and forty-two? *Oh my gosh, people are reading it. Not just people in school. People!*

"Whoo!" The shout echoed through their downstairs, past the soldier mannequin, past Wax Lincoln, all the way to his soldier in the photo. It felt amazing. Like he was being heard.

Wyatt shut the browser, in case anyone walked in, and headed over to his soldier, who was smiling out at him. No weapon in his hands at all. How do you fight without a weapon? Maybe . . . with words. Like Lincoln's speeches, or a blog.

And maybe, all those years ago, Wyatt's soldier had been Gay, too. *Like me. Like Lincoln. And now people are finding out.*

But . . . Wyatt didn't want to get three weeks of detention. Or get suspended. Or have to redo ninth grade! If he dropped the whole thing and deleted his post before midnight, Principal Jackson, Mayor Rails, and Mr. Clifton would be happy. As long as none of them tuned in to yesterday's Q Satellite Radio news, which seemed unlikely.

And even if his parents heard it, nothing in it said anything about his being straight—or not. Roz had been good to her word. He might still get away with his dad and mom never finding out how he really felt about girls . . . and guys, at least until he was out of high school. He and Mackenzie could stay together as a couple, keeping Jonathon and his sharks at bay. He could get Mackenzie's help doing a new book report. Maybe even share her book about Abe and Mary, and they'd lean over it and kiss . . .

A mental record scratch stopped the fantasy. He wasn't that guy. He wasn't that straight guy.

He'd been working all week on his new proof post. And if he didn't put it up by midnight, Mr. Guzman was going to make him start all over. And deleting that first post would be like admitting he'd made up the whole thing about Lincoln being Gay, when it was the truth!

But . . . if he kept going with this, if he blogged more about Abe loving Joshua, Jonathon would keep calling him Gay.

Then he could keep denying it. After all, he'd never even kissed a guy, and he'd kissed Mackenzie—twice! So that *kind of* made him straight, in action, at least.

The words came to his mind unbidden:

In judgment but not in feeling . . .

He needed to talk to someone. His mom would just say, "Don't make any waves." And how could he explain to her or his dad why it was so important to tell the world about this, without explaining everything? And Mackenzie's ultimatum had been pretty clear. . . . His soldier just kept smiling—he was cute and all, but what Wyatt needed was an impartial friend to talk to.

And he didn't have one.

The mail slot rattled, and Wyatt heard stuff drop in the basket. His dad hated their personal mail sitting out for everyone to see, so he headed over to get it and put it on the desk in his parents' bedroom. Before he even got to the basket, the doorbell rang, making him jump.

The mail carrier was bobbing to the rapping Wyatt could hear through her headphones as he opened the door. "Registered Express Mail!" she shouted. "Needs a signature." She held out a pen.

Once he signed the green slip of paper, the mail carrier tore it off and gave him the cardboard envelope. It was addressed to him. He had a bad feeling about it, and didn't open it until he got to his room.

Office of the Head Librarian
Lincolnville Public Library
100 South Lincoln Boulevard
Union Square
Lincolnville, OR 20252

January 15

Wyatt Yarrow
542 Hayes Street
Lincolnville, OR 20252

Re: Your Violation of Our Lending Agreement:
Financial Obligations & Legal Repercussions

Dear Mr. Yarrow:

We regret this letter is necessary, but your refusal to return *Joshua Fry Speed*, a rare reference book in our library's collection that was erroneously circulated on January 7 and checked out to your account, has left us no choice.

You are in violation of our lending agreement, and pursuant to the laws of the State of Oregon (Oregon Revised Statute (ORS) 375.975, regarding the willful or malicious detention of library property), if the title is not returned by 9:00 a.m. on Monday, January 19, your standing as an unemancipated minor and your willful and malicious misconduct will constitute grand theft from our library facility and will result in both civil and criminal actions against you.

Civil action may also be taken against your parents in this matter, pursuant to ORS 163.577. Specifically, you and your parents will be held jointly and severally liable for damages of the maximum $360.00, plus the replacement cost of the book: well over $12,000.00, given its rarity. Only 250 copies were ever printed, only 225 of which sold. The last available copy came up at auction in 1954.

An additional levy of 10% of the civil penalty will be assessed for every 24-hour period you delay beyond this Monday, January 19, in returning the library's rightful property (accruing at $1,236.00 per day).

This is not to speak of the criminal action that may still be filed against you for this theft. You should note that the value of this rare book escalates this infraction beyond petty theft to a full grand theft crime, which, as a potential felony charge, would go on your permanent record.

The deaccessioning of *Joshua Fry Speed* is of our library's greatest priority, and we urge you to return the book immediately to avoid this future unpleasantness. Of course, if you return the book forthwith, all will be forgiven.

Gravely,

Mr. Ira Clifton, MLS

Mr. Ira Clifton, MLS
Head Librarian

Wyatt's voice was still shaking as he finished reading the letter over his cell phone to the guy at Legal Advocates of Oregon. After Wyatt had read it to himself the first time, he remembered that hot guy singing about the Revolutionary War general being Gay—and how the next video to come up after that had been some civil rights organization. . . .

He'd found them online, and the second he'd seen the Gay Pride Rainbow flag on their website, he'd called. When the guy had answered, "Hello, Legal Advocates of Oregon," Wyatt had barreled into it.

When Wyatt was done, the guy whistled, long and low. "Wow, they're really trying to scare you, aren't they?"

"It's working," Wyatt admitted.

The guy asked, "What's in the book?"

Wyatt paused. What if this lawyer was going to get all mad at him, too? Lincoln was a lawyer—maybe there was some all-lawyers-stick-together pack mentality and they wouldn't want to help Wyatt after all. Maybe they'd think he was messing with a national hero. . . . But it was already after five on a Friday—he was lucky he hadn't gotten voice mail. And who else was he going to ask for help from before midnight? Maybe he could get some general advice, without having to go into it. He'd been quiet too long and knew he had to say something. "I don't see what that has to do with anything—"

The guy cut him off with a scoff, like he was just some dumb kid. "It has everything to do with it!" Then his voice got kind again. "Come on, Wyatt. You can tell me. What are they so afraid of?"

It felt like jumping off a cliff, but Wyatt told him. Everything. The guy just listened. Wyatt even told him how to find his blog online, and waited while he read it. Then Wyatt could hear him watching the video. The guy started chuckling. Wyatt wasn't sure if it was at him.

"No way! Wyatt, that's awesome!"

The guy, even if he was a lawyer, was cool with it. But Wyatt was still a mess. "I don't feel awesome. That letter—"

He cut Wyatt off again. "Lincoln, Queer! I love it!"

"About the letter?"

"Ahem." The guy cleared his throat and got back into lawyer mode. "It's not about the book. Snap some cell-phone shots and give them the book back. All you really need is the proof, right?"

Wyatt hadn't thought of that—it was a pretty genius idea. "Yeah, I guess. . . . What about being suspended? I have another post I want to do, one that really proves Abe was in love with Joshua. I was going to put it up this afternoon, 'cause my teacher gave me this deadline, but the principal said if I don't take the blog down by tonight, he might even suspend me . . ."

"Well, if you're asking for legal advice, I . . . uh . . ."

"Martin?" Wyatt heard a woman's voice, like someone was shouting at the guy from another room. "Did I just hear you say *legal advice?*"

Wyatt could hear her voice getting louder. "Did you get my cell to work, or are calls still forwarding to yours? Who are you talking to?"

"Wait. You're *Martin?*" Wyatt asked. "The guy who sang on that video?"

The hot guy?

"Uh . . ."

"Dude! You're a lawyer? You're, like, my age." If Martin was just playing him for a fool, then maybe he wasn't so hot after all.

"No! I'm not . . . I was just trying to . . ."

There was noise, some rustling, and Wyatt heard the woman say, "Shh!" And then she was on the phone with him. "Hello?"

Wyatt wasn't sure what to say. "Hi . . ."

"I'm terribly sorry about that. My son is not qualified to be giving legal advice until he goes to law school and *passes the bar exam!*" That sounded more for Martin's benefit than for Wyatt's.

Wyatt heard Martin's "I wasn't—" but it stopped short as the woman spoke.

"I'm Rhonda Sykes—and no, not the comedienne, she's Wanda. I'm the attorney of record and field representative for Legal Advocates of Oregon. How can I help?"

"He got a threatening letter!" Martin's voice—he must have still been right there. "He outed Lincoln as Queer for an online book report, and now the library's threatening to sue him for thousands of dollars so they can get the book back and hush it up! And his principal wants to suspend him!"

Wyatt could hear Rhonda put her hand over the phone, but he could still make out, "I told you to hush."

"He's right," Wyatt told her, thinking that at least the hot guy was a good listener. "That's pretty much what's going on. Can they do it?"

"How about you email me the letter and we'll see? Are you a minor? They can't be sending a minor a threatening letter."

Wyatt almost laughed with relief. This time, he didn't want to be any older. He'd need to tell her about the Q Satellite Radio show, too. "Yeah."

"And if it's an issue of free speech, it sounds like your principal's just blowing hot air. Don't worry. You're not in this alone."

Sometimes, it was good to be a kid.

Wyatt snapped a photo of the letter with his cell and emailed it to Rhonda. They spent the next hour before Wyatt had to go down for dinner going over it. From "You are in violation" to "permanent record," it turned out Martin was right—they were just trying to scare Wyatt. He legally had thirty days after their written notice to return the book before they could do anything to him—something Mr. Clifton hadn't mentioned about ORS 357.975.

Sneaky jerk.

But Rhonda, and even Martin, were pretty cool.

Wyatt's parents thought he was getting a "good night's sleep"—after all, tomorrow was his first "big date" with Mackenzie; he was taking her to their high school's Purple and Gold Pep Rally. But instead of sleeping, Wyatt sat at the window seat in his room, holding the old-fashioned key to the bookcase downstairs. The midnight deadline was approaching, and he was trying to figure out what to do.

Rhonda had said it was his choice, and that if Wyatt wanted to, he could let it go—return the book, delete the blog, let life go back to normal. At that suggestion, Martin had shouted to him in the background, "No! Blog more about Lincoln being Gay!" Rhonda had stopped Martin, saying it was Wyatt's life, and Wyatt's call. But it felt pretty great that someone wanted him to keep talking about it. . . . He bet Roz would want him to keep talking about it, too.

And if Wyatt did decide to blog more about Abe loving Joshua, Rhonda had promised to back him up and make sure he wasn't suspended for simply speaking his mind and exercising his First Amendment right of free speech.

Wyatt pushed the registered Express Mail envelope and the official-looking letter from the library farther away from him on the cushion. It was crazy how he could be so freaked out by it one minute, and then, a couple of hours later, the same thing didn't bother him so much. It was just an adult being a bully on paper, trying to get his way. Well, the letter's *we* probably meant Mayor Rails was behind it, too.

What were they even going to do with the book once they got it back? Just put in on the reference shelf to make sure it didn't leave the building again? Would they even let people see it?

Why give the book back till he had to? Thirty days gave him until Sunday, February 15—and their final blog assignment was due February 12. So he was good. He'd return it after he finished that last post, in plenty of time before it was really due, and they couldn't do a thing to him.

Or he could just take those photos, like Martin had said, and return the book. Maybe he'd post the whole thing on his blog. After all, Martin had pointed out, it was long out of copyright. And Rhonda had said Wyatt didn't even need to "dignify their threats with a response."

He decided to put the letter away. Why have it out for his dad or mom to stumble on and get all freaked out themselves? They sure didn't have an extra $12,360 lying around. Wyatt grabbed the letter to put it back in the Express Mail cardboard sleeve, when his eye caught on the first line of the last paragraph:

> The deaccessioning of *Joshua Fry Speed* is of
> our library's greatest priority . . .

He'd forgotten to ask Rhonda about that, but it was already 10:43 p.m. Too late to call her again tonight. But she must have seen it—he'd sent her the whole thing. It couldn't be that important. Still, he wished he knew what *deaccessioning* meant.

He crept downstairs to the reception computer to look it up.

Deaccessioning: The process of disposing, selling, or trading objects from a museum collection.

The hair prickled on the back of Wyatt's head. They didn't want the book back to keep it safe. They were going to get rid of it. They wanted to destroy the evidence that Lincoln was Gay! And if they did, maybe no one would be able to prove the truth, ever again.

Wyatt couldn't let that happen.

Abe loving Joshua was important. It could change everything. And if all Wyatt had was words and a blog, then that was how he'd fight.

A hint of a smile played on Wyatt's lips as he thought of Principal Jackson's gun-firing advice. If their trying-to-scare-him letter was the bullet, then they deserved one hell of a kickback.

Chapter 12

Wyatt Yarrow's Book Report Blog
for Mr. Guzman's 9th Grade History Class,
Lincolnville High School

Book: *Joshua Fry Speed: Lincoln's Most Intimate Friend,*
by Robert Kincaid

QUEER AS A FIVE-DOLLAR BILL

Blog Post: Friday, January 16, 11:18 p.m.

More Proof President Abraham Lincoln Was Gay:
An Annotated Letter!

Okay, Mr. Guzman. Here's the letter Abraham Lincoln sent to Joshua Fry Speed on February 13, 1842 (from pages 47–48 in my book). I've added my own comments alongside Abe's lines. And the post after this is photos of my whole book, where you can see the letter yourself.

"Springfield, Illinois,
February 13, 1842

> Abe is 33, and it's just over a year since he broke his engagement to Mary Todd by being a no-show on their wedding day.

Dear Speed:
Yours of the 1st instant came to hand three or four days ago. When this shall reach you, you will have been Fanny's husband several days. You know my desire to befriend you is everlasting; that I will never cease while I know how to do anything.

> In the letters before this one, Abe has been trying to convince Joshua that they should both marry women, even though they're in love with each other. Now, Joshua has just married Fanny. "**My desire to befriend you is everlasting**" is Abe saying he still loves Joshua.

But you will always hereafter be on ground that I have never occupied, and consequently, if advice were needed, I might advise wrong. I do fondly hope, however, that you will never again need any comfort from abroad.

> Abe's hoping marrying a woman will satisfy Joshua so he won't need Abe's love in the same way any more. Abe is hoping this is true for him, too. He's hoping he can live in the closet.

But should I be mistaken in this, should excessive pleasure still be accompanied with a painful counterpart at times, still let me urge you, as I have ever done, to remember, in the depth

> The pleasure is their getting married to women and living *acceptable* lives. The pain— the depths, "**even the agony of despondency**"—is that Abe and Joshua have to be apart even though . . .

and even the agony of despondency, that very shortly you are to feel well again.

. . . they love each other, because society won't accept them as they really are: Gay and in love.

I am now fully convinced that you love her as ardently as you are capable of loving. Your ever being happy in her presence, and your intense anxiety about her health, if there were nothing else, would place this beyond all dispute in my mind.

Abe is trying to convince Joshua that Joshua loves Fanny, at least as much as Joshua is "**capable of loving**" a woman.

I incline to think it probable that your nerves will fail you occasionally for a while; but once you get them fairly graded now, that trouble is over forever.

Joshua's "**nerves**" failing him is that he doesn't really love Fanny, he loves Abe, but he went through with marrying Fanny because that's what society expected him to do. Abe is giving him a pep talk, saying he can do it, he can pretend, and that the longer he does it, the easier it will get. And now that he's married a woman, everyone will think Joshua is straight and "**that trouble is over forever.**"

I think, if I were you, in case my mind were not exactly right, I would avoid being idle. I would immediately engage in some business, or go to making preparations for it, which would be the same thing.

Or maybe Joshua just shouldn't think about it too much, and should distract himself with something else—anything else.

If you went through the ceremony calmly, or even with sufficient composure not to excite alarm in any present, you are safe beyond question, and in two or three months, to say the most, will be the happiest of men.

This is the smoking gun: Abe is reassuring Joshua that if he was able to get through the marriage ceremony without anyone becoming alarmed—if he stayed calm, if he kept his composure—then he is now "**safe beyond question.**" How much more obvious do we need Abe's words to be? What else could Joshua have been so panicked about, in marrying Fanny? What else about Joshua would Abe have been concerned would "**alarm**" the people who were at the wedding? They're talking about Joshua being Gay, about Abe and Joshua being in love, and about no one being the wiser about it at the wedding. It was no accident that Abe wasn't at his *best friend's* wedding! If he had been there, would . . .

. . . Joshua have been able to go through with it? Would they, together, have excited "**alarm**" in everyone present? You bet.

I would desire you to give my particular respects to Fanny; but perhaps you will not wish her to know you have received this, lest she should desire to see it. Make her write me an answer to my last letter to her at any rate. I would set great value upon another letter from her. Write me whenever you have leisure.

Abe knows Joshua will want to keep this letter secret from Fanny. Neither of them wants Fanny to know the truth, which this letter pretty much spills!

Yours forever,
A. LINCOLN.

He signed it, "**Yours forever**"—he loves the guy! It's pretty interesting that the letters Abe wrote Mary once they got married (like the one he wrote her on June 12, 1848) were signed, "**Affectionately**," which sounds a lot less affectionate!

P.S. I have been quite a man since you left.

Check out the P.S.! This is like some secret code between Abe and Joshua, where being **"a man"** is acting straight, or dating women. **"I have been quite a man since you left"** is all about Abe letting Joshua know that since Joshua left Springfield—since Joshua left Abe and the bed they shared for those four years—Abe has been doing the same thing Joshua has: covering up the truth about his being Gay and going out with ladies. Maybe he's even hinting here that he might get back together with Mary. Which Abe does, marrying her on November 4 of this same year! By marrying Fanny, Joshua is now **"safe,"** and Abe won't be **"safe"** until he gets married to a woman, too.

You wanted proof that Lincoln was Gay? That he was in love with Joshua Fry Speed?

There you have it—in his own words!

Oh, and one more thing: February 13, the day Abraham Lincoln wrote this letter? That's the day after Abe's birthday. The day before Valentine's Day.

And it's one heck of a love letter.

Chapter 13
Saturday, January 17

"OKAY, YOU TWO, let's try it again. And smile this time!" His mom used Wyatt's new video camera to record Wyatt and Mackenzie, arm in arm, coming down the stairs to the B and B's entryway. Like their own private paparazzi, Mackenzie's dad joined in, snapping photos with his cell-phone camera.

Mackenzie hadn't mentioned anything about his blog all day, and Wyatt sure wasn't going to bring it up. But she hadn't called him Honeybear, either. He figured either she was giving him another chance or she hadn't seen it yet—maybe she'd been too busy with karate and shopping with Wyatt's mom. Whichever it was, Wyatt felt like he was juggling sticks of dynamite around her and it all might explode any second.

This time, he remembered to stop on the last step. Mackenzie stepped down to the ground floor and swiveled so they were eye to eye. She smiled, but Wyatt couldn't tell if it was for the cameras, for their parents, or for him.

"Gregory! You don't want to miss this!" Wyatt's mom called to his dad, who was still working on the "full and complete" inventory of their store for the bank. Wyatt's dad came over, clipboard and plastic bag of rifle pens in his hands. He gave Wyatt a proud *that's my son* wink, which made Wyatt feel even worse.

Mackenzie's dad said, "It's funny how teens date at night and old people like us meet for 'coffee' on Sunday."

"Dad . . . now?" Mackenzie criticized.

Wyatt's dad asked, "Hey, you got a date?"

"It's just coffee." Mr. Miller put up his hands defensively to Mackenzie. "We're only as sick as our secrets, and I'm not going to have any new ones. We're all like family, anyway."

"It's perfect, their dating, isn't it?" Wyatt's mom asked Mackenzie's dad, then turned back to her directing: "Now, Wyatt, slip the corsage on her wrist . . . slowly!"

"You do know it's recording sound?" Wyatt asked. His mom was totally overreacting, treating the pep rally, where everyone had to wear some purple and some gold, like it was junior prom or something. She'd gone dress shopping with Mackenzie that morning in Corvallis. They'd found Mackenzie's sparkly gold dress at a thrift shop, and Wyatt's mom had even arranged for the purple-orchid corsage he was putting on his girlfriend like a bracelet.

Wyatt, for his part, was in his nice black jeans and an also-new-from-the-thrift-shop purple button-down shirt. But instead of the horrible gold-sparkle cummerbund his mom insisted was "perfect" but that he knew he'd never live down, that afternoon he'd used some of the gold-colored nail polish they had to touch up frames in the exhibits to make his shirt buttons gold. He thought it came off pretty slick.

His mom moved her head out from behind the camera. "Have some faith. Your dad and I had a wedding video."

"I've never seen it." Wyatt wondered why.

"Your father didn't want to transfer it to DVD, or even video."

His dad made a note of the number of pens. "Eight-millimeter film should be seen on an eight-millimeter projector."

"Which we don't have," his mom cut in. "I don't even know if we could track down the film canister after all these years."

"It was beautiful," his dad recalled. "They even sepia-toned the whole thing."

"What I remember," Wyatt's mom said, "is that they shot the picture and replaced all the chitchat with our song. As soon as you two tell me what your song is, we'll do the same."

Wyatt knew his parents' song: "At Last," by Etta James. They slow-danced to it in the kitchen every anniversary. And he'd bet that Mackenzie's parents had had a song, too, but when he saw that pained expression on Mr. Miller's face, he wasn't about to ask.

Wyatt looked at Mackenzie. "Our song?"

She shrugged. "I guess that's one of the fun things couples get to figure out."

Couples. Like us.

Maybe they were okay, after all.

Lincolnville High School electric sign:

Purple and Gold Pep Rally
Tonight!

Wyatt's mom pulled into the school driveway, right behind a jacked-up pickup Wyatt couldn't help but recognize. *Jonathon's.* Dangling from the undercarriage was an eight-inch-long polished chrome scrotum.

"Classy," Mackenzie said.

Wyatt could feel the heat starting at his neck. Was that about him, and the mosquito-ball joke? Jonathon had to prove he had the biggest balls . . . or that his truck did?

"Mom, just drop us off here, okay?" Wyatt said. That way, they could avoid Jonathon, who'd have to park.

"You sure?" his mom asked.

"Yeah." Wyatt looked at Mackenzie and offered her his hand. "Ready?"

Amid a stream of decked-out students, Wyatt and Mackenzie walked into the crepe-papered gym. Cheerleaders chanted:

>Gold and Purple!
>Purple and Gold!
>Fighting Soldiers,
>Never Grow Old!

There was scattered applause, and Coach Rails's band struck up "Sweet Home Alabama."

"Mr. Yarrow! Miss Miller!" Spiffy in a 1950s tuxedo, Mr. Guzman walked up to Wyatt and Mackenzie as they entered. The woman on Mr. Guzman's arm had neon pink hair and otherwise was dressed for the same 1950s sock hop he was. He clicked his tongue and then told her, "Nikki, these are two of my best students!"

Nods all around.

Mr. Guzman said to them, "I've been thinking of starting a debate program, and I wanted to sound you out about it. The state speech championships are in April, which, of course, isn't a lot of time. But next year you'll be sophomores, and we can grow the program. You have to start somewhere, right?"

Wyatt had to ask about his blog post. "Mr. Guzman, did you get a chance . . . ?"

Mr. Guzman nodded. "I read your blog, Mr. Yarrow. I'll be heading to U of O's library tomorrow to do some research of my own. Nikki lives in Eugene, so that will work out."

Nikki mocked offense. "How easy a woman do you think I am?"

Mr. Guzman made a clicking sound, "Not easy. Delightful." He kissed her hand like she was royalty. "Delightful enough to join me chaperoning a high school pep rally on a Saturday night." He turned back to Wyatt and Mackenzie. "I must attend to my lady fair. . . . We'll talk more on Monday. Tonight, you two enjoy!" Leading Nikki away, he suggested, "Let's get some punch, shall we?"

"That was crazy," Wyatt said, to make conversation. Jonathon and Charlie walked by with the freshman basketball team, all in uniform. Jonathon slowed down to scan Mackenzie top to bottom and back again.

"Classy," Wyatt joked under his breath, but Mackenzie just stared at Wyatt.

"You can't let the Lincoln-being-Gay thing drop, can you? Not even for one day."

"What? I just—"

"I saw your blog, too, Wyatt." Mackenzie's voice amped louder. "You're choosing that stupid idea of Gay Lincoln over me!"

It's not stupid, he thought, but he didn't dare say it. It was like Mackenzie had lit the dynamite and he couldn't juggle fast enough.

"Did you ever really care about me in the first place?"

In judgment but not in feeling . . .

How could he explain? Wyatt was keenly aware that Jonathon had stopped to listen. People were starting to look their way.

Mackenzie's words bit the air. "Do you know what a beard is?"

Wyatt tried to keep it light. "You mean like Coach Rails is growing out?"

"No. I mean like your ridiculous blog is saying Mary was to Lincoln. And Fanny was to Joshua. Everyone's thinking that's what I am to you!"

Play stupid. "What?"

The song ended with a drum roll and cymbal crash. In the moment of quiet that followed, Mackenzie's words were practically a shout. "I don't want to be *the girl with the Gay boyfriend!*"

"You're not—I'm not!" Wyatt protested, then lowered his voice. "Can we talk about this later?"

"No!" She lunged forward, lips puckered, and Wyatt pulled back.

Mackenzie gave a short laugh, but it sounded bitter. "You don't even want to kiss me now, do you?"

Wyatt looked everywhere but at her. "Well, you really set the tone there."

Her nostrils flared in anger. "A real guy doesn't need *tone*! He always wants to kiss a hot girl. And I'm hot, Wyatt. Whether you appreciate it or not, I'm hot." She swung her arm to include everyone in the gym. "Which guy do you want to kiss, Wyatt? Because it's never been me!"

Alarms screamed in his head as every skin cell burned with heat. Did she know? Was it a guess? Or was it just the worst thing she could come up with to hurt him?

"That's his girlfriend asking!" Jonathon crowed, and laughter pealed around them.

The burning fuses on the dynamite were nearly gone, and the only thing Wyatt could think to do was to get angry back at Mackenzie. "You know what? I don't want to date someone who's so intolerant."

"*No!*" Mackenzie reared back, eyes wide. "I'm breaking up with you! You have no idea . . . You don't even care what I'm losing here. Again! You want to say Lincoln was Gay? Fine. Then why don't you date *him?* Because you and I are done!"

Boom.

The dynamite blew up as Mackenzie stomped away in Wyatt's mom's purple pumps—the ones that reminded him of butterfly wings.

No more juggling.

Wyatt stood there, alone, in a sea of people.

Mayor Rails's voice carried in the postdetonation quiet. "I like that girl."

"All right, enough soap opera!" Coach Rails said into the microphone from the stage. "How about some good ole country rock and roll to get this party started, before we present our Fighting Soldier teams?"

The crowd roared its approval.

Wyatt noticed Coach Rails was clean-shaven—how was he going to be Lincoln in the parade now?

"This one made the top one hundred country songs!" Coach Rails adjusted the mic stand. "I'm sure you know it. It's called 'That Dog Don't Hunt'. . . ."

As Coach Rails's band launched into the song, Wyatt walked as fast as he could to the exit. His eyes took a last, wild spin around the gym. He didn't see Mr. Guzman or his date. There was Mayor Rails, frowning at her husband, singing up onstage. And over by the punch table, Jonathon was talking to Mackenzie. Mackenzie's friend Jennie was with them and caught Wyatt looking their way. She scowled at him.

Not a single friendly face.

Outside, the night air slapped the heat in his skin. And it hit Wyatt that he didn't have a girlfriend anymore. Or a best friend. And now everyone at school was going to think he was Gay. Know he was Gay.

What was he going to do?

It was a long walk home.

Four Outlets That Picked Up the Q Satellite Radio Story That Night

1. *San Francisco GLBT Times*
2. *Pacific Northwest Queer Consortium*
3. *Weird News of Western Washington*
4. *Gay Guide ATL: Atlanta's Rainbow-Hued News*

THE BUZZING VIBRATION of Wyatt's cell woke him. He fumbled for it in the pocket of his pants on the floor and squinted at the time. 8:00 a.m. But it was Sunday! He'd wanted to sleep in. Forever.

It vibrated again, and he peered more closely at the screen in his hand: "Lgl Adv Or."

He pressed TALK, panicking. "Hello?"

"Hey, Wyatt! It's . . . Martin."

Wyatt sat up. His room was a freezer. He shivered. "Is everything okay? Am I in trouble?"

"No, nothing's happened about your case! I'm sorry to bother you. I just wanted to say I'm sorry for kind of making you think I was a lawyer—I didn't mean to! I want to be one, a lawyer, I think, if the singing and songwriting don't work out. Anyway, I've been up, all night actually, and I was thinking . . ."

Martin kind of trailed off and didn't say anything more. Wyatt didn't know what to say. They were both silent, for twenty seconds.

"This was a bad idea. I'm sorry," Martin said. "Go back to sleep.

I mean, you weren't asleep, but . . ."

"Well, I was, but it's okay. I'm not. I'm awake." Wyatt let himself yawn. "What's up?" He settled under the comforters, where it was warm.

Martin took a deep breath and let it out. "I just wanted to tell you I think you're really brave. To buck the system and all. I mean, we help a lot of adults, but not guys our age. You're standing and fighting. . . . You're . . . kind of a role model."

Grateful Martin couldn't see him turn red, Wyatt said, "I liked your von Steuben 'Yankee Doodle' song."

"Thanks! I liked your new blog post about Lincoln and Joshua."

There was another pause, but this one was almost cozy. And Wyatt didn't really want to go back to sleep. He wanted to keep talking. "What school do you go to?"

"I don't. Homeschooled. I'm just going to skip the whole high school thing and go to college early. I mean, high school's just a factory. College is, too, but at least it's a factory where you can be yourself. And music school, if my mom will let me, should be better than a regular college."

Wyatt wondered if *be yourself* was code for *be Gay*—Martin had seemed so out in the video. He wanted to ask but had no idea how. Martin saved the moment with his own question: "So, what's new?"

Wyatt wasn't going to say anything about breaking up with his *girlfriend,* that was for sure. "Nothing much. You?"

"I've actually been doing some stuff about your blog. . . . You had some traffic, but you deserved more."

"More?"

Wyatt could hear Martin click at a keyboard. "I've been linking and posting it in comments all over the Web since yesterday. And the radio show, their archive's linkable, so I'm getting that out there, too. It's just starting to get some traction in the Queer blogosphere and a few local outlets. There's some traffic from the Civil War–buff sites, too. And I cloned it, just in case. With luck, we'll get you picked up by an aggregator."

We'll.

Wyatt stumbled downstairs to the reception computer to see for himself. He loaded the stat counter page: 4,920. People!

"You did this?" he asked Martin.

"You're the one who's saying what they're excited about. I'm just trying to help make sure people hear it."

"It's, um, I . . . I gotta go." Wyatt hung up, and for the rest of the day, he felt like he was sleepwalking. He tried to not think about Mackenzie, and how everyone at school would know she'd broken up with him at the pep rally, and why.

Mackenzie didn't come over for their Sunday "homework club," not that Wyatt had thought she would. When his mom asked where Mackenzie was, he didn't want to get into it, so he made up some extra-credit project she was doing with Jenny.

Wyatt dodged his parents' questions about the pep rally and stayed busy catching up on algebra worksheets, doing a load of laundry, and taking a trip to the lumber yard with his dad to get the two-by-fours for a new display case. And the two times he allowed himself to check, his numbers grew: 6,603, then 9,042.

It was like some magic beanstalk.

After the James Bond movie that night—without Mackenzie—Wyatt checked his stats one more time: 10,978.

It was exciting. And scary. That was a lot of people. He went to bed that night with the same nervous anticipation he used to have with a tooth under his pillow, wrapped in a tissue and zipped inside the little embroidered red-and-gold Chinese change purse. What was the tooth fairy going to bring him? Only this time, it was the *truth* fairy.

First thing Monday morning, Wyatt raced downstairs, and it felt like Christmas and tooth fairy and New Year's and the first day of school all rolled into one. He got to the stat page and hit "Refresh": 42,317.

Oh. My. Gosh. Part of him wanted to tell Mackenzie, but he knew he couldn't. She wouldn't want to hear it. He didn't even know if they'd ever talk again.

But he had to tell someone!

And then he thought of it—he could text Martin.

Seven More Outlets That Picked Up the Q Satellite Radio Story That Sunday

1. *New York Reenactment Society LGBT Forum*
2. *Kansas City Queers* newsletter
3. *Los Angeles Lesbian Times*
4. *Vermont Teen Power*
5. *Austin LGBT History Club*
6. *Shout! National Newsmagazine*
7. *Rocky Mountain Newswire*

Chapter 15
Monday, January 19

ON THE WAY in to History, Wyatt nearly stopped in the doorway. For some reason, Mr. Clifton was sitting at their teacher's desk, absorbed in paperwork.

Where's Mr. Guzman?

Wary, Wyatt made his way to his own desk and pulled out his notebook.

Jonathon was standing over by Mackenzie, talking to her. They caught Wyatt looking at them, and Jonathon raised his voice. "So, Mackenzie, you wanna go out sometime? Maybe catch a movie?"

His ex-girlfriend smiled at the guy who'd tormented Wyatt for the past six years. "Sure. Sounds fun."

"Awesome!"

Pretending to read his notes, Wyatt shut his eyes, trying to ignore the whispers and laughter at his expense. The bell rang, and Wyatt heard Jonathon high-five Charlie on the way back to his seat.

Mr. Clifton's chair scraped as he stood up, finally acknowledging they were there. Wyatt raised his head as their town's librarian spoke. "What you see is self-evident: Mr. Guzman is not here, and I have been assigned to be your substitute." Murmurs of surprise bounced around the room. Mackenzie whipped around and glared at Wyatt like it was his fault.

The worst part of it was that he knew it was.

"Consequently, there will be new temporary hours at the library, some early, some late."

New hours? How temporary is this going to be?

Mr. Clifton laid stacks of flyers on the five front desks and had people pass them back. Wyatt gave one a quick glance and then shoved it in his backpack, passing the stack behind him.

Their new teacher walked toward Wyatt's desk. "And, Mr. Yarrow, before I forget, Principal Jackson asked me to make sure you understand that you are expected after school in detention, starting today, for three weeks."

"Ooohs!" of *he's in trouble now* swirled in the air.

Wyatt fought the heat in his face.

Heading back to the front of the classroom, Mr. Clifton continued, "The more observant among you may have noticed that your ill-fated school blogs are no longer on the World Wide Web." He made a face like it was distasteful to refer to technology. After all, the one computer in the library was practically an antique. "But this does not mean your President Lincoln book reports are no longer due. On the contrary, you will complete them the traditional way and hand in your three-thousand-word papers on paper."

The class exploded at that, everyone trying to figure out how many pages that was.

Holding up a book from his desk, Mr. Clifton said, "Once again, *Mr. Yarrow,* I have your new book on President Lincoln here, which you can pick up at the end of class. Really, we've all made enough exceptions for you already."

Wyatt stared at the wall, telling himself to keep it together while Mr. Clifton bragged about how he used to be a teacher so he knew all about proper formatting. *Wait.* The walls were bare. All those motivational posters Mr. Guzman had put up were gone.

One person can't make a difference.

Grabbing his stuff, Wyatt shot out of his chair for the classroom door. As he raced past, Jonathon snickered with a hissing noise and whispered, loudly enough for everyone to hear, "Fag!"

"Where do you think you're going?" Mr. Clifton challenged Wyatt.

"I'mgonnabarf!" Wyatt flung the door open and tore into the hallway.

Mr. Clifton shouted after him, "I expect a note from the nurse!"

Panting, Wyatt stopped at his locker. He put his forehead against the cool metal, trying to figure things out. *I should have played sick and not come to school at all.* If he cut out again, the nurse would never buy it. And it would just give Principal Jackson more ammunition for his "serious consequences."

Stalling for time, Wyatt spun the combination. When he opened his locker, sitting on top of his bunched-up orange-and-black Oregon State Beavers sweatshirt was a large yellow envelope. "Where did that come from?"

Floating fake-breast woman wasn't going to tell him, so he picked it up.

There was nothing written on either side, but it was sealed shut. Feeling like he was living in a Bond movie, Wyatt snuck it into his backpack and didn't open it until he was locked in a bathroom stall.

No note. Just photocopies. Four thin stapled packets.

He looked through the first one, past the image of a book cover: *A. Lincoln, Speeches and Writings: 1832–1858.* On the second page was a highlighted circle around a date. It was a reprint of a letter:

Springfield, Illinois, February 13, 1842
Dear Speed:
Yours of the 1st . . .

It was his letter! The one Wyatt had written about on the blog.

He checked the next packet. Another letter circled with yellow highlighter, from *Abraham Lincoln: Complete Works:*

February 13, 1842

And the third, from *Herndon's Life of Lincoln,* circled in the same neon yellow:

February 13, 1842

They were all copies of the letter. The same letter, in three different books.

Who would . . . ? Mr. Guzman! He proved I'm not making it up!

There was one more packet. The cover was *The Routledge Dictionary of Modern American Slang and Unconventional English,* followed by a copy of the dictionary's page 607. Highlighted at the bottom was a word with its definition:

lavender *adjective*
effiminate, homosexual *US, 1929*

What's that about?

The next page was another book cover, *Abraham Lincoln, The Prairie Years—I. Volume 1.* By Carl Sandburg, 1926. And after that, a copy of the book's page 266. This time, a few sentences were highlighted:

Their births, the loins and tissues of their fathers and mothers, accident, fate, providence, had given these two men streaks of lavender, spots soft as May violets. **"It is out of this that the painful difference between you and the mass of the world springs."** And Lincoln was writing in part a personal confession in telling Speed: **"I know what the painful point with you is at all times when you are unhappy; it is an apprehension that you do not love her as you should."**

An arrow was drawn from "two men" to the circled names Lincoln and Speed.

He knew! The rush of being believed was heady. And Wyatt wasn't the first person to see that Abe loved Joshua. This guy Sandburg wrote about it—even if it was sort of in code—in 1926! And Mr. Guzman wanted Wyatt to know he knew about it!

But then, as fast as the rush had come on, it deflated. It didn't matter anymore if Mr. Guzman believed him—he was gone.

Now, it seemed like it was all for nothing. They'd gotten rid of his blog, along with everyone else's. The whole idea of Lincoln being Gay would probably disappear, again, into history—just like no one cared that some guy hinted at it back in 1926.

He'd have to write a whole new book report—there was no way Mr. Clifton would accept one on Abraham Lincoln maybe being Gay. Mr. Clifton and Principal Jackson and Mayor Rails had won.

He had no idea what to do. But he couldn't go back to that classroom. Jonathon knew about him. Everyone knew. And now Mackenzie was going to start dating Jonathon? Some best friend.

Maybe he could transfer to another school.

He needed to call Martin.

He needed to get out of there.

Wyatt snuck away and made it to the stream. Fifteen minutes past the ford, he dialed.

"Hey! We hit sixty-eight thousand before they pulled the plug," Martin said, before Wyatt could say anything.

Sixty-eight thousand?

There were only 5,818 people in all of Lincolnville. Wyatt held the phone in the crook of his neck and picked up a big rock, half the size of a basketball. He heaved it into the stream. It splashed huge, making some damn good ripples that traveled the whole twelve feet to the other bank. For a couple of seconds, it was all churned up, and some water even went backward, but then the stream kept flowing and the ripples faded out—almost all of them, except he could see his rock, just under the surface, still creating little white-water eddies of current around it.

The splash had gotten him, too. His jeans from the knees down, and his sneakers, were soaked.

"Wyatt?" Martin's voice on the phone.

"Yeah."

"It sounded like you jumped in a pool or something."

Now that the blog was gone, Wyatt thought maybe his life could get back to normal. Like none of it had happened. Do his three weeks of detention and then go back to no one knowing about him. Let it all die down and try to get over Mackenzie betraying him. He swallowed hard. "At least it's over."

"Over?" Martin scoffed. "They don't own the Internet. I told you I cloned the site, right?"

"What's that mean?" Wyatt asked.

Martin couldn't seem to get the words out fast enough, "It means Lincoln's still out and all your posts are up, just at a different URL: QueerAsAFiveDollarBill.com. I've been relinking to it all morning. I left comments disabled, like on your school blog, because we don't want to get hit with a wave of stupid. We're already up to thirteen thousand page loads! And if I can get the two aggregators that picked us up to redirect their traffic, we'll be golden. It's our—your—First Amendment right of free speech in action. The fact that your school tried to kill it is a story itself, and I submitted *that* to six more aggregators, plus the two that carried us in the first place. We'll be blowing up again by this afternoon at the latest. You should feel great!"

Wyatt didn't feel great. He thought about Mr. Guzman. What had happened to him? Had Wyatt gotten him fired?

His phone buzzed with a text coming through.

Mom   8:23 a.m.

Where are you? School called. Get home now!

"Get home"? Not "get back to school"? He was in so much trouble. *Should I tell Dad and Mom about me? They're probably going to hear it from someone at school. But if I come out, what if they don't . . . What if they stop loving me? What if they suddenly hate me, just for being me?*

The familiar dread felt like someone trying to hold him underwater, and Wyatt had to thrash to the surface of his fear just to breathe.

"Hey, did I lose you?" Martin asked.

"I gotta go." Wyatt's voice sounded squeaky. He pressed END CALL and headed for home, socks squishing every step.

Ripples, it turned out, could get you soaked.

WYATT FOUND THEM in the kitchen, hovering over the speaker-phone. His mom was in a workday skirt and blouse, but her hair was still wet from the shower. There was a half-inch stack of papers that looked like legal stuff in her hand. Wyatt's dad, in his messy-job overalls, held up a finger for him to be quiet.

Wyatt's mom was talking. "First it was two—two!—tickets on my truck, which made no sense, then the library's letter, and now you're suing us, too?"

The speaker crackled with Mayor Rails's voice. "On behalf of the town. You're not giving me much choice here. It's your family spreading this destructive rumor that's getting completely out of control. They'll be coming for my head soon if I don't act for the common good."

"But this is crazy!" Wyatt's mom attempted a laugh, but it didn't quite work. "It's just a book report, for heaven's sake."

Mayor Rails's voice was knife-edge serious. "Five organizations have dropped out of our parade. Five! Our grand marshal just canceled, and it's not even nine a.m.! Businesses are screaming at me to fix this, our local economy stinks, what am I supposed to do?"

Wyatt slunk over to one of the chairs around the table. Sitting there in the center next to two parking tickets signed by Mackenzie's dad—one for being too far from the curb, and the other for mud on their license plate, which was ridiculous because everyone in Lincolnville had mud on their license plate—was the letter from the library saying Wyatt owed them all that money. That the library was going to sue them.

Did they find it? Heart pounding, he leaned forward to check and saw it was stamped SECOND NOTICE.

Oh, crap. The bookcase key Wyatt was still carrying around in his pocket like a good-luck charm suddenly burned like it was radioactive.

His mom checked the papers in her hand. *A lawsuit.* "So you want us to pay . . . a thousand dollars a day, for *lost tourism revenue?*"

The mayor scoffed. "If you read it more carefully, you'll see that the amount is tied to lost revenue. A thousand's just an estimate, but whatever businesses lose, you'll be on the hook to make them whole."

"She knows we can't afford any of that," Wyatt's dad said quietly.

"Greg, I'm glad you're on the line with us," the mayor said. "If you can't pay for the damage you're causing, then your only choice is to wipe this story off the Internet, destroy the radio program files . . ."

At that, Wyatt's mom shot Wyatt a *What exactly have you done?* look.

"And get Abraham Lincoln's—and our town's—good name back." There was a staticky pause on the mayor's end of the line. "Look, Elizabeth, I don't want to be unreasonable. If you can make this whole thing go away and have the parade be the success it needs to be, I'll let you keep your job as my assistant. But if it all crashes and burns, so do you."

A dial tone filled the kitchen as the mayor hung up on them.

Wyatt's mom put her forehead in her hands. His dad's eyes darted from object to object like he was figuring out what they could save and what they'd have to sell once they were homeless.

Neither of them looked at Wyatt.

He knew why. He'd done this. Speaking up. Telling the world about Abe being Gay. He'd ruined their lives.

He stared at his wet feet. It wasn't ripples—it was a storm at sea—and he needed things to calm down. He was never going to be able to come out to them.

"It's the third offer, Gregory. *The Von Lawson Report.* I think we should do it." Wyatt's mom was holding the phone in the kitchen, some producer on hold. The B and B line hadn't stopped ringing since they'd gotten home from returning *Joshua Fry Speed: Lincoln's Most Intimate Friend* to the library's drop box. Wyatt could just imagine Mr. Clifton looking all smug when he found it there after school. At least the entire book was still online and they couldn't hide it anymore. But the whole seven-block ride home, Wyatt's dad and mom had been on him to call Martin the minute they got back to take down the new blog.

It was the last thing Wyatt wanted to do.

That call had had to wait because his phone was at home in his mom's purse. His parents had confiscated it—"No more technology for you, young man"—as part of their big lecture about how could they ever trust him again after he hid the library's we're-going-to-sue-you letter from them and lied about being eighteen so he could do the radio interview. About how hurt they were that they had to find out from Mackenzie's online profile that he'd broken up with his girlfriend. About how honesty was so important.

And he sat there in the truck's backseat and couldn't say anything.

Then they got home and the phone calls started. Two news outlets, and now this TV show, wanted his blog up.

Wyatt's mom kept trying to sell it to his dad. "It's a nationally syndicated show. The book's returned, and we couldn't buy this kind of publicity. Maybe this is how we get through this—the silver lining. If we can make the B and B support us, then I don't need to work for Kelly!"

"Liz, you don't believe Lincoln was Gay any more than I do," Wyatt's dad reminded her.

"If we're smart, we can spin this!" His mom held her hand over the phone. "Wyatt can take the line that intelligent people can disagree about Lincoln. The main thing is not to pass up this chance. It's once in a lifetime!"

Wyatt's dad twisted the strap of his overalls. Neither of them asked Wyatt what he thought. He just sat there, as they decided his fate.

"Seven million viewers!" His mom's eyes were lit up with hope.

Wyatt's dad asked her, "Are you sure about this?"

She was. "If we can get to their studio in Portland by seven, Wyatt will have a chance to talk up the B and B, coast to coast."

His dad said, "We'll need to coach him on exactly what to say—to not make a big deal of the bed or anything that makes people think about what Lincoln might have done in bed."

Wyatt tried to keep his face a mask and not show the flash of pain he felt. *Anything Gay, you mean.*

His mom nodded. "Kelly gets prepped before all of her public speaking engagements. And we'll have two and a half hours in the car. But we have to go now if we're going to make it."

"All right," his dad agreed. "Tell them we'll do it."

"Coaching" Wyatt took nearly two hours. He was supposed to talk about the tours they did, about Lincoln and how important he was to their town, and he wasn't allowed to say anything about who he thought Lincoln slept with or loved. And if he could get in how comfortable the rooms were, that would be good, too. *And* the Civil War–Era Suppers.

"And don't mention the bed at all," his dad insisted.

Wyatt thought that was crazy. "We're the Lincoln Slept Here Bed-and-Breakfast. How am I not going to say the word *bed?*"

"Just say *B and B!*" His dad changed lanes even though he didn't need to. "Stress the other stuff."

His mom agreed, "It's like the social media updates I do for Kelly. If you want people to like you, or vote for you—or stay at your B and B—you can't talk about anything bad or anything that's going to make people uncomfortable."

But then you end up with a world that's all fake.

Instead of arguing, Wyatt just bobbleheaded it and went back to repeating what they wanted to hear.

When they were finally satisfied, his parents started talking about all the things they'd do if the B and B were a success, his mom didn't have to work for the mayor, and they had some extra money. Be one of the sponsors for the big summer Civil War battle reenactments on Asgur's farm. Go to Hawaii on vacation at Christmas. Put aside money for Wyatt's college.

They were dreaming, and Wyatt didn't want to burst their bubble.

One of the photocopies Mr. Guzman had left him turned out to be from a book they had a copy of in the glass bookcase. Wyatt had noticed it when his dad and mom made him get *Joshua Fry Speed* out of hiding to return it. So he'd grabbed *Herndon's Life of Lincoln* for the ride and was flipping through it when he found a poem Lincoln wrote, on page 48:

> **For Reuben and Charles have married two girls,**
> **But Billy has married a boy.**
> **The girls he had tried on every side,**
> **But none he could get to agree;**
> **All was in vain, he went home again,**
> **And since that he's married to Natty.**

It turned out Natty was a nickname for Nathaniel. Abe wrote it as a mean joke when he was in his twenties, but Wyatt thought it was pretty wild that Abe was thinking about this kind of stuff. That he wrote a Gay poem, about two guys getting married, back in the 1830s. Something he and Joshua couldn't do when they met and fell in love.

Maybe I should read this on the TV show. He snorted at the thought. *Dad and Mom would freak.*

He needed to talk to Martin.

His mom's purse was on the floor between the two front seats, and his cell was in there. They were exiting the freeway, and his mom was squinting at her smartphone's map for shortcuts. His dad was cursing the traffic and the rain, even though it wasn't much more than a drizzle. They were both busy, and Wyatt went for it.

He pretend-dropped his book on his mom's purse and, hand fumbling around, managed to grab his phone. He pulled his knees up. Blocking his phone with the book, he saw he had four new voice mail messages. All from Martin. He couldn't listen to them or call him back. He'd have to text him.

Wyatt   6:39 p.m.

> hey! returned book after all.
> on way 2 von lawson report –
> I'll b on live show 2night!

Wyatt turned off the sound, pressed SEND, and waited, hoping for a response. Outside the window, downtown Portland was all lit-up buildings and shiny asphalt streets. The funny step pattern of Big Pink winked by. A city of skyscrapers, full of strangers, caged off from nature. He swallowed against the thought that he'd have to live someplace like it someday.

Come on, Martin!
A text flashed silently on his screen.

Martin   6:42 p.m.

hey! wondered if u were ok.
bad idea 2 go on vlr. stop it if
u can.

Wyatt looked at how intense his dad and mom were about just getting him to the studio on time. There was no way he was getting out of this.

Wyatt   6:43 p.m.

can't.

Martin   6:45 p.m.

ok. never told you this, but
knowing about von steuben,
& lincoln & joshua, it makes
a difference. makes it easier.
for me. for a lot of us. don't
forget that. speak truth to
power. & know

I'm cheering u on.

His chest felt warm as Wyatt powered down the phone. *Truth to power.* Maybe Martin was right. Maybe, in the middle of everything his parents wanted him to say, Wyatt could make the argument.

Convince some more people. Keep the real story of Abe and Joshua alive. After all, like his mom said, intelligent people *could* disagree. . . .

"Take a right here!" his mom ordered.

His dad protested, "It's an alley!"

"I know! But traffic is blocked up ahead and I can get us through."

He had to put the phone back. "How much longer?" Wyatt leaned forward like he was trying to see out the windshield as his dad turned them away from a mass of red brake lights. Wyatt slid his cell back into his mom's purse without their seeing.

His mom's eyes flicked to the dashboard clock: 6:47 p.m. "We'll get there."

His dad's fingers were tight on the steering wheel as they picked up speed.

MS. EAGLE'S BIBLE CHEAT SHEET:
Phineas (also *Phinehas*)

NUMBERS 25:1-5
The people of Israel were whoring around with the daughters of Moab, and starting to follow *their* gods, and the LORD told Moses he was pissed off.

NUMBERS 25:6-9
Phineas, the son of an Israelite priest, saw his countryman Zimri, the prince of a chief house of the Simeonites, getting it on with Cozbi, a high-born Midianitish woman. Phineas got a spear, went into their tent—where the couple was getting busy—and ran them through.

NUMBERS 25:10-15
God was pleased with Phineas, because he had been zealous for the sake of the LORD. Good things happened for the Israelites after that, because God wasn't angry with them anymore.

The announcer's voice boomed around Wyatt and his parents as they stood just offstage. "A conservative in the heart of the liberal Pacific Northwest . . . A thorn in their backside . . . Your friend, and mine . . . And a great American . . . Ernest Von Lawson!"

The studio audience of seventy screamed like they were at the Super Bowl as Ernest Von Lawson walked past Wyatt onto the set in a dark blue suit, white shirt, red tie, and green-and-black cowboy boots that Wyatt would have bet ten bucks had never seen a horse. "Hello, Real America!" Von Lawson waved like a rock star and sat at his desk.

The show started with a couple of jokes that Von Lawson read off a teleprompter. They went over big. Someone with a clipboard tapped Wyatt on the shoulder. "You're on in two."

Wyatt's mom straightened his thin black tie, something his dad had from college, and pulled at the sleeves of the gray dress shirt Wyatt had gotten for his great-aunt Freida's funeral last summer, like that was going to make it fit. The whole time, she was reviewing Wyatt's robot programming. "Okay, sweetie. Remember to call him *Mister* Von Lawson. Be respectful. Get our points in: Tours. Lincoln heritage. Cozy rooms. Yummy food. A real taste of the Civil War era."

His dad soft-punched him in the arm. "Knock 'em dead, soldier." *Soldier?*

He guessed he was. And the battlefield was national TV.

Someone pushed Wyatt to start walking. His mom whispered urgently behind him, "Make sure someone says *The Lincoln Slept Here B and B in Lincolnville, Oregon,* or they won't be able to find us!"

Von Lawson wound up his introduction. "He's one of our youngest guests ever, blogger and ninth-grade student at Lincolnville High School in—where else?—Lincolnville, Oregon. Please welcome Wyatt Yarrow!"

There was applause for Wyatt, which he thought was cool, and he followed the line of red tape on the floor out onto the set. He shook

Von Lawson's hand and sat in the black leather armchair nearest the desk. The lights were really bright, and the makeup ("so you won't be shiny") made his face feel tight, but he was pretty pumped up.

"Wyatt." Von Lawson leaned forward on his desk, all friendly. Wyatt tried to focus on what Von Lawson was saying and not on the cameras. Which one was on?

"It seems you've decided to try and single-handedly destroy the Republican Party."

What?

"Destroy the memory of the greatest president the United States of America has ever had." Von Lawson paused, making sure he had everyone's attention. He had Wyatt's. "Destroy the proud legacy of Abraham Lincoln."

Boos. The crowd was booing him.

Oh no.

Von Lawson turned to the audience. "Let me tell you what this young man has done. He started a blog, an innocent enough thing, to do a book report on President Lincoln. Honest Abe. Sounds okay so far, right?" Cautious nods. "Gentlemen in the audience, who here has a best friend? Can I get a show of hands?" Men who looked like truckers and farmers and high school coaches put their arms up. Every guy in the audience had a best friend. So did Von Lawson. With a leer, Von Lawson lowered his hand. "Now, tell me, are you having carnal, unnatural, immoral relations with him?"

The studio audience bellowed like a zoo full of furious, injured animals.

Von Lawson patted the air to get the audience to listen. "Well, Wyatt here, he thinks you probably are!" The people in the front row made faces like Wyatt was a steaming pile of poop. A shot of Wyatt's school blog was projected on a screen behind Von Lawson's desk, Wyatt's blog header shouting QUEER AS A FIVE-DOLLAR BILL in ten-inch-high letters.

Von Lawson kept going. "In fact, his blog—paid for with our taxpayer money—says that our sixteenth president was doing the nasty nightly with his best friend, Joshua Fry Speed. His best friend! Have you ever heard something so disgusting?" Hisses and boos. Someone yelled, "Pervert!" One woman crossed herself as a guttural growl traveled through the audience.

People started shouting, and Wyatt struggled to make himself heard. "It's not your tax money anymore. . . . The school deleted the blog!"

Von Lawson turned on him. "Ah, but you, with your deviant homosexual agenda, put it up on another site, didn't you? QueerAsA-FiveDollarBill-dot-com. These images are live from the Internet." Von Lawson signaled over the audience, and the image behind them changed to Wyatt's new blog. It scrolled down the posts about Lincoln being Gay, the letter, and the video. Von Lawson continued, "He even included his so-called 'proof,' stealing images from the book about Lincoln's best friend and posting them illegally!" The website showed those pages, too.

Words flashed at the bottom of the monitor that showed Von Lawson what was being broadcast. Wyatt couldn't help but read it:

LINCOLN. UNDER. ATTACK!

"You know, it's such a crazy idea, that we here at *The Von Lawson Report* did a national survey." On the screen, graphics appeared by Von Lawson's head as he spoke. "And it turns out that two percent of people think Lincoln might have been 'sweet' on another guy—as absurd and toxic a lie as that is. But that survey has a plus or minus error of three percent! Which means that something less than zero percent of people actually believe our President Lincoln, founder of our Republican Party, was a limp-wristed fairy."

Sitting there, Wyatt knew he had to say something, but Von Lawson wasn't about to stop. "Even with more than a hundred-and-one percent of people knowing it's nothing short of historical terrorism, Wyatt and his attack on Lincoln are getting quite a bit of attention. As Lincoln isn't here to defend himself, it falls to me. To all of us. To stand up"—here, Von Lawson got up and walked around his desk to be right in front of the audience—"and say, repeat it after me, *hell no!*"

"Hell no!" The studio audience roared to its feet.

Von Lawson relished every shouted syllable. "Lincoln was great!"

"Lincoln was great!" It flashed through Wyatt's mind that the only thing that kept them from being a mob was that they didn't have lit torches and pitchforks.

Von Lawson slashed the air like his arm was a sword and he would have first blood. "Lincoln was *straight!*"

"Lincoln was *straight!*" It was pandemonium, and Wyatt wished he could just disappear.

With a satisfied expression, Von Lawson shook his head from side to side. After a long time, he motioned them to settle down. He got a solemn look on his face. "It's at moments like this that we need to ask ourselves . . . what would Phineas do?"

A roar exploded out of the crowd.

What? What did that even mean?

"What would God ask of us, in the face of this plot to make an idol of their perversion, to flush our country down into the sewers of chaos and madness, to destroy the very foundation of this Christian nation?"

A photo of Wyatt's family's B and B appeared on the screen behind them.

Oh no.

Von Lawson gave a sly smile. "Would *He* want you to visit the place that's saying that Lincoln had this lethal addiction, spending four years doing terrible things against God's moral order with his best friend? Well, if you think *He* would, then you go visit Wyatt's family's bed-and-breakfast, amusingly enough called the Lincoln

Slept Here Bed-and-Breakfast. Though, after hearing what they're saying went on in that bed, I know I've lost my appetite.

"But here's an idea for you heathens out there: Why don't you make a day of it?"

The screen behind Wyatt and Von Lawson started showing photos of the different businesses in Lincolnville, with Photoshopped drag queens and Gay Pride Rainbow flags and shirtless guys holding hands in front of them. Von Lawson said, "How about, after getting your Queer history at their Lincoln Was a Sexual Deviant B and B, you get your homosexual Civil War photo taken at Woo's Historic Photo Shop? Do some Queer shopping on Johnson Street and the Gay ole stores on Union Square?"

The studio audience howled, eating up the pictures and every word. "Hungry yet? Get your homo food at the Lincolnville Pantry and your how-to-be-Queer books at the Lincolnville Public Library. And, evidently, you can get your nothing's-too-sacred-to-be-Gay-for-us education at Lincolnville's very own public high school. You want to know what's wrong with our country today, Real America? The radicalized and destructive homosexual agenda coming out of Lincolnville, Oregon!"

The audience cheered.

Wyatt felt pummeled. He was trapped there in the chair by Von Lawson's desk, cameras on him and nowhere to hide. He could feel himself sweating through his shirt and hoped it didn't show.

Wyatt noticed someone with a clipboard give Von Lawson a thumbs-up, and then the host changed gears. "But the news out of Lincolnville isn't all bad. Another young man—a Real American!—has courageously stepped forward to respond to these allegations about our beloved sixteenth president. . . ."

There was a drumroll, and Von Lawson flung his hand to the side of the stage as a cymbal crashed.

Wyatt whipped his head up in time to see a spotlight hit *Jonathon*, standing there in jeans and a blazer over a yellow T-shirt. The audience fell silent.

Jonathon's voice rang out across the stage: "If you think Lincoln was Gay, then I'm a proud member of the John Wilkes Booth Appreciation Society!" He took off his jacket so the cameras and everyone could see his T-shirt, with black letters that said that very thing:

IF YOU THINK LINCOLN WAS GAY
THEN I'M A PROUD MEMBER OF
THE JOHN WILKES BOOTH APPRECIATION SOCIETY

Then Jonathon turned around so they could all read the back:

. . . AND YOU'RE A BIG FAIRY

The crowd went wild as Wyatt tried not to freak out.

Wyatt watched a red light–topped camera push in on Von Lawson as the host laughed. "I want one of those!"

"I've got one for you!" Jonathon strode across the stage and, from the side of the leather chair next to Wyatt, lifted a small shopping bag. He presented it to Von Lawson, who pulled out a T-shirt of his own. To whistles and huge applause, Von Lawson took off his blazer and pulled the T-shirt on over his shirt and tie.

Time seemed to slow as Von Lawson got back behind his desk and Jonathon sat in the chair to Wyatt's right. Wyatt could see the two paths ahead:

If he admitted he was Gay, no one would ever believe him about Lincoln. The whole thing would disappear again into history.

Or he could stay on the path he was on. Stay "straight" and, like Martin said, let the story of Abe and Joshua make a difference. In lots of people's lives—just not his own.

Steeling himself, he spoke as soon as the noise dropped down enough to be heard. "Believing Lincoln was Gay doesn't make you a fairy!"

Jonathon stared accusingly at him. "But you are!"

Wyatt stood his ground. "I'm not. But Lincoln might have been. Not . . . not a *fairy*, but in love with another guy!"

Jonathon's comeback was whip-quick. "Where's the real proof? All you have is stupid letters. They had kids! Lincoln and Mary had this pretty beautiful, traditional family—and there's power in that!"

Wyatt tried to sound confident. "Why can't intelligent people—intelligent straight people—disagree?"

Von Lawson cut them both off, standing to model his new T-shirt for the cameras. "Well, Wyatt, if you think Lincoln was Gay, then I believe that makes me a proud member of the John Wilkes Booth Appreciation Society!"

Hoots and applause.

Von Lawson turned to Jonathon as he sat back down. "I suppose that makes me your first official member?"

"There's no formal society, yet. . . ." Jonathon shrugged. "It's really more to show just how *stupid* it is to think that Abraham Lincoln was anything other than a red-blooded, woman-loving, Real American!" He looked at Wyatt, then over at Von Lawson. "But sure. You can be member number one!"

"Then I guess that makes you president of the society," Von Lawson said to Jonathon.

Jonathon laughed in surprise. "I guess it does."

The studio audience loved that and applauded again.

Von Lawson eyed the camera. "See? I told you he was a good kid. Now, as for this awesome . . . You teenagers still say *awesome*, don't you?"

Jonathon nodded.

"As for this awesome shirt," Von Lawson addressed the people in the first rows, "a way to speak back to this shameful attack on all that's right and honorable about our history, and the answer to 'What would Phineas wear?' . . . I bet you all want one, too!"

Enthusiastic nods.

Von Lawson stood up and walked around his desk, signaling Jonathon to join him. They stood in front of Wyatt, blocking him, as Von Lawson put an arm around Jonathon's shoulder. Wyatt considered running offstage, but didn't want to call any more attention to himself.

His voice all conspiratorial, Von Lawson said to Jonathon, "You have something to tell them, don't you?"

Jonathon grinned. "There's a free T-shirt under all their chairs!"

The crowd exploded, like they'd all just won the lottery. Everyone reached down to pull out a shirt and then started putting them on—over dresses, over sweaters, over dress shirts. In a minute, the audience was a sea of yellow T-shirts, all shouting their membership in the John Wilkes Booth Appreciation Society.

Von Lawson crowed. "There you have it! Remember Phineas, hold great and straight Lincoln in your heart"—he pounded his own chest—"and we'll be right back with this . . ." He clapped Jonathon's shoulder. "How did you put it? Red-blooded, woman-loving, Real American Teenager!"

The show's going-to-commercial theme music blasted, and the studio audience leaped to their feet, screaming their cheers.

The red on-air lights above the three cameras and the set doors went off, and an earsplitting buzzer sounded. The noise dropped to a dull roar. Wyatt was pushed offstage as makeup people and Von Lawson's staff hurried on set. Someone yanked Wyatt's body microphone cord off so hard, it left a red line across his neck. People were jeering, yelling at him.

The producer who had welcomed them and given them free drinks in the green room before rushing them to the set waved as Wyatt's mom hurried his dad and him past the makeup room. "That will be great ratings! And hey," she shouted after them down the corridor, "any publicity's good publicity, right?"

As they passed a different green room then the one they'd been in, Wyatt heard a voice he knew: "When's the best time to give Von

Lawson my demo? I want to make sure he hears it and it doesn't just sit there." Wyatt glanced in and saw it was Coach Rails, talking to another producer. A large-screen monitor was on the wall behind them, showing the set. Von Lawson was getting his face touched up by a makeup person while someone handed Jonathon a soda.

Against his will, Wyatt's feet slowed. Mayor Rails was on her cell phone. "He knows how to work a crowd, all right. But this could be a disaster for local businesses. . . ."

Becca was there, too, on the room's couch, folding a stack of yellow T-shirts and putting them into individual plastic bags, which already filled two large cardboard boxes. She glanced up and caught Wyatt's eye. She gave him this small smile, like it was all some big game and not his whole life on the line.

Of course she'd seen it. His complete humiliation, and Jonathon's star moment.

And then, Wyatt remembered: *millions* of people had seen it.

He ran to catch up with his dad and mom, and they didn't even stop to put on their jackets as they burst out the door to the parking lot. It was pouring rain.

The door shut behind them, and the three of them just stood there in the downpour. Stunned.

Chapter 18
Monday, January 19

NO ONE SAID anything for the first half hour of the ride home, while Wyatt used nearly half the box of tissues trying to wipe the makeup off his face. Wyatt's mom was driving, because his dad was too much of a mess. His mom's cell rang, and his dad answered it. He talked for barely a minute, saying only, "I understand" and, "Okay" and, "Yes, we'll refund your deposit."

He hung up and stared at the phone for a long moment. "The Collier wedding. Seems they're big fans of *The Von Lawson Report.*"

"That was all eight rooms!" Wyatt's mom glanced over from the road. "For this weekend! How are they going to find another venue in time?"

The rain beat on them and the rest of the freeway traffic.

"That's not really our problem, is it?" Wyatt's dad turned in his seat. "You get this friend of yours to take down that other website pronto!"

"I'll need my cell," Wyatt said.

Wyatt's dad pushed the purse at him.

Wyatt fished out his phone and tried dialing Martin. Four rings, and it went to voice mail. "He's not answering. Should I leave a message?"

His dad and mom chorused, "Yes!"

There was the beep. "Hey, Martin. It's . . . Wyatt. Call me, okay? It's kind of important."

He pressed END CALL and sent him a quick text.

> where are u? we need 2 talk!
> u were right. about not going
> on the show.

Finger snaps got him to raise his head. His mom held out her hand for the phone. Wyatt surrendered it and watched it drop back into her purse.

The three of them rode in silence for the next two hours, until they got home. They staggered inside from the kitchen porch. No guests tonight.

Maybe no guests ever, after that.

Wyatt noticed the voice mail light blinking on the B and B line, showing they had six messages. But no one hit PLAY or said anything.

In his room, Wyatt peeled off his fancy clothes. They were still damp. He pulled on sweats and crawled into bed, wanting to do a Rip Van Winkle —fall asleep for a hundred years and have it be a totally new world when he got up. Or maybe he was mixing that up with Sleeping Beauty.

Tuesday, January 20

Wyatt woke up more than an hour before he had to. By now, probably everyone at school had seen online replays of *The Von Lawson Report*. He buried his head back under the comforters. He wasn't moving from this bed.

His eyes opened, and he scrambled to his backpack, on the floor by his desk. Digging in it, he found the flyer and uncrumpled it to check. Yeah, he was right. Tuesdays meant early hours at the library.

The B and B was quiet. Wyatt snuck out the front door, past the Confederate and Union flags in their holders on either side of their B and B sign. The flags were limp from last night's rain. With everything going on, he had forgotten and left them up overnight. Well, he figured, it saved him a chore this morning.

He did a slow warm-up run the five blocks to Union Square. Nobody was around, and it was dark, since it wouldn't be daylight for another two hours. But Wyatt had fire inside him. As he cut past the square's metal arch that spelled out LINCONVILLE, his breath puffed into the cold air like steam—like a dragon on a warpath. When he got to the library parking lot, he jogged in place behind a hedge. The streetlamp light was just enough to make out that the lot was empty. He didn't have a phone to check for the time, but it didn't matter. It wouldn't be long.

Figuring working out again wasn't such a bad idea, he'd done two sets of ten push-ups and was just about to try for more when Mr. Clifton's half-size smart car made the turn from Route 37. Mr. Clifton didn't see him. He pulled into a spot right by the loading-dock door, triggering the yellow motion-detector floodlights. Wyatt waited until Mr. Clifton was getting out and headed over.

"Why did you give me the book in the first place?"

Mr. Clifton turned from picking up his briefcase. "Wyatt!" He wasn't happy to see him. Which was fine with Wyatt, since that made two of them.

Wyatt thought Mr. Clifton might make a run for the door, and he stepped forward to block his way. "Did you guys destroy it yet?"

"I . . . I'm afraid I'm not at liberty to say." Mr. Clifton fidgeted with the keys in his hand. "Though I'm not sure it matters, as you've put the whole thing online."

"Why, Mr. Clifton? Why let me know about it and then slam me for saying it?"

"I was trying to be kind!" Mr. Clifton jerked his head both ways to check the empty parking lot, but no one had heard him. It was just the two of them in the amber-lit darkness. "I wanted you to know that you're not alone. That . . . *we're* not alone."

Wyatt's mind spun. *He's Gay? And he knows I am, too?*

But that meant Mr. Clifton thought they were the same. That Wyatt was like him. "You mean, in the closet?"

"Sometimes, you have to do what you have to do, to get by. Fly under the radar. Keep quiet. Surely you can understand that."

"I'm not like you!" Wyatt shouted.

"Shhhh!"

Wyatt stared at Mr. Clifton. His eyes showed white, all around the irises. His nostrils flared, breaths shallow and fast. He was a cornered animal, posing as a grown-up.

Wyatt didn't want to be afraid. Or quiet. Not anymore. But he couldn't come out—not now, not when the whole truth about Lincoln hung in the balance.

But did that mean . . . Wyatt couldn't bear to look at Mr. Clifton anymore.

Was that going to be him, in forty years?

The idea was like a punch in the gut, and Wyatt stumbled away.

Mr. Clifton cleared his throat. "I'm sure you won't tell anyone. I suppose it's a bit like the USSR and America during the Cold War. All those nuclear weapons pointed at each other. And it turned out the best deterrent was mutually assured destruction."

Anger flared inside Wyatt, but he didn't turn around. Instead, he started running, pounding his fury into the ground with each step. *It's probably a good thing they don't give teenagers the nuclear codes.*

IT WAS STILL dark outside, but the not-quite-period grandfather clock by the stairs said it was 6:15 a.m. Wyatt hung back in the kitchen doorway. His dad and mom were at the table, with the ledger book. His dad put down the phone and crossed out another name. "And that last one was the junior high from Albany." He said it like someone had died. "That's two tours and eleven room nights canceled. And we haven't booked anything since Saturday."

His dad's eyes traveled to some papers on the table in front of them. Wyatt recognized the logo: Lincolnville National Bank. They had the loan on this place. The payments that Wyatt's family couldn't miss even one more of. Whatever fire he had left inside him fizzled out. Damn ripples.

His mom glanced up and saw him. "There you are." She came over and kissed Wyatt on the forehead, then pulled him to the table. She reached into her purse and pulled out his cell phone. "We'll come up with a different consequence. This is *not* for interviews, but for now, don't use the landline." She handed the cell over to him.

Wyatt gave her a *What's going on?* look.

"There were some pretty nasty messages this morning." His mom looked away, like just talking about them hurt. "You don't need to hear that."

Wyatt tried to swallow past the lump in his throat. He'd done this. Gotten them into this mess. How was he ever going to fix it?

"Excuse me."

They all turned to stare at the teenager standing in the kitchen doorway, a blue guitar slung over his shoulder and a rolling carry-on by his side.

"Martin?" Wyatt had trouble believing it.

But the smile he gave Wyatt felt like the sun when you get out of the cold ocean and you're all goose-bumpy. "Hi, Wyatt."

Wyatt couldn't help checking Martin out. His teeth and eyes were electric white against the deep, river-stone brown of his skin. He was wearing jeans and a tight blue tie-dyed Superman T-shirt that was a *G* instead of an *S*. Wyatt wasn't sure what it stood for, but it did show that Martin was in really good shape. Scratch that—he was hot.

Martin pointed over his shoulder to the front of the house. "My mom says she won't come in while the Confederate flag is flying outside."

"Oh, uh . . ." Wyatt crossed to the doorway. "I'll take it down."

Wyatt tried to pass him, but Martin went to his left just as Wyatt went to *his* right. Then they did it the other way, and Martin laughed low. "Wanna dance?" He flashed his impossibly bright grin at Wyatt.

"I . . . uh . . ." Wyatt could feel his face get lava-hot and couldn't get any words out. He slipped past him, nearly brushing against his shoulder as Martin held his guitar out of Wyatt's way.

Wyatt darted down the corridor, through the entry hall, and out the front door, taking the stairs in a rush. A woman stood there by a pile of luggage. Martin's mom. Rhonda. She was staring at the flags like they were stopping her from taking even one more step forward. Like they were Kryptonite.

Wyatt yanked the Confederate flag out of its holder and started to roll it up on its four-foot-long stick. "I'm really sorry about the flag—it's not meant to disrespect African Americans. It's just that we're a Lincoln *and* Civil War site, and having both flags seemed kind of . . . fair . . ." *Did that sound terrible?*

Rhonda pulled out a camera and aimed it at their Lincoln Slept Here Bed & Breakfast sign. The flash went off as she snapped the picture. "Documenting everything is critical."

Wyatt glanced to see if it was that different without the slaveholding states' flag, and saw what she had *really* photographed. Someone had crossed out the Here on their sign with pink spray paint and had written in *WITH GUYS*.

Making them the Lincoln Slept WITH GUYS Bed & Breakfast.

Wyatt cringed, wondering if he could get that off before his dad saw it. While he was busy with the flag, Rhonda lifted her carry-on and started up the front porch steps. Wyatt grabbed the other two bags and hurried to join her. His parents and Martin were in the entry hall.

Rhonda glanced around her at the exhibits, and Wyatt felt a flash of relief that their military mannequin was still in his Union blues. *That* could have been awkward.

Martin's mom's eyes lingered on the Martin Luther King Jr. quote above their The Great Emancipator display case. She read it out loud: "Five score years ago, a great American, in whose symbolic shadow we stand today, signed the Emancipation Proclamation. This momentous decree came as a great beacon light of hope to millions of Negro slaves who had been seared in the flames of withering injustice. It came as a joyous daybreak to end the long night of their captivity." She frowned. "You're missing the next line."

Wyatt checked the wall. That was where their quote ended.

Rhonda said to her son, "You know it."

Martin recited from memory, "But a hundred years later, the Negro still is not free." He said it with force, and meaning. His mom gave him a *well done* dip of her head. He looked down, kind of shy.

He was mighty cute. But Wyatt was going to be straight. He had to.

Rhonda turned to him. "You must be Wyatt? TV is always so deceptive."

Wyatt gave a nod.

"Forgive us," Wyatt's dad said, "but do we have a reservation for you? We certainly have room; it's just that . . ."

She pulled out three business cards, handing one each to Wyatt's mom, dad, and Wyatt himself. "I'm Rhonda Sykes, attorney of record and field representative for Legal Advocates of Oregon."

Wyatt looked up from the card in his hand. "They're here to help."

"The new blog picked up right where the old one left off!" Martin had put his guitar on the far side of the kitchen table and was setting up his laptop, running the Internet over some cellular data card because the B and B's setup was "quaint." "It took me a while to relink stuff, but three more aggregators picked us up, and one of them was huge. We were at nearly two hundred thousand hits when we left Idaho. . . ."

Wyatt had gone over how he'd contacted Rhonda twice already, but his mom still studied the business card clutched in her hand. "It says *Oregon?*"

"We were in Boise, helping out with a class-action gender-discrimination suit," Rhonda explained.

"Let's make it load on top of the old visits. . . ." Martin grabbed a muffin from the basket Wyatt's dad offered as he worked. "Drove all night to get here. Did it in just under nine hours!"

Rhonda pulled out a chair and sat heavily. "I'm so glad Martin has his provisional license. I couldn't have done that by myself."

"Coffee?" Wyatt's dad asked.

Rhonda stretched her neck side to side. "Please."

"Me, too," Martin said, left hand up as he typed. "Halfway."

He drinks coffee?

Wyatt's mom got a second mug for Rhonda while his dad poured Martin half a cup. Martin filled it the rest of the way with milk and seven packets of sugar. He took a tentative sip.

Well, I like coffee ice cream, too.

Martin hit a final key and whistled. "I thought so! Von Lawson's show was like rocket fuel."

Wyatt leaned over Martin's shoulder to check out the new stats. His nose picked up the waft of sweet coffee and bright citrus, like the way your hand smells after you peel a tangerine. Was he wearing aftershave? *Focus, Wyatt.*

The new statistical readout page showed a bunch of big vertical lines. Page loads per day. Today's was shorter. Wyatt was trying to make out the numbers, when Martin moved the cursor to point out the total.

"We're over a million?" Wyatt asked. That couldn't be right.

"One million, two hundred and thirty-two thousand, one hundred and seventy-nine!" Martin raised his hand for a high five, and their palms connected. Wyatt's was suddenly sweaty. He wiped it on his sweatpants.

Wyatt's dad frowned. "Unless we're somehow getting a dollar for each of those visits, that TV show—and that blog—actually destroyed our business!"

Wyatt didn't mean to flinch, but the truth hurt.

Martin shrugged. "We can't get a dollar, but we could probably get some fraction of a cent per hit if we put advertising on it."

"We're going to lose this place!" Wyatt's dad fumbled his coffee, and it spilled across the table. "Can we close the computer and focus on what's going on in the real world?"

"Hey!" Martin leaped up with the laptop and grabbed his guitar into the air, too, even though the spreading puddle of coffee was still a foot away from where the blue instrument had been.

Rhonda used some paper napkins from the holder to blot the spill. "We're here now. And we can help."

Martin still held the laptop and guitar, like he didn't want to put them down.

Wyatt's dad just sat there, motionless, staring at the chipped handle of his now-empty Jefferson Davis mug.

Wyatt's mom squeezed his dad's hand and spoke to Rhonda. "There are already one-point-two million people who won't be staying with us. You want to help? Get your son to take that website down."

What if his mom was right? Who knew if anyone visiting his blog even agreed with him about Lincoln? It was probably just looky-loos. Or Von Lawson's audience, working themselves up. Getting to know who they needed to hate. *Him.*

Over a million people hated him.

Wyatt's voice cracked oddly. "Are they going to come after me?"

"We won't let them," Rhonda said. "But let's take things one at a time."

The adults decided Rhonda would take the case pro bono—which meant Wyatt's family wouldn't have to pay her. In return, Wyatt's parents would let Rhonda and Martin stay with them for a week or so. And, instead of the Confederate flag, the B and B would fly the thirty-three-star *and* the thirty-five-star Union flags, from the beginning and end of the war. And the blog could stay up, for now.

Room 1, down the hall from the Lincoln Room and in the front of the house with a big bay window, would be Rhonda's room and temporary office. Martin would stay in Room 2, closer to the stairs. Closer to Wyatt's room, one flight up and down the hall.

Outside, the darkness had lightened to an inky blue. Wyatt spent a half hour in the B and B sign's light, trying to remove the pink graffiti. It wouldn't come off. Dumping the useless cleaning stuff in the downstairs closet, he peeked in the kitchen. Rhonda sat at the table with Wyatt's dad and mom, using a red pen to scribble notes on the lawsuit the mayor had hit them with. After Von Lawson's show, local businesses were going to lose a lot of money. Money they didn't have if they lost the lawsuit. What would happen then?

He wondered where Martin was. Probably in his room . . .

Wyatt searched his brain for a reason to go up there. *Clean towels!* He raced up the stairs to the laundry room on the third floor. Then, arms loaded with a pretty good excuse, he walked down the flight of stairs to Martin's room.

The blue guitar was outside the doorway, propped against the blue-gray and orange-brown leaves of the hallway wallpaper. Wyatt wondered if he should pick it up and carry it in for him, or if that wouldn't be cool. He was about to ask but froze when he saw him. Martin was wearing plastic gloves and a white face mask with yellow rubbery head straps. He had the mattress off the bed and a giant silk bag halfway over it.

"What are you doing?" Wyatt asked.

"Dust mites," Martin said, carefully pulling the bag all the way over the mattress and then zipping it shut along the side. "You ever seen one in a microscope? They're like aliens."

He finished with the mattress, and then, like it might bite him, cautiously fit another silky bag over the room's pillow. Once that was zipped shut, he pulled his gloves inside out, careful not to touch any of the parts that had been on the outside. Putting the gloves in a plastic bag, he knotted it and put that in the trash can under the antique desk. Then he took off the face mask. "Mom says it's like I go all Howard Hughes, but we're in a different place every couple of days. . . ." He shrugged, zipped open his rolling carry-on, and pulled out his own sheets.

"We do wash things here," Wyatt said, putting the towels on the desk.

"It's just allergies. I've kind of got it down."

Wyatt helped him push the hermetically sealed mattress back on the bed. *He's weird. Cute, but weird. Or maybe . . . weird, but cute.*

Martin's mom came up the stairs. "Wyatt, you need to get to school. We can't be giving them any excuses to suspend you. Martin, I need our system up and running an hour ago."

"I'm on it," Martin said.

Man. Wyatt had been hoping no one would bring up school. He checked his cell phone. It was 7:25 a.m. He was already thirteen minutes late.

Once he'd locked himself in the third-floor bathroom, Wyatt closed his eyes against the day he knew was ahead:

Sharks in yellow T-shirts, saying they'd rather celebrate the guy who killed a hero than acknowledge a hero might have been Gay. Basically saying they'd kill Wyatt if they knew he was Gay, too. And then celebrate it with custom T-shirts printed for the occasion.

Mackenzie, getting all lovey-dovey with Jonathon.

And probably some camera crew following Jonathon around, for the new reality TV series he was probably going to star in.

Wyatt ran the hot water until it gave the glass-and-mercury thermometer a high enough "fever" to be convincing. Sometimes his dad's insistence that old-fashioned things were better was useful.

There was no way Wyatt was going to school.

Just thinking about all of it made him feel sick.

So it wasn't a total lie.

Wyatt holed up in his bedroom until lunchtime, when hunger got the better of him. He was heading down to the kitchen when Martin called out from his room, "Hey, it's you."

Martin came to his doorway, running a hand back along his close-cropped hair. His T-shirt rode up, and Wyatt could see a line of skin pulled taut over muscle. *Wow.* He needed to look somewhere else, anywhere else, and recognized the stripey cover of the book in Martin's hand. It was *Absolutely, Positively Not . . .* He must have bought it! And Wyatt guessed Rhonda was okay with that.

Did that mean . . . ?

Maybe it didn't mean anything. After all, he wasn't wearing a rainbow bracelet like he had in that video. Maybe he was just cool with Gay people.

But maybe . . .

Martin's smile was a little lopsided. "Feeling better?"

Wyatt's mouth was suddenly dry. "You wanna get out of here? I'll show you our town."

The house was empty, and Martin explained that the adults were off in Corvallis at the Benton County Circuit Court. They snagged two granola bars and were out the door. Martin wanted to bring his guitar along, but Wyatt said no—they didn't want to attract any attention on this mission.

"So, being homeschooled must be heaven, huh?" Wyatt thought it would be sweet never to have to set an alarm again. Never to have to see Jonathon, either. They were on the school side of Jenson's Stream, since the near side was too overgrown with Himalayan blackberries. But they were walking along the bank at the bottom of the ravine—it wasn't like anyone would see them. Wyatt was thinking he would take Martin all the way to the covered bridge into town. They could pop up there, and Wyatt could show him Union Square and stuff without getting caught cutting school.

"It's all right," Martin said, picking up a pine cone by the path.

They were both quiet for a bit, but it was okay. Martin stopped to put the pine cone gently into the water, like he was launching a boat. They watched it bob along. "How many seeds do you think are in there?" Martin asked him.

Wyatt had no idea. "Fifty? A hundred?"

"That could go all the way to the ocean and travel to New Zealand. Start a forest there. That would be cool to see."

It would, but Wyatt knew his future was in some big, anonymous city, where he could just disappear. The pine cone was almost out of sight, and Wyatt wondered if it would make it past the ford. His voice got quieter, and a bit sad. "The second high school is over, I'm out of here."

Martin seemed like he wanted to ask a question, but didn't. Instead he said, "Being homeschooled? My mom only gives me a hard time about doing my work, not about being myself."

"You were getting crap at school for being Black?" Wyatt didn't think that was it, but he had to ask.

Martin scoffed. "I was getting crap for thinking Daniel Craig coming out of the ocean in *Casino Royale* was hot. Instead of Ursula Andress in *Dr. No.*"

"Craig is completely the best Bond!" Wyatt said, but inside he was screaming, *He's Gay! He just said he's Gay! Act cool.*

"You watch them, too?" Martin asked, his smile like a superpower that short-circuited Wyatt's brain.

Wyatt managed to squeak out, "Yeah," and they started walking along the bank again. Did Martin know about him? He couldn't. Could he?

Wyatt turned, hoping to see it again. Feel it again. They caught eyes, and the look Martin gave him made Wyatt feel like his stomach had dropped out of his body. Like Martin wanted Wyatt to stop everything and just look at him. Let him look at Wyatt.

Wyatt's breath caught, and he plunged ahead.

Why didn't I ever feel like this with Mackenzie?

After a while, Martin started humming. His voice fit, somehow, with the birds and the gurgle of water, even their crunching footsteps on the path. Wyatt didn't talk anymore. He just wanted to listen, hoping to get his pulse to stop pounding in his neck.

Ten minutes later, they were climbing the bank by the covered bridge to top out on Route 37. As they gained altitude, Wyatt saw there was only a single car by the log cabin. Usually there were at least a couple of tour vans and buses. Martin touched his arm as they got to the road.

"Wyatt," he started.

Wyatt jerked his arm away—anybody could see them.

"Look."

Wyatt followed to see where Martin was pointing, at the WELCOME TO LINCOLNVILLE—REAL AMERICA sign.

But the sign on the red bridge had the same pink graffiti as the B and B sign at home. This time, the word REAL had been crossed out, and QUEER was scrawled over it instead.

Wyatt felt sucker-punched. Trapped. He couldn't get away from it. Any of it.

Martin pulled out his cell phone and snapped a photo of the sign. "My mom will want that." He saw the sick expression on Wyatt's face and gestured back to the stream trail. "Let's get out of here."

Wyatt's feet obeyed. But as they headed down the ravine, and the whole walk back, he couldn't get the image out of his head. The sign shouting:

WELCOME TO LINCOLNVILLE—QUEER AMERICA

Hiding out in his bedroom for the rest of the week, Wyatt felt like he was caught in an avalanche, and the whole hillside was sliding out from under his feet.

IT WAS PAST noon, and a knock on Wyatt's door, followed by the sound of the key in the lock, got him to sit bolt upright in bed. "Yeaahhhh?" he said cautiously. He'd left it unlocked—he wasn't hiding anything.

After it got locked and then unlocked again, in walked his dad, mom, Rhonda, and Martin.

Yikes. There were piles of clothes and papers scattered everywhere. Martin hadn't seen Wyatt's room yet, and this wasn't the best first impression.

Martin avoided his eyes, "Hey. This is . . . an intervention."

What?

Wyatt's mom straightened the edge of his top comforter. "We've been making a mistake, sweetie, letting you hole up at home. You can't hide from life."

Rhonda took her turn: "Monday, you have to go back. If you miss another day of school without a notarized doctor's note, they're threatening to expel you for truancy. And there won't be anything I can do about it."

His dad looked him square in the eye. "We Yarrows don't hide from our problems. Time to get up and face them."

Martin's face was serious, but there was a teasing glint in his eyes. "You do know I've been here for four whole days, and you've been a terrible host?"

Wyatt had to laugh at that one. "Okay, okay!" Hands up, he slid out of bed to stand. "I'm up."

His mom ruffled his hair. "I've got an open house to set up for tomorrow, your dad will be busy going through the attic, and Rhonda has to work. So I'm dropping you two off by the junior high, and you can walk back. At least that way I'll know you've made it out of this room."

Twenty minutes later, Wyatt climbed into the backseat of their green pickup, letting Martin and his guitar ride shotgun. As his mom made the turn to Johnson Street, Wyatt saw a whole bunch of yellow-and-black flyers on the utility poles. Someone having a yard sale, he figured.

But what he really noticed was that the Lincoln businesses and the Log Cabin were a ghost town. The only human being they saw was Mr. Woo, sorting through the period costumes on his outdoor clothing rack. He spotted them but didn't smile or anything. Just turned his back and went into his store. Like they were lepers. Wyatt guessed they kind of were. Or at least *he* was.

His mom punched the radio's ON button to cover the awkward moment. It was talk radio, and it was like the shock-jock hosts of the show couldn't spin their words out fast enough as the truck headed into Union Square.

ROB: Hey, Amy, did you hear about the Sapphic mayor of Lincolnville?

AMY: Rob! What are you talking about?

ROB: It's all over. See, now that it's been revealed that Lincoln might have been secretly Gay, there's talk that everyone in Lincolnville is a closet case. Their mayor? I hear she's a big Lesbian.

AMY: So, you're saying high school coach and sometimes country singer Bryan Rails, her husband, is a bit . . .

ROB: Limp in the wrist? Well, if the pump fits . . .

AMY: How about the other people in their town?

Wyatt's mom slowed them to a near stop as they listened. Wyatt stared at the library, just up ahead.

ROB: They're saying it's not true, that they're all straight, but science disagrees.

AMY: Science?

ROB: Statistically, the people who know these things are saying that between three and twenty percent of the people in Oregon are Gay.

AMY: Three and twenty? That's some kind of "knowing things."

ROB: Well . . . what if everyone who's Gay in Oregon is there?

AMY: In Lincolnville?

ROB: You hear about them in Portland, and Ashland, of course, and I hear there's some bent folk over in Bend, but . . . maybe all the closeted ones are living right here in Benton County—you know, in the town with possibly the most famous closeted Gay man of all, Abraham Lincoln!

AMY: I used to get the best pancakes at their Pantry restaurant . . . or was it Pansy? Who'd have thought? Lincolnville.

ROB: I hear they're calling it Queerville now.

AMY: A rose by any other name is just as . . . Gay?

ROB: Is that what Shakespeare said?

AMY: Just call me the Bard of Stratford-on-AM radio!

Martin shut the radio off, but it was like Wyatt could hear their words still echoing in the truck cab.

How many people listen to that show?

The silence stretched, as taut as the space between lightning and thunder. Wyatt's mom drove them forward again, made the right onto Route 37, and accelerated under the covered bridge. Wyatt checked in the side-view mirror as they cleared the roof. QUEER AMERICA—the graffiti was still there.

Two blocks past the high school turnoff, Martin cleared his throat. "You know, Shakespeare was Bi."

Wyatt's mom swerved the truck onto the shoulder of the road and slammed to a stop. She let her head drop to the steering wheel. Wyatt wasn't sure if she was crying or not.

Guitar rescued from the floor, Martin turned and caught Wyatt's eye, looking guilty.

Wyatt gave the slightest shrug. He didn't want to make him feel worse. "Mom? You okay?"

She didn't say anything. Wyatt was about to unbuckle his seat belt to check on her, when she took in a shuddering breath. "Kelly told me she can't wait to fire me the Monday after there's no parade. We only had thirty-one entries, and I have twelve voice mails that I'm afraid to listen to. My emails are . . . I can't even . . . The B and B is going under—I don't think we can save it. Which means the bank will foreclose. Rhonda says we can fight the lawsuit, but . . ." She raised her head and looked at Wyatt in the rearview mirror. Her eyes were puffy. "This has gotten so out of control."

"I didn't mean for it . . . ," Wyatt started, but he didn't know what to say. Martin fidgeted in his seat.

"I know," Wyatt's mom said. After a moment, she dug into her purse. "Why don't you two get out here? I'll give you some money for Sandee's." She held out a five-dollar bill.

Wyatt's eye caught on Lincoln's face, and his mom forced a smile. "There's no escaping it, is there? Go. Have some fun—someone should."

"You going to be okay?" Wyatt asked her, as he pocketed the five.

"Your dad told me this great thing last night." She checked her reflection in the rearview mirror and wiped under her eyes with a knuckle. "Winston Churchill, in the middle of World War Two, said, 'If you're going through hell, keep going.' And that's what we have to do. Don't stop; just keep going."

A minute later, Wyatt and Martin stood in the weeds by the roadside. Under Wyatt's mom's truck, the tires spit gravel as she pulled back onto the road.

Martin turned to Wyatt. "I guess . . . we should keep going."

"Those foreign commercials can be a riot." Martin was speaking over the sound of the soccer match broadcast in Spanish as they browsed the shelves of Sandee's Liquor and Candy Mart. "Ooh—there's this one French Orangina ad where an opera singer is on a plane. She has a sip, starts singing high C, rips the door off, and skydives out!"

Martin mimicked the falling opera singer, "Orangin—aaaaaa!" He hit a falsetto note and crumpled to the floor. Wyatt cracked up.

"You've got to see it—I'll show you online when we get back," Martin said.

"¡Fue falta! ¡Idiota!" Sandee yelled at her screen.

Martin looked up at Wyatt. "You going to help me up, or am I just going to lie here?"

Wyatt put out his hand, and Martin grabbed on. It was almost electric, the current that shot through Wyatt's arm from where they held each other. Wyatt yanked—stronger than he meant to—and Martin soared up, bumping into him. They caught their balance and steadied out, faces inches from each other.

The door jingled. "I'm pretty sure it doesn't list the pH . . . ," Jennie was saying, as she and Mackenzie, still in the white pants and T-shirt from her karate class, walked in.

Three of the four of them froze, watching each other. Wyatt's face shut down. Martin looked from the girls to Wyatt, like he was trying to figure out what was going on. Breaking the moment, Wyatt stepped back, bumping into the shelf of shaving creams and Band-Aids.

Jennie started to head for the sodas, but Mackenzie pulled her toward the shelves of gum opposite Wyatt and Martin. "Indoor glow-in-the-dark mini golf. And in the dark, Jonathon could hardly keep his hands off me!" She was talking to Jennie, but Wyatt knew it was for his benefit. "We had such a great time! He's busy tonight, but wants to see me again tomorrow. Now that my Sunday days are free, we're meeting at eleven to watch a movie in their screening room and have a catered lunch. Did I tell you he sent roses? They came this morning. You wouldn't believe how fancy they are."

Wyatt made a beeline for the freezer and snagged an ice cream sandwich. Martin was taking his time, browsing the shelves of crackers and chips.

"Hey!" Wyatt leaned in close and whispered to him. "Grab something and let's get out of here."

"Why? What's up?" Martin asked.

Wyatt's eyes pointed out Mackenzie, who at that second turned with a packet of gum in her hand to scowl at them. He said under his breath, "That's Mackenzie. My ex- . . . friend."

Martin's eyes darkened. "And her Jonathon's *Jonathon*?"

"Yeah," Wyatt breathed.

Jennie touched Mackenzie on the arm. "What are you thinking?"

Mackenzie spat the words out, "That I've had enough." She slapped the gum she'd been holding back on the shelf and strode over to them. "Who's the stranger, Wyatt? We don't get a lot of outsiders who aren't tourists here."

Wyatt gave her a look like she'd gone crazy. "Uh, Mackenzie? We're all outsiders, unless we're Paiute Indians."

"Name's Martin." Martin crossed his arms, which, Wyatt noticed, made his arm muscles pop. "I'm staying with Wyatt for a few days."

Mackenzie's eyes flashed at Wyatt. "You didn't waste much time getting a *boy*friend."

"He's not my boyfriend!" Wyatt was nearly shouting and told himself to chill. "I'm not Gay. Martin and his mom, they're staying at the B and B. That's all."

Martin snagged a bag of almonds and slipped past Mackenzie, like he was done with the conversation. "What are you getting, man?"

Wyatt held up his ice cream to answer and tried to pretend that the lasers in Mackenzie's eyes had no effect on him, either. He joined Martin at the counter, put his ice cream sandwich by the almonds, and topped it with the money his mom had given him.

Sandee stood there, watching them, ignoring the penalty kick happening on-screen. "It would be a shame to break that." She pushed the green portrait of Abraham Lincoln back at Wyatt. "This one's on me. Just, go home, and be safe."

Wyatt blinked, surprised. Did that mean Sandee believed him about Lincoln? Was she a Lesbian? Or did she just want to be nice?

He looked at her. Whatever the reason—he was grateful. "Thanks."

Sandee gave him the slightest dip of her head, then turned back to her soccer match. "*¡Ja! ¡Patea la pelota!*" she yelled at the TV.

Not risking another glance in Mackenzie's direction, Wyatt got them out of there.

They were heading down Hayes Street, back to the B and B, and Wyatt could feel Martin's eyes on him.

Finally, Martin said, "Ex-friend or ex-*girl*friend?"

"Uh . . . ," Wyatt stalled, trying to figure out what to say about him and Mackenzie. "Kind of . . . both?"

"Oh." Martin said.

"No! It was never like that; it's just . . ." Wyatt stalled out. "It's kind of hard to explain."

Martin nodded, like he understood. *Did he?*

"Well, thanks for standing up for me with the *un*welcome committee," Martin said, ripping open the bag of almonds and popping a few in his mouth.

Wyatt took another bite of spongy chocolate and velvet-cool vanilla, but he felt all torn up from everything. Mackenzie had been so mean. And she and Jonathon . . . he didn't want to think about it. And Martin was right here—he finally had a friend who was Gay!—but Wyatt couldn't even be real with him. . . . And Martin was thanking him for standing up for him?

Wyatt shrugged. "That's what friends do, right?"

Martin put his hand on Wyatt's shoulder. "Yeah. That's what we do."

They were in public!

Wyatt stepped away so Martin's hand fell. Wyatt kept going, pretending the reason he'd moved was that he wanted to read one of those yellow-and-black flyers stapled to the utility pole on the corner ahead.

Martin covered the moment by pocketing the bag of almonds and swinging his guitar around. Like he had only been trying to pat Wyatt on the back.

But Wyatt was hyperaware that they both knew what had happened, and they both knew the other knew it, too.

Awk-ward!

Martin plucked out some notes as they passed under another one of the banners announcing the town's upcoming parade.

It felt weird, and Wyatt didn't want it to. *If I were walking with a girl, no one would care if she had her arm around me. Why does this have to be so much harder?*

Martin strummed a chord and started to sing. The melody was familiar to Wyatt: it was a Civil War song from one of the CDs they played in the exhibit rooms. But the words were new:

> *Two brothers on their way,*
> *One wore blue and one wore gray,*
> *One was straight and one was Gay,*
> *All on a beautiful morning . . .*

"Whoa—those aren't the lyrics I know!" Wyatt spoke over his shoulder as he neared the flyer.

"I've been playing with them." Martin fingered the strings, plucking out the wistful melody.

Wyatt turned back to see who was having a yard sale. The letters shouted,

> WORRIED ABOUT THOSE PEOPLE
> WHO THINK LINCOLN WAS GAY?
> JOIN
> THE JOHN WILKES BOOTH APPRECIATION SOCIETY

The uneaten half of Wyatt's ice cream sandwich squished in his fist. Reading it over Wyatt's shoulder, Martin stopped playing.

There was a line of them. Wyatt saw that the flyers went all the way down Hayes Street. He scraped the mess off his hand and threw it to the asphalt as he hurried to the corner of Union. More yellow flyers.

"Wyatt!" Martin ran behind him, guitar bongoing against his hip, trying to keep up. But Wyatt couldn't stop. Grant Street, yellow flyers. Johnson Street, yellow flyers. Buchanan Street, yellow flyers.

It was the whole town.

Back home, they found out that the afternoon tour, a Boy Scout troop from Philomath Christian Day School, had canceled. So had Tuesday's tour for Mother of Sorrows Elementary, who had told Wyatt's dad they weren't going to bring their children to a place that "promoted homosexuality." But it wasn't like Wyatt had expected any of them to show, not now.

All frazzled, his dad went back up to the attic to keep looking for hidden treasure. Martin's mom was still knee-deep in legal documents, and Wyatt's mom wouldn't be home till nearly dinner, so they were on their own. "You want a tour?" Wyatt asked Martin, pointing to their exhibit rooms.

"Ahhh. You're making an effort to be a better host," Martin teased. "I better play along."

Wyatt tried to keep his face serious. "You better."

He kept thinking it was his first Gay-friendly tour and he should change stuff, but the facts about Lincoln and the war pretty much stayed the same. Just . . . how Wyatt felt about it was all different.

Martin pointed to Wax Lincoln's hat. "In kindergarten they told us he kept papers in there—but it sounded crazy."

"He did! Tucked in the lining." Wyatt took the imitation beaver-fur hat off Wax Lincoln and handed it to Martin so he could see the coffee-aged Emancipation Proclamation Wyatt kept inside it for tours. "It left his hands free."

Martin reached up to put the hat back on Wax Lincoln. "The hat made him even taller."

"That was probably the point. So he would stand out even more." It struck Wyatt that while Lincoln had been willing to stand out about some things, like being super tall and leading their country through the Civil War, he hadn't been willing to stand up about loving Joshua. A wave of sadness washed over him, and he shook it off.

As they walked by the weapons case, Wyatt thought about introducing Martin to his soldier but decided that would have been too weird.

He just snuck a wink at the photo and led Martin to the flat-screen monitor in what used to be the dining room. At the end of the *Civil War in Four Minutes* DVD, Martin gave a low whistle at how many people had died during the war. The casualty numbers on the screen topped out at North: 702,000, South: 621,000.

"One-point-three million," Martin said. "Just think, nearly triple that have read all about Lincoln being Gay, thanks to you."

Triple? Wyatt hadn't asked about or checked their blog stats all week. *That's more than three million. . . . Thanks to me?* He shook his head. "Thanks to *us*." He was glad they were in it together.

They finished the tour upstairs in the Lincoln Room. The bed stood at the far end like some altar. Wyatt made himself busy, moving the bronze plaque's wooden stand and the three metal stanchions with their velvet ropes to the side—it was a better view without them.

"Can I get on it?" Martin asked.

"We're not supposed . . . ," Wyatt started, then changed his mind. "Sure." He picked the three Wax Lincoln hairs off the pillow and put them on the lip of the china washbasin. Wyatt slid his palm in the air for Martin to try the bed out.

"I'll be right back." Martin ran across the hall to his room. A minute later, he returned with a plastic dropcloth and eased the door shut. "Those are going to be some old dust mites. Help me?"

Wyatt wanted to tell Martin he was being paranoid, but he just took one end. They unfolded the thin plastic and laid it over the bed like they were getting ready to paint the red-striped wallpaper behind it.

Martin carefully climbed on, plastic crinkling underneath him. He looked over at Wyatt. "Lie down."

Wyatt cleared his throat. "Nah. I mean . . ."

"Come on! Let's see if they could really be in this bed together without, you know . . ."

"I tried it!"

Martin shook his head. "You just put those mannequins on it."

He patted the plastic space next to him. "This way, you get to experience it."

Wyatt walked over to the edge of the bed and hesitated. Martin's right arm was thrown back under his head, which made his bicep in his tight T-shirt . . . perfect. He was so hot. *Damn.* Wyatt turned around and lowered himself onto the thin plastic. It was like lying down on his mom's dry cleaning or something. *Stop thinking about Mom!*

"You're going to fall off." Martin's voice was soft.

"I'm okay."

Martin's hand came around and rested on Wyatt's chest, pulling him back toward him. And Wyatt let him, covering Martin's hand with his own. And then Martin was spooning him, and even with the plastic under them it was warm and safe and crazy and—

Wyatt jumped away, keeping his back to Martin. His face burned, and he couldn't catch his breath. "I . . . I gotta go!" He raced to the door, flung it open, and took the stairs two at a time to his bedroom. He got the door closed behind him and sank to the floor.

Oh, man . . .

Blood pounded through Wyatt's body as he tried to get it under control.

There was no way they'd been in that bed together without getting it on.

And now, for sure, Martin knew about him, too.

Mackenzie   8:14 p.m.

Jonathon's on The Von Lawson
Report. You might want to watch.

WYATT WAS SO furious with her and Jonathon, he didn't want to see it. But Martin said they had to and yelled for his mom. Wyatt's parents came, too. Moments later, they were all crowded into Rhonda's room, watching the live broadcast on one of the three computer screens on the antique rolltop desk.

Jonathon was there on TV, wearing his yellow John Wilkes Booth Appreciation Society T-shirt, sitting across from Von Lawson. They were laughing about something. Words under them read:

LINCOLN. UNDER. ATTACK!

"It's hard to shove that Gay genie back in the bottle!" Von Lawson said, then faced the camera. "It's been just about a week since our last national survey, so we did another, asking, 'Do you think Abraham Lincoln and Joshua Speed might have been more than just "friends?"' This time, eight percent of people believed it. What scares me here—and there's not much that scares me, Real America—is the growth. Last week, two percent. This week, eight. Following that same line, next week we'll be at thirty-two percent of people believing it. . . . And the week after that? Everybody! Except you"—he pointed at Jonathon, and then at himself—"and me. In a bunker. Hiding from this radiation poisoning of history. That's what they want: drive us underground, into their old closets—where they should be! And it's starting now, right this minute, with this poor, stupid eight percent."

Jonathon and the audience booed the 8 percent.

"It's their First Amendment right to be asses!" Rhonda commented from the edge of the bed, her left hand working a silver ring with a jade stone around in circles.

"We're very glad you're here," Wyatt's mom said to Rhonda. She and Wyatt's dad were watching from the room's Victorian couch. Tensed up in a ball in the armchair, Wyatt caught eyes with Martin, who was sitting on the wood desk chair next to his mom. *Count me glad, too.*

Martin winked at him.

Wyatt felt the flush rising in his face and tried to focus on the TV show. He wasn't sure how he felt about Mackenzie tipping him off that her boyfriend was on *The Von Lawson Report* again. Was that her being kind or just rubbing his face in it?

Von Lawson continued, "Now, I've been getting some flack, people saying that I shouldn't even be talking about this on my show, that we're giving them a platform for these obscene lies, but I ask you, Real America—if someone's burning down your house, should you just walk away and not say anything?"

The studio audience yelled, "No!"

"That's right. If someone's trying to burn down *my* house, I'm going to stop them, with a fire hose on full blast!"

Jonathon chimed in, "An air tanker, dropping a *[beep]* load of water to put it out!"

Von Lawson drummed the air at Jonathon, building on what Jonathon was saying, "Not water—fire retardant!"

Jonathon laughed. "Retard! They're retards!"

"I know! I'm with you." Von Lawson leaned back and put his cowboy boots up on his desk. "I want to get us back to a simpler America. Where we don't have all these minorities shouting about wanting what we have, when we earned it. . . . In the good old days, you didn't see freaks, and 'disabled' people, and retards, and people practicing bestiality and necrophilia and homosexuality, running around, making all this noise: *Gimme, gimme, gimme!* And it's the professional homosexualists— they're the ones who want to make our thoughts a crime. They're the ones perverting not just today, but history! Nothing's safe from them! We need to just clean our country out!"

"Holy crap," Wyatt whispered.

Martin met his gaze and nodded.

"Um . . ." Jonathon hesitated on-screen. "I'm not really talking about getting rid of anyone—"

Von Lawson cut him off. "But when it's an enemy from within, you have to control the outbreak! If someone you love has cancer, you get doctors to cut it out, and then use drugs to kill it, cell by cell. Should we do any less for the country we love?"

Jonathon looked lost. "I guess it's important to, uh, stick together? I wanted to say that not *everybody* in Lincolnville thinks Lincoln was a Queer. I mean . . . most of us don't, and if—"

Von Lawson cut him off again by slapping his desk. "But the numbers are rising! What's it going to take before this country wakes up?" A new camera angle let him speak directly to the viewers. "What's it going to take before *you* wake up?"

Maybe Mackenzie had been warning Wyatt?

Von Lawson was on his feet, shouting, "Make no mistake about it,

Real America! This is a war. A war for the very soul of our country. They are trying to weaponize history against us. We have to save Lincoln, and save the nation!"

Huge applause and fist pumping as the image pulled back to show the studio audience. Von Lawson shouted over the going-to-commercial music, "We'll be right back, with our Prayer for America!" Wyatt watched Von Lawson shake Jonathon's hand heartily. For a second, he thought Jonathon looked dazed. And then Von Lawson said something in Jonathon's ear and the two of them were laughing again, waving at the camera.

Martin hit MUTE. No one said anything.

How did Martin do it? Being Gay—with everyone knowing—seemed like walking around with this giant target painted on your back. Did Martin need to be afraid? *Do I?*

Wyatt's dad was the first to speak, but he didn't say anything about Gay genocide or a war for the soul of the country. All he said was, "Dinner's getting cold."

WITH NO GUESTS coming, Wyatt was heading out to their B and B sign before dinner to take down the two flags for the night. When he opened the door, he found a giant shopping bag of his mom's shoes right outside. Each of the ten or so pairs was packed neatly in its own clear plastic bag, but there was no note or anything. He picked up the oversize shopping bag and carried it to his parents' room, leaning it against his mom's shoe wardrobe.

He sighed, not wanting to have to explain to her about Mackenzie and her laser beam eyes. Grabbing a sticky note from the mail desk, he wrote: Left by the front door

"Wyatt?" his dad's voice called out. "We're starting!"

He stuck the note to the bag with the butterfly wing–colored shoes inside and hustled back outside to get the flags.

Five minutes later, as Wyatt jiggled cheesy broccoli off a serving spoon and onto his plate, his cell vibrated once in his pocket. An incoming text. He passed the dish to Martin and then, pretending to adjust the napkin in his lap, got his phone out.

Mackenzie   8:32 p.m.

Can we talk?

Wyatt   8:33 p.m.

text

Things felt tense around the table. No guests meant no money. Which meant Wyatt and his parents were fast on their way to being homeless.

Martin broke the silence. "I just wish Lincoln wasn't such a racist—then this whole his-being-a-Gay-hero thing would sit better."

"What are you talking about?" Wyatt remembered the quote pretty well. "Lincoln was the guy who said, 'Whenever I hear anyone arguing over slavery, I feel a strong impulse to see it tried on him personally.' He wasn't a racist."

The phone under Wyatt's napkin vibrated again.

Martin speared a piece of chicken. "Lincoln wanted to deport all us Blacks out of the US. He even said he didn't see us as equals."

"He said 'all men are created equal' should apply to everyone!" But even as Wyatt defended Abe, his thoughts dashed ahead. Was Lincoln really a racist? He'd never heard that, about Lincoln wanting to deport Black people . . . but he knew Martin wouldn't lie about it.

"It's a bigger issue," Rhonda cut in. "Should a hero's flaws overshadow the tremendous good they brought about?"

Wyatt snuck a glance at his phone.

Mackenzie   8:35 p.m.

I'm so sorry. What they said was terrible.

Wyatt   8:38 p.m.

but ur still going out with him

Wyatt hit SEND and took a huge bite of broccoli. He chewed, nodding at Rhonda like he'd been listening the whole time.

She was saying, "Frederick Douglass wrote that Lincoln treated him with great respect. That's pretty high praise for the 1800s."

Martin asked his mom, "But don't you wish Lincoln had been an abolitionist? A fierce opponent of slavery?"

Rhonda took a sip of wine and then said, "Perfect people don't exist."

Wyatt's mom snorted a laugh. "No matter what their online profile says."

Rhonda put her hand on Martin's arm. "It's something I had to come to terms with years ago, when I named you."

Wyatt's mom was curious. "What did Martin's father want to name him? Gregory and I had quite a time coming up with *Wyatt.*"

Rhonda's face was carefully neutral. "Martin doesn't have a father."

Wyatt's mom started, "But everyone—"

Martin cut her off. "Sperm donor."

Wyatt looked at him. He hadn't expected that. But maybe that explained why Rhonda wore multiple silver and stone rings on every finger, except the ring finger of her left hand. Kind of like the opposite of being married.

"I prefer the term *genetic contributor,*" Rhonda said sternly.

"But no one knows what that is," Martin said, like they'd had the argument before. "*Sperm donor* is really clear. You didn't need a guy; you just needed the sperm."

"I'd rather we didn't use that kind of language."

Martin rolled his eyes. "It's just a word! *Sperm!*"

Rhonda gave him a *you're pushing it* glare. "We are guests in this home, and we should respect other people's comfort zones."

"It's okay," Wyatt spoke up. "We say *sperm,* too." But then he got the giggles. Martin did as well, and soon the two of them were laughing so hard they could barely catch their breath.

Tucked under his leg, Wyatt's phone vibrated.

"As I was saying . . ." Rhonda exaggerated a turn away from the teenage boys and spoke to Wyatt's dad and mom. "The lack of perfect people is something I had to accept when I named my *son, who has no manners!*"

"I'm sorry . . ." Martin dissolved into giggles again.

"Well, it's an incredibly important decision." Wyatt's mom nodded like she understood, "It's a given that everyone's a little fake. . . ."

At that, Wyatt had a surge of hope. Would she understand about him when it finally came out? When *he* finally came out?

His mom finished her thought. "But what if someone did something really terrible? You don't want to build a whole life on the crumbling foundation of a lie!"

Wyatt's emotions plunged like the drop on a roller coaster, and he could feel his face heat up. He was saved from being noticed by his dad coughing, like some food had gone down the wrong way. While his dad waved away everyone's concern, saying he was fine, Wyatt snuck a glance at his phone.

Mackenzie   8:40 p.m.

No. I can't believe he didn't speak up for Becca. Or anyone else. I'm going to break up with him.

Wyatt   8:42 p.m.

when

Mackenzie   8:42 p.m.

Tomorrow. And then we'll talk. Okay?

Wyatt   8:43 p.m.

k.

Wyatt hit SEND, and his chest felt a little less tight about things. Mackenzie still owed him some major apologies—like, how could she date that jerk in the first place?—but at least they were communicating, and it wasn't all laser-beam hate stares.

Rhonda was on the third flawed person she had considered: "But then even Malcolm X had that drug-and-larceny background—"

Martin cut in, "So you named me after an adulterer."

"Martin!" Rhonda put down her fork. "What is with you tonight?"

"Kidding. Sort of," Martin acknowledged. He glanced over at Wyatt, who was slipping his cell back in his pocket. The muscles that had been so tight in Martin's face relaxed.

"Martin Luther King?" Wyatt asked.

"Junior." Martin nodded.

"That's why you knew the speech by heart!" Wyatt said, taking his last bite of ketchup-drenched chicken.

"Have you seen it?" Rhonda asked Wyatt. "The I Have a Dream speech?"

Wyatt shook his head no.

Rhonda inclined her head to Martin. "You could recite the whole thing. . . ."

"I don't want to be the trained seal," Martin protested. "Anyway, he should watch the original." He checked Wyatt's plate and saw he was pretty much done, too. "Come on. I've got it on my laptop, from when she made me learn it by heart."

They left the adults downstairs. Up in Martin's room, Martin slid his computer onto the foot of the bed and hopped on the mattress with his guitar. Wyatt hesitated. He didn't want to be weird about it, so he took a spot by the pillow, as far away as he could get. Leaning back against the headboard, he didn't recognize the flannel comforter they were sitting on and realized Martin must have brought that with him, too. *Weird.*

Martin found the video file, and Wyatt wondered if he was going to play along. But Martin just held the guitar, and they watched.

After images of marchers, a chorus of people singing "We Shall Overcome," the Mall in Washington, DC, packed with people, and an introduction calling him "the moral leader of our nation," Dr. Martin Luther King Jr. was there, in black and white, starting his speech.

> "I am happy to join with you today in what will go down in history as the greatest demonstration for freedom in the history of our nation."

After the words painted on their wall downstairs, and the line about Black people still not being free, he said:

> "When the architects of our Republic wrote the magnificent words of the Constitution and the Declaration of Independence, they were signing a promissory note to which every American was to fall heir. This note was a promise that all men, yes, Black men as well as White men, would be guaranteed the 'unalienable right' of 'Life, Liberty, and the Pursuit of Happiness.'"

Yes.

> "Now is the time to make justice a reality for all of God's children."

Martin turned back to Wyatt. Their eyes caught, and Wyatt felt something stir inside, a connection, but he couldn't think about it. Instead, he moved his eyes back to the screen.

> "But there is something that I must say to my people, who stand on the warm threshold which leads into the Palace of Justice: In the process of gaining our rightful place, we must not be guilty of wrongful deeds. . . . Again and again we must rise to the majestic heights of meeting physical force with soul force.

The words were so powerful, Wyatt had to say them out loud. "Soul force."

Martin moved the pillow aside and scooched back to lean against the headboard next to Wyatt. Wyatt told himself it was no big deal. Martin probably just wanted to get more comfortable.

Dr. Martin Luther King Jr. was saying that not all White people were bad. That many of them were there that day, listening to him, because they had

> "come to realize that their freedom is inextricably bound to our freedom. We cannot walk alone."

Out of the corner of his eye, Wyatt glanced at Martin—his mouth was moving along to the words. And Wyatt saw him. It was a gift, his mom naming him after this amazing man. Even if Dr. Martin Luther King Jr. hadn't been perfect.

Martin was pretty awesome, but he wasn't perfect, either—that whole weird dust-mite thing.

And I'm sure not perfect.

And Lincoln? Closeted Gay man . . . Racist? But maybe it was okay that Abe wasn't perfect, too.

Dr. King was telling them about his dream of everyone being equal, and was saying that they should

> "let freedom ring!"

from all over the country.

> "And when this happens, when we allow freedom ring, when we let it ring from every village and every hamlet, from every state and every city . . ."

The side of Martin's hand brushed against the side of Wyatt's hand and stayed there. Nerves fired from where their skin touched all the way through Wyatt, like the fireflies he'd seen dancing in the air in Pennsylvania last summer.

> "we will be able to speed up that day when all of God's children, Black men and White men, Jews and Gentiles, Protestants and Catholics, will be able to join hands and sing in the words of the old Negro spiritual: Free at last! Free at last! Thank God Almighty, we are free at last!"

Thunderous applause.

Wow. Wyatt was so glad to have seen it. "That was amazing."

"He had his good points," Martin admitted. His face was so close, Wyatt could feel Martin's breath against his own cheek.

Wyatt got up, breaking the skin contact and the moment. "We just need to add Gays to his list."

"Yeah." Martin closed his laptop. "Travel back in time, add it in the speech."

Wyatt knew Martin was being sarcastic, but after he said it, the idea hung in the air for a long moment.

"They were pretty similar," Wyatt said.

Martin fingered chords on his guitar's frets. "Who?"

"King and Lincoln. Both minorities—Black and Gay. Both assassinated."

"Both left our world a better place," Martin added.

"I'd like to do that, too. Just"—Wyatt grimaced—"not the getting-killed part."

"You are! With the blog."

Wyatt paced the small room. "Am I? Is it making any difference? There's all this hate out there. . . ."

Martin strummed his guitar. "There's this great song about how the best place to start making a difference is inside yourself. 'Man in the Mirror.'" He launched into the chorus.

But as Martin sang, Wyatt knew he needed the world to change first. If he came out now, it would all be for nothing. Nobody would believe his story about Lincoln loving another guy anymore—they'd think the whole thing had been a lie. And it had gone so far, all those millions of people who watched *The Von Lawson Report* and went to the blog would hate Wyatt even more than they already did.

Wyatt backed up to the doorway. Martin stopped playing as soon as he noticed.

"We should get back for dessert," Wyatt said, and turned to hustle down the stairs. It wasn't going to do him any good to hang out in Martin's room. It didn't matter if he was a little weird—the guy was way too cute.

WYATT WAS STILL awake at 11:00 p.m., when there was a light knock on his door.

A soft voice, "You asleep?"

Martin.

Wyatt's palms got sweaty.

"One second!" Wyatt whispered, and changed fast to jeans. He didn't want to seem like he'd been about to go to bed. He didn't even want to *think* about being with Martin anywhere near a bed.

Wyatt opened his door just enough to peer out. Martin was wearing jeans and his Super *G* shirt and carried a lime-green down jacket and work gloves.

"Hey." Martin grinned at him, and Wyatt felt temporarily blinded.

"Going somewhere?" Wyatt asked.

"Yeah. So are you."

Wyatt pointed at Martin's shirt. "What's the *G* stand for? Is your middle name Gabriel or something?"

"The *G* is for *Gay*. Sort of . . . superhero Gay." Martin shrugged. "I like it."

Wyatt pulled the door all the way open. Martin sure looked the part. By Martin's feet, Wyatt noticed the plastic bin of painting supplies his dad had used to degraffiti their B and B sign. "What's with the paint?"

"Von Lawson gets more than seven and a half million viewers for each show. We're getting outgunned with just the blog." Martin glanced at the paints and then up at Wyatt with a mischievous twinkle in his eyes. "I figure it's time for another front in this war."

An hour later, they were standing under the streetlamp at the corner of Garfield and Route 37, with its banner, eight feet up:

CELEBRATE FEBRUARY 14!
ABE AND MARY: A GREAT LOVE
PARADE 9:00 A.M. @ UNION SQUARE

Once Martin had explained the plan, it turned out they didn't need the paint after all. Instead, Wyatt had used the entire stack of do-it-yourself bumper stickers from their store. Usually they printed a Lincoln quote, with his picture, and sold about two a week, but for this they needed only one word, printed big.

Martin shimmied up the pole and, holding on with his legs and one arm, reached down. "Ready," he said.

It was hard to peel the backing off the bumper stickers with his weeding gloves on, but Martin had insisted: no fingerprints. Wyatt finally got two of them and handed them up, and Martin slapped them onto both sides of the banner. He climbed down, and they inspected their work:

CELEBRATE FEBRUARY 14!
ABE AND JOSHUA: A GREAT LOVE
PARADE 9:00 A.M. @ UNION SQUARE

"Awesome," Martin said, and Wyatt couldn't have agreed more.

Hiding the few times a car passed them, they used all forty-six of their bumper stickers on Route 37 and in front of the library on Union Square. While that "fixed" only about a quarter of the ABE AND MARY banners, it would have to be enough.

There was hardly any traffic now, and Wyatt and Martin walked through town, tearing off every last yellow-and-black John Wilkes Booth Appreciation Society flyer and stuffing them in the plastic yard-trash bag Wyatt had brought along. Eighteen blocks in and out, around Union Square. When they finished, the only line of more flyers went east on Route 37. Martin used a flashlight to help them not fall on their faces as they crossed the covered bridge and made the turn onto Polk Street, following the trail and ripping them down as they went.

The flyers marked every light and utility pole down to the high school. Their bag was stuffed, and it was supposed to hold thirteen gallons! *Thirteen gallons of hate.* It seemed to Wyatt that it weighed a lot more than that.

Opposite the school rock, Martin ripped down the final flyer and stuffed it in the bag. A flashlight check didn't show any more within view. Wyatt knotted the top, slung the sack over his shoulder, and cut across the lawn to the Dumpster by the gym.

Wyatt huffed, "It's like we're Santa Claus, only instead of giving presents"—he paused as, together, they heaved it off his back and into the metal container—"our gift is taking away the ugly."

"That's pretty brilliant," Martin said.

The compliment made Wyatt feel suddenly shy.

They headed back to the street, and Wyatt noticed one of the lights on the corner of the gym lit up the words PADDLE, RATTLE, SKEDADDLE on the school rock. *Stupid.* He walked toward it, staring. And he got this crazy idea. *Crazy awesome.* "We're going to need the paint after all."

The light in Martin's eyes danced. "You thinking what I'm thinking?"

And then Wyatt wasn't thinking about the rock, or how they

needed to go back home to get paint. He just wanted to touch his lips to Martin's.

Let him know what it meant, doing this together.

How he felt.

Was Martin leaning in?

Wyatt thought so. He knew he wasn't breathing. Neither was Martin.

Martin had gently closed his eyes, and he was so beautiful. Did he look like that when he was asleep?

Wyatt couldn't believe this was going to happen. He leaned in, too.

Headlights raked across the front of the school as a car turned into the main driveway. Wyatt pulled Martin down behind the school rock a split second before they were caught. Wyatt's breath came fast, and he tried to pant silently. He waited for the lights to pass, then peeked over the top of the boulder. A police car. No—a Parking Enforcement car!

Mackenzie's dad, stifling a yawn as he scanned both sides of the driveway. Like he was a patrol officer or something.

Wyatt felt like he'd just outrun a speeding train. *That was close.*

Too close.

Sneaking back into the B and B for the paint, Wyatt expected everyone to be asleep—it was nearly 2:00 a.m. But when he and Martin tiptoed to the cleaning-supply closet opposite Wyatt's parents' room, he could hear they were still up. Talking.

"Gosh, you're tense." His mom's voice. "You need to go bowling again."

"We can't afford it." His dad's.

"You should go anyway."

"One tour, Liz. That's it. And only eight room reservations left, unless more cancel tomorrow."

"I was on the phone all day—no one wants any part of the parade," his mom said. "I can't believe Kelly already told the bank I was going to be fired! And how dare they send us a letter warning us they're going to foreclose, when we haven't even missed the payment yet!"

"I did promise Benny we wouldn't miss another, and they won't let us do a third mortgage. We don't have the equity. But it's just a warning. We have until February sixteenth."

"Did you find anything we can sell to help make it?" his mom asked.

"Not much—most of the good stuff's on display, and if we sell any of that, then what's the point? We'll be just like the Morris Lodge Express, except they have that pool!" He sighed. "I did pull some of the older books that were tucked here and there. I'll have Wyatt check auction prices. Maybe there's a first edition that will surprise us. . . ." He didn't sound convinced. "We could sell the pickup, but that's no solution. How are you going to get around? And what am I going to do, bicycle to Costco?"

"It's hard enough with just one car," his mom agreed. "Maybe we *should* sell this place. Move, and start over somewhere else. . . ."

They were silent a long moment. Then Wyatt's dad said, "I don't know how to fix this."

"How could you?" His mom's voice was tender. "You didn't break it."

Wyatt swallowed hard. Was he making things worse? But being silent didn't solve anything. It just made you a punching bag. It made you Mr. Clifton.

Martin leaned in to Wyatt, his breath tickling Wyatt's ear. "That Churchill line about going through hell? It's also a country song." He sang the line real low.

Wyatt knew Martin was right. The blog was north of 3.8 million hits. And earlier, Martin had showed Wyatt all these cloned blogs. People from all over the country, and the world, who had copied everything on Wyatt's blog and put it up on websites they controlled. At first Wyatt was kind of pissed off. *I mean, plagiarize much?* But then Martin explained it was kind of like insurance—this way, if Wyatt's blog went offline again, the truth would still be out there.

Which meant that even if they took down their own blog, there was no way to stop this anymore.

All Wyatt could do was keep on going. And if he was straight, then no one could say he was just saying Lincoln was Gay because he was Gay. That meant no more thinking about Martin like that. No more almost kisses.

Wyatt handed the brushes to Martin and silently grabbed the quick-dry white primer and the can of green left over from redoing the fence in back.

They had a rock to paint.

Chapter 24

Sunday, January 25

WYATT GOT UP thinking about how it was his mom's pick for their Sunday movie. Outside, the sky was cloudy but bright. He wished they hadn't seen the Bond movie yet, since Martin would have probably wanted to see it. Maybe his mom would let him switch weeks and they could watch 007 save the world again. He pulled on yesterday's jeans to go ask Martin what movie he'd want to see. After all, his parents had wanted to give Mackenzie a turn, and she hadn't been living with them!

He spotted the envelope on the floor, like someone had slipped it under the door while he'd been sleeping.

Wyatt opened it and read:

> *Wyatt,*
>
> *3,986,017*
> *Went to get some daylight pics for the blog,*
> *to take us over 4 million.*
>
> *Yours Forever,*
> *Martin*

Yours Forever? Abe's words to Joshua. And now Martin's to him. . . . But Wyatt wasn't going there. He couldn't.

He stumbled to his door and swung it open to head down to the kitchen. His mom was standing there, like she'd been about to knock.

"Hey," Wyatt said, rubbing one eye and hiding Martin's note in his back pocket.

"Sweetie." His mom was way serious. "We need you to come downstairs."

The air seemed to slow Wyatt down when he saw Mackenzie's father standing in the entryway with Wyatt's own dad. Mr. Miller was all dressed up like a police officer, which Wyatt had always thought was funny, since he was just a parking-ticket cop. But nothing about this looked funny.

Was it about Mackenzie? Or had Mr. Miller seen them last night?

Behind Wyatt on the stairs, his mom prodded him to keep walking.

Looking like he hadn't gotten enough sleep, Mr. Miller didn't even say hello, just stared at Wyatt's jeans. Wyatt glanced down. There was a smear of green paint by his left knee.

"I guess I've caught you green-handed, huh? Should I just cuff you here, or are you going to come peacefully?"

Wyatt's voice cracked. "You're arresting me?"

"No one's arresting anyone." Rhonda had followed them down the stairs and walked forward to hand Mr. Miller her card.

He read it and gave her a wary look. "Counselor."

Rhonda noted his badge. "Parking Enforcement Officer Miller."

He bristled. "I'm in training! I've got him on vandalism and defacing public property."

"Where's your proof?" Martin came in the open front door and walked around to stand at Wyatt's side. Wyatt thought it was a pretty superhero move, even with the guitar strapped across Martin's chest.

Mr. Miller was all suspicious about Martin and the backpack in his hand. "What else did you and your friend vandalize? What's in the bag, young man?"

Martin shrugged. "My stuff." He didn't seem that freaked out. Maybe Wyatt was freaking out enough for both of them.

"Care to show me?" Mr. Miller reached for the bag.

Rhonda put out a hand to stop him. "I'll thank you not to interrogate or illegally search my clients without probable cause. That would be police—or parking enforcement officer—harassment."

Mr. Miller glared at Rhonda. "You want to see probable cause?" He went down the front porch steps to his car, parked by the curb. Wyatt saw that the back of Mr. Miller's car was stuffed with cream-colored fabric.

Yanking out a rectangle as big as he was, Mr. Miller stomped back up the steps. He thrust the material at them. "How's this?"

It was one of the ABE AND MARY banners, chopped off top and bottom, with their JOSHUA bumper sticker over Mary's name.

"So that's where they all are," Martin whispered to Wyatt. He turned to Mr. Miller. "Cutting them down's a little extreme, isn't it? Couldn't you have just taken the stickers off?"

"Stop talking!" Rhonda snapped at Martin, and cut her eyes to Wyatt, ordering the same.

"They don't come off!" Mr. Miller tugged on a sticker edge to prove it. The banner fabric tore, leaving a ragged gap.

Oh . . . Wyatt realized it would have to be some pretty strong adhesive to stay on a car bumper. He hadn't really thought of that.

Rhonda stepped between Mackenzie's dad and Wyatt and Martin. "You can't prove my clients did that."

"Your . . ." Mr. Miller's face reddened. "Who else would it be?" He tried to get past her to their Lincoln and Civil War Memorabilia Alcove by Reception. "They sell bumper stickers here, don't they?"

They had used up all the bumper sticker paper, but Wyatt realized the empty box was still in the trash can right under the computer. Mr. Miller would see it if he went behind the counter! A trickle of sweat slid down Wyatt's back.

Rhonda stayed on Mr. Miller like it was man-on-man defense and backed him up to the front door. "You'll need to come back with a warrant."

Wyatt's cell vibrated in his pocket. He stole a glance at the text.

Mackenzie   10:28 a.m.

> emergency! I need you here 1 pm.
> about my mom.

Her mom? Wyatt pocketed it before Mackenzie's dad could maybe see it.

Wyatt's lingering anger at Mackenzie—waiting for an apology after she was going to break things off with Jonathon—suddenly felt petty. She had news about her mom? Wyatt should be there for her. He would be there. That was, if he wasn't in jail.

"Really?" Mr. Miller stared at Wyatt's dad and mom, who were standing as still as Wax Lincoln. "You're going to make me go bother the chief and a judge on a Sunday morning to get a freakin' warrant, when anyone can just walk in there and buy a bear? Who is this crazy woman?"

Wyatt's dad cleared his throat. "Ms. Sykes is our lawyer."

They stood in a silent face-off. Then Makenzie's dad said, "I'll be back" and clomped down the front porch stairs.

Rhonda called after him, "No, you won't!"

Wyatt liked how she didn't give him the last word.

But the second Mr. Miller drove off, the adults were all talking at once.

"What were you thinking?" Wyatt's mom.

"We're trying to put out the fire, and you're pouring kerosene on it?" Wyatt's dad.

And Rhonda: "What's the paint about?"

Wyatt tackled Rhonda's question, since it was the safest. "We just painted the school rock. Everyone's allowed to—it's the rules."

Rhonda gave her son and Wyatt a pained expression. "They're not going to be playing by the rules. You both need to be model citizens moving forward. Understood?"

They nodded, Wyatt thinking how the bumper sticker box would make the perfect kindling for the fire he was about to start in the living room fireplace.

Mackenzie looked surprised that it wasn't just Wyatt at the door. Martin was with him, guitar in hand.

"What's he doing here?" Mackenzie asked.

Wyatt ignored that. "Your dad's not here, is he?"

"No. He's 'having coffee' in Philomath."

"Good." Wyatt caught eyes with Martin, and they both relaxed.

Mackenzie didn't move from the doorway.

"Can we come in? Jeez." Wyatt pushed his way past her. "Is your power out?" He reached for the light switch, but Mackenzie put her hand out to stop him.

"It's supposed to be dark."

Wyatt gave her a strange look as her cat, Tali, drawn to the warm sunlight, rubbed by her leg. Martin noticed, and Mackenzie snapped at him as she scooped up the cat. "It's not a singalong, you know."

"I don't know what it is," Martin answered her. "I'm here because of Wyatt."

Mackenzie turned and whisper-hissed at Wyatt, "I thought it was just going to be you!"

"Well, is this an emergency, or isn't it?" Wyatt asked. "We can both go, or we both stay. You said it was about your mom."

"Fine." She whipped around on Martin. "But this is serious. You have to be respectful!"

Martin put up both hands, all innocent. "I'll give what I get."

Mackenzie pushed the front door closed with her shoulder and let Tali go. She gestured to the entry bench. "You can leave your guitar and shoes there. You won't need them."

She nodded a late welcome to Wyatt as he kicked off his sneakers. He gave her a half smile. "How did it go with Jonathon?"

Mackenzie made a face. "I can't talk about it. I have to concentrate on what we're doing."

"What are we doing, again?" Martin asked, settling his guitar on the bench and lining up his loafers neatly under it.

"Did you hear from her?" Wyatt asked. "Your mom?"

Wyatt had filled Martin in on Mackenzie's missing mom on the way over, and they both looked at her expectantly.

"Follow me." The shades were down, and Mackenzie led them along the darkened hallway to her bedroom.

Wyatt took it all in. Unlit candles set up in the four corners: north, south, east, west. Ivory Scrabble game letters *A* through *Z* arranged faceup on the back of a game board in the middle of the floor. She'd used black marker on the blank sides of ten extra tiles for the numbers 0 to 9. And then, on two pieces of paper, she'd drawn a sun with the word *yes* next to it, and a moon by the word *no*. There was also a pink plastic heart, about the size of Wyatt's palm, probably an old preschool toy, sitting on the board.

Another unlit candle, with three wicks, sat on the board, near a pen and paper, and a photo of Mackenzie's mom laughing. Wyatt remembered that birthday party, when Mackenzie had gotten a trampoline—she'd been twelve. Mackenzie's hair today looked exactly like her Mom's in the picture: red and super long.

"We're going to do a séance," she told them.

"What?" Wyatt thought for a second that she was joking, but that was a lot of prep for a joke. "Why?"

"Mary had eight séances in the White House. Why more than *once* if it didn't work?" Mackenzie lit the vanilla-scented candle on the board. "I think it *did* work."

"Doesn't it need to be dark out?" Wyatt asked.

"Why would ghosts care?" Martin shrugged, walking around the room and checking it out. "They don't need sunglasses or anything."

"Not ghosts, spirits," Mackenzie corrected, as she lit the other candles.

Martin picked up a two-sided, framed postcard of Machu Picchu, Peru, and turned it over. He read aloud, "Dearest Mackenzie, the Incas were amazing! Hope to show you someday."

"Hey! That's personal!" Mackenzie raced over and took the framed postcard from him, resetting it on her bedside table.

"It was just sitting there. . . ." Martin looked at Wyatt. "The next line was 'happy *birthdays*.' Not 'happy birthday.'"

"It's the last card she got from her mom," Wyatt told him. "Right after she turned thirteen."

Martin made a face like he'd really messed up. "Sorry . . ."

"You know what, let's just focus," Mackenzie said, heading back to her setup in the middle of the room's white carpet. "This is a spirit board." She plunged into explaining. They were each to sit on one side of the board, fingertips of both hands on the pink plastic heart, which she called a planchette. She gave them strict instructions that they weren't supposed to move it but should let the spirits move through them.

"You really think you can find out about your mom this way?" Wyatt tried to keep his voice gentle, but this was crazy.

Mackenzie just nodded yes.

Wyatt shared a dubious look with Martin, and they sat down.

Mackenzie started, "Sensei Jodi in karate says that if you play a string on a *biwa*—"

Martin interrupted, "What's a *biwa?*"

"It's like a Japanese guitar," Mackenzie explained. "Anyway, she was saying that if you play a string on it, it will make the same string vibrate on another *biwa*. It's sort of about teamwork and how the dojo has an energy you can tap into."

Wyatt looked over and caught Martin nodding.

Mackenzie gave a nervous smile. "I'm thinking a séance probably needs an energy, too."

She took a moment to focus, then sang a clear G note: *"Ahhh . . ."* She motioned for Wyatt and Martin to join in.

Martin's lips twitched, like he was fighting back a laugh, and she stopped singing and gave him a stern look. "You promised." She turned to Wyatt. "I'd do this by myself, but I can't. It won't work."

Wyatt gave Martin a *come on, let's try it* look and they settled back in their places.

"Ahhh . . . ," Mackenzie sang again, and this time they joined her. The air vibrated in harmony.

"Spirits, speak to us!" Mackenzie called out. They fell silent, staring at the plastic heart. "Is my mom there?"

Wyatt thought Mackenzie sounded like she was eight years old again.

They waited a long minute. No response.

"Maybe, ask it in a different way," Martin suggested.

Mackenzie tried again. "Is there . . . a message for me?"

Another long wait. Wyatt was about to say he didn't think it was going to work when their hands suddenly slid as the planchette scraped three inches along the board to rest its point against the *D* tile.

Wyatt jerked his hands away like it had burned him. Mackenzie and Martin let go fast, too, knocking some tiles off the board.

Wyatt's eyes were wide. "I didn't move it."

"I didn't, either." Martin seemed stone serious now.

Mackenzie's words sounded like they were squeezed out of her throat. "I know I didn't."

Wyatt stood up and paced. "I don't know, Mackenzie. I don't think this is such a good idea."

"Please. I need to know." Mackenzie blinked hard. "Please, Wyatt."
Martin reset the letters on the board and gestured with his head
for Wyatt to sit down again. "Come on. We said we'd help."
Wyatt wasn't happy about it, but he sat. Mackenzie nodded at Martin.
She put out trembling fingers to once more join theirs on the planchette.
"Nobody let go," Martin instructed. "Ask them again."
Mackenzie spoke the words slowly. "Is. There. A. Message. For. Me?"
Four long seconds passed, and then the planchette swung into
action, touching its point at

D

E

V

It moved faster, and Wyatt saw that the hair on Mackenzie's arms
was standing up.

O

L

Mackenzie fought for breath.

R

U

Suddenly, the planchette shot off the board, hitting her trash can
and making a hollow gong sound.
Martin scrambled to write it all down.

D E V O L R U

"Does it mean something to you?" Martin asked her.
Mackenzie shook her head.
The three of them stared at the message.
It didn't make any sense. But then, suddenly, Wyatt saw it. He gasped.
"Look at it backward." He pointed as he spelled it out. *"U. R. LOVED."*
Mackenzie stumbled up with a wild animal scream. Then her body
seemed to crumble. Tears washed her onto her bed, and she clutched a

pillow to her stomach as waves of loss tossed her about.

"I know that's true." Wyatt sat as close as he could to her, not sure she could hear him over her sobs. "She loves you. Wherever she is, your mom loves you."

Mackenzie just kept repeating, "She's gone. She's gone. She's gone."

Wyatt held her now, rocking her back and forth. "I know. But she loves you, still."

It was all he could think to say, all he could give Mackenzie to hold on to amid the crosscurrents of grief that wracked her, until finally, sleep came for her.

Careful not to let the cat out, Wyatt eased the condo door closed and he and Martin headed down to the street. Someone had tilled the dirt around the thorny-fingered, cut-back rosebushes in the front planter, and something about the smell reminded Wyatt of a freshly dug grave. He shivered.

Martin made sure his guitar was wedged carefully on the floor behind the driver's seat, then got in. The second he'd closed the door and they were alone, Wyatt turned on him. "How could you lie to her like that?"

"What?" Martin started up his mom's Volvo to get them back to the B and B. Their moms had agreed he could drive the few blocks as long as they were extra careful.

"Tell me the truth." Wyatt crossed his arms and leaned against the door. "You moved the thingy."

Martin did a slow three-point turn to get them heading South on Grant before he said anything. "Otherwise, we were just going to sit there all day."

"I knew it! Martin, now she thinks her mom is dead!"

"I didn't sign it from her mom or anything. It could have been a message from a great-great-grandmother. Or . . . Cleopatra, for that matter."

"Ha . . . ha."

Martin slowed them down as they got to the four-way stop at Sixth Street. "Right?"

"No, one more. She's sure the message was from her! Oh, *grawww!* And *I* broke your stupid code." Wyatt pushed Martin's arm. "I can't believe you made me part of it!"

"I'm driving here!" Martin scolded.

Wyatt rolled his eyes. There was no traffic, they were going about thirteen miles an hour, and it wasn't like he'd punched Martin and made him lose control of the car or anything. *He drives like an eighty-year-old.* Wyatt seethed as he directed Martin through the painfully slow sequence of turns. Right on Seventh. Left on Hayes. And right again into the B and B lot.

Martin's foot jerked against the accelerator, and the old car staggered into the spot. Wyatt braced himself, hoping they wouldn't hit the foundation latticework. He didn't want to have to repair it.

Once they were safely landed and Martin got the car into park, he asked, "She's not really going to believe it was her mom, will she?" He sounded a little guilty.

Wyatt ran a hand through his own hair. "I'm going to have to tell her tomorrow that you lied to her. That *we* lied to her!"

"I didn't. We didn't. She *is* loved." Martin shut the car off. "You love her. Anyone can see that."

Wyatt sat up taller and tried to peek sideways. Was Martin maybe . . . jealous?

A Sampling of Op-Ed Pieces and Headlines from National Papers That Saturday

Queerville Problems in Oregon

Teen Catches Lincoln with His Pants Down

If Lincoln Were Alive Today, Would He Get Gay-Married?

Small Town Rewrites History, One Gay Bedbug at a Time
Could Lincoln Be a Hero for a Whole New Generation?
If Lincoln Had Gay Orgies in Springfield, Then Hitler Was
   Santa Claus's Brother
Homosexuals Kill Lincoln . . . Again!

Martin was on his laptop in the kitchen, reading Wyatt and his parents the headlines.

Rhonda walked in, cell phone by her ear. "My contact at *The John Stevens Show* is calling again. . . . John really wants Wyatt to come on his show."

"No!" Wyatt said it fast.

Martin made a face like Wyatt was making the wrong call, but Wyatt wasn't going to be set up again. Rhonda left to tell whoever was on the phone that the answer was no. For the third time. No to them and to everyone else who had been asking.

The B and B line rang. They all froze. It had been nonstop since they had gotten back from Mackenzie's. Either people screaming at them or cancellations. Wyatt and Martin weren't allowed to pick it up.

It rang again.

Wyatt's dad's face sagged like a condemned man's as he walked over and picked it up on ring number four. He listened. "Yes." Listened some more. Hung up. And then he just stood there, staring at the phone. Finally, he said, "That's it" and pulled the phone jack out of the wall. Then he walked out of the kitchen.

This is my fault!

Chair scraping, Wyatt jumped up to follow his dad. He heard him on the stairs. Where was he going?

Wyatt found him in the Lincoln Room, stripping the sheets off the mattress. His dad usually washed them on the first of the month, but Wyatt guessed he was keeping busy.

The hairs on the pillow! Wyatt remembered in a panic, then found them on the lip of the china washbasin . . . where he'd left them when he'd been in here with Martin. Wyatt's cheeks blazed just thinking about it. He tipped the hairs into the basin for safekeeping.

Wyatt's dad carefully pulled the flat bottom sheet out of the far corner. "Maybe we should call this place something else. Go back to being the Civil War Bed-and-Breakfast. Sell off all the Lincoln stuff while it's still worth something." Wyatt's dad scanned the room with a sour expression. "Let someone else deal with this headache."

"B-but," Wyatt stammered, "what about the bed? Isn't it always going to be worth a ton?"

His dad folded the sheet on top of the others, in a neater pile than Wyatt did his clean clothes, then crossed the room and shut the door. Wyatt flashed on Martin closing it, and wondered if his dad somehow knew about their having been in here yesterday afternoon. If he knew about Wyatt. And then his dad said, "It's not real."

Wyatt wasn't sure what he was talking about.

His dad gestured at the wood bed frame, which seemed naked without its sheets and pillow and quilt. "Well, it's a real bed. And it's from the same era, more or less. But it's not Lincoln's bed. Not from those years in Springfield. No one knows what happened to that bed."

Wyatt felt his dad's words knock the air out of him. "So this whole thing is . . . a fake?" He had really believed it. And he'd been telling everyone it was real. For years . . .

"You've got to sell people what they want," his dad said, like that explained it.

Lies. He'd been selling lies. *Wyatt* had been selling lies.

"Wyatt? You can't tell your mother."

He had to get out of the room.

"I never meant for it to make you think Lincoln was Gay!" his dad was calling after him, but Wyatt was through the door and already halfway down the stairs.

"You have to understand . . . Wyatt!"

He let the front door slam behind him and pumped his legs. Zigzagged to Grant Street and then down Jenson's Stream Road. He made a right at the ford and raced along the bank. Going with the water away from town. Away from everybody.

Away from all the lies.

AFTER THIRTY MINUTES, Wyatt was way downstream, and his run downshifted to a walk. The bank on this side wasn't much more than a footpath, and that petered out at a jumble of boulders up ahead. They formed an eight-foot waterfall that dropped into a swimming-deep pool before the stream narrowed again. It wasn't dramatic enough to be on any tours, but it was pretty beautiful all the same.

He'd miss this when he got to San Francisco. Or maybe New York.

Wyatt climbed over the rocks, still out of breath as he picked his way down the far side. The off-center flat stone in the pool was bright with sun, too far to get to without swimming. A flash of silver in the water caught his eye. A steelhead.

He was already all sweaty.

Wyatt kicked off his muddy, too-small sneakers, stripped down to his boxers, and put his clothes high on a rock. He was starting to feel cold, but he couldn't think about it too much or he wouldn't do it.

"Aaahhhh!" With a shout, he long-jumped in, and it was like some crazy ice plunge as the water swallowed him up. Thrashing to the surface, he whipped the hair out of his eyes. Arms pumping, Wyatt kicked fast, and the ripples didn't stop him. Six strokes, and he pulled himself up on the flat, sun-baked boulder. The air cooled down his wet skin, and Wyatt shivered. But the sun was bright and hot. He looked around. This place was hidden in the woods, and even in the middle of summer, it was rare to see anyone—only the occasional hikers. And while it was warm for January, it was January. Wyatt listened carefully, but there was only the rush and fall of water. The high *ta-ta-tah-ta* trill of some red-winged blackbirds. The drip of his wet hair on the rock. He was alone.

Go for it.

Stripping off his boxers, Wyatt wrung them and spread them out in the sun next to him. He lay back.

The wash of it.

The sun on his body, on his closed eyelids.

And he unknotted, bit by bit.

The bed was fake. His proof was fake.

But Lincoln was Gay. Or Bi. Or whatever you called it, he'd been in love with Joshua. Even if they didn't have *the* bed. The letters proved it! And when Wyatt had gone to the online site for the Lincoln Home in Springfield, Illinois, there had been photos showing that Abe and Mary had not only separate beds, but separate bedrooms! But Abe and Joshua had shared a bed, even if it wasn't *that* one, for four years.

Wyatt started to warm up.

Their whole town and everyone in it was being called Gay. *Queerville.* And everyone was blaming Wyatt. But all he was doing was telling the truth about history.

The solidness of the rock under him made him feel like he was solid, too. If only there were some way to make this part of Oregon Gay-friendly so he wouldn't have to move to a big city to be himself. . . . That would be the fantasy.

He inhaled the mineral-rich smell of the water. The mud on the bank. Squinting his eyes open, he caught the kaleidoscope of greens and browns all around him. Wyatt leaned back again and let the sun, radiant, fill him up.

It felt good to be this free. Not hiding, not even behind clothes. And, lying there, Wyatt didn't feel vulnerable being naked. He felt powerful.

His thoughts went to how his parents were on the defensive. How *he'd* been on the defensive, his whole life. It was maybe a way to avoid losing too badly, but defense was not how you won the game—any game. You won with offense.

Wyatt sat up. He wasn't even all dry yet, but he knew what he had to do. Holding his boxers high, he slipped back into the freezing water and swam-kicked to the bank. Dripping, he grabbed his cell phone out of his jeans pocket and speed-dialed Legal Advocates of Oregon.

Rhonda picked up. "Hello? Wyatt?"

"Can we sue them?" Wyatt asked her, toweling off with his sweatshirt and trying not to get the phone too wet.

"What? Slow down."

"We should sue all of them—Principal Jackson, Mayor Rails, the school board, the people who write the history books! I mean, they're all lying about Lincoln!"

"If there's any doubt about that, and there is, you have no case," Rhonda said.

"I don't have any doubt!"

She was quiet a moment. Wyatt tucked the phone between his ear and shoulder and pulled on his jeans. Finally, she said, "Answering their frivolous lawsuit with our own isn't my style. It just alienates the same judges you want on your side another day."

Wyatt plopped down on a boulder. "But then how are we going to play offense? How are we ever going to win?"

"We do what civil rights activists do: speak truth to power. And trust that truth is our strongest weapon. We can talk about it more tonight."

Wyatt mumbled, "Yeah," but what was the point of talking anymore if she wasn't going to do it? His thumb was on END CALL when he heard her again.

"Wyatt? You're doing it with your blog."

He hung up and pulled on the rest of his clothes, thinking about what she'd said.

Truth to power?

He wasn't. Not completely.

He'd been telling the truth on the one hand and lying on the other. Just like Lincoln.

But, maybe, the truth about Abe and Joshua was strong enough on its own. Wyatt stood up, nerves jangling with energy at the thought. If the truth didn't need the *bed* to still be true, and it didn't, maybe it didn't need *him*, either.

And that meant . . . he had the chance to do something Abraham Lincoln never did.

As Wyatt jogged back, carrying his wet boxers and sweatshirt, he decided to head past the school rock. It was Sunday, no one would be there, and he'd get to check out their ABE LINCOLN LOVED JOSHUA SPEED in giant green and white letters. Charge himself up to do this.

Moving got Wyatt warm again, and he crossed over at the ford and cut up the ravine. The parking lots and outdoor basketball court were empty, and the place seemed abandoned. Wyatt slowed down as he neared the corner of the gym—he didn't want to run into a big group of people by the rock. He just needed to see it for himself.

He peeked around the corner to scope it out. No cars. No people. But the school rock had been completely repainted. The whole thing. A light brown.

Wyatt walked out slowly to the giant piece of caramel on the lawn. A few flecks of green and white paint were still on the grass, but otherwise it was like what he and Martin had painted last night had never been there.

They had erased it. Like the truth about Abe had always been erased.

Wyatt spun around and broke into a run.

He was not going to be erased.

Wyatt paused just outside Martin's doorway. Martin was playing his guitar and singing softly, like he was figuring out the words as he went along.

Two lovers on their way
One wore blue and one wore gray
With their love locked safe away . . .

He stopped, then strummed the opening chord and tried again, voice shimmering:

Two lovers on their way
One wore blue and one wore gray
No one knew that they were Gay . . .

Sitting on the bed, Martin leaned forward to type on his laptop. He glanced over and saw Wyatt standing there. "Hey!" He hit a key, and a screen saver popped up.

"Sounding good," Wyatt told him, but his eyes were on the transformed computer screen. It showed an old-fashioned painting of . . . Wyatt moved closer to make sure. It was! Some naked guys by a river! Did Martin know he had just . . . ? "What's that?"

"Still trying to work out new lyrics for the 'Two Brothers' song."

"No," Wyatt said. His eyes drew a line to the naked guys. "That."

Martin turned and saw what Wyatt was staring at. "Thomas Eakins. Don't laugh, but it's called *Swimming Hole.*"

Wyatt could only imagine how much a guy could get teased for that.

He leaned in to study it. It wasn't . . . sexual. They just weren't wearing clothes. It was a bunch of guys hanging out. Swimming. Being themselves.

Wyatt put a hand on Martin's arm. "Dude, you know I'm . . . ?" It was so hard to knock down the wall he had spent forever building.

Martin pulled off his guitar and stood to face him. "You can say it, Wyatt. I am, too."

"Okay." Tears were in his eyes, and Wyatt whispered it. "I'm Gay."

Martin put out his arms and Wyatt fell into him, sobbing. He didn't have to hold it all in so tight anymore.

After a minute, Wyatt pulled back, wiped his nose with his sleeve. "I need to tell my folks." He checked out the painting on Martin's computer screen again. "They look . . . free."

Martin didn't take his eyes off Wyatt. "Yeah, I think they are."

"You sure you want us here?" Martin whispered, as Wyatt led him and Rhonda down the corridor to the living room, where Wyatt had his dad and mom waiting.

With Rhonda, who accepted her Gay son, and Martin there with him, Wyatt figured it was insurance against his dad and mom freaking out too badly. They couldn't disown him, or kick him out, or tell him they hated him—with witnesses. At least . . . that was the plan.

Wyatt bobbed his head nervously. "Yeah."

Telling Rhonda had taken two minutes. He'd gotten a hug, and a little advice. "You might need to give them some time to get used to the idea. Think how long it took you to feel good about it." But Wyatt couldn't stop and think. This was like jumping into the stream—he had to do it fast, or he'd get cold feet.

Wyatt's dad and mom looked up as they entered, and before Martin and Rhonda could even sit, Wyatt blurted it out: "I'm Gay."

The room was silent. For what seemed like forever.

Wyatt stole a glance at his dad, who had stopped restacking the wood in the iron log holder. Then Wyatt took a quick peek at his mom in the lounge chair by the glass bookcase. They seemed afraid to move—like they were china and might break.

"It's not actually a bad thing. . . ." Wyatt's words faded out. He wanted to scream, disappear, explode. Was this the end of everything he knew? Were they going to hate him now? Would he lose them? Why didn't they say anything?

Wyatt's dad cleared his throat. Twice. "So, this whole Lincoln thing was your way of . . . ?"

"I don't know." Wyatt stood there, squirming. "It's true, about Lincoln and Speed, and I thought it was like . . . a way to see how it would go?"

"And it's gone so spectacularly well that now you're telling us you're Gay, too?" His dad tossed the log he was holding onto the stone hearth. *Thunk.*

Oh no.

"Well, maybe it hasn't gone that well, but . . . more people know the truth about Lincoln, at least." Wyatt's voice got really soft. "I wanted you to know about me, too."

"But, what about Mackenzie?" his mom asked, like she knew Wyatt was wrong. About who *he* was.

Wyatt shook his head. "We were just friends." Now wasn't the time to feel guilty about Mackenzie and how he'd lied to her, too. About himself *and* the séance. Blood pounded in his ears.

His dad sighed. He and Wyatt's mom exchanged a silent look, but it was parent language, and Wyatt couldn't read it. Had they expected this? Or had he hidden it too well all these years?

What were they going to do?

"Lincoln did the right thing," his dad started.

No—the right thing by being closeted? By never speaking his truth? Wyatt's eyes burned.

His dad continued, "Even when it wasn't popular." And then his dad's mouth slowly wrenched into a pained smile. "Maybe you learned that lesson better than I did." He exhaled, buzzing his lips. "I guess, better to know the truth now than never."

What? Was he talking about the bed or Wyatt?

His dad continued. "I'll always admire President Lincoln, Gay or not. And I'll always love you."

Wyatt didn't want to ask it, but he had to. "Even if we lose this place because of me?"

His dad looked right at him. "Even if this B and B comes crashing down around our ears."

"But, it's your dream. . . ."

His dad shook his head and gazed up, as if seeing the whole building around them. "Maybe this will never be the success I want it to be. But my son? My *Wyatt?*" His dad's voice caught for a moment. "You will never cease to make me proud."

He put his arms out, and then Wyatt did something he hadn't done since he was a little kid. He rushed into them, wanting the reassurance of the hug, wanting to know it would all be okay.

"Why are you wet?" his dad asked, but Wyatt just laughed and held him tighter.

"It's going to be such rougher seas for you." Wyatt's mom stared into the empty fire grate. "I always thought that if I could just avoid making waves, my boat would never capsize. And I wanted that for you, too." She scoffed. "But it doesn't even work for me."

She stood up, awkward. "I think my mother's sister was a Lesbian."

"Great-Aunt Freida?" Wyatt was stunned.

His mom shrugged. "She lived with this other woman for more than thirty years."

"How come I've never heard this story?" Wyatt asked.

"Well, they didn't advertise it," his mom said. "But you met Shara at the funeral."

Wyatt had no idea which old woman it had been. But it blew his mind to know that even in their family, he wasn't the only one. . . .

Wyatt's mom picked up the log from the hearth and placed it carefully with the others in the holder. "There are going to be so many mean, uneducated people to deal with. . . ." She turned to Wyatt, wiping bark debris from her hands. "Are you ready for that?"

"I don't know," Wyatt said. "I guess . . . I have to be."

"*We* have to be," his mom corrected. "And we will. Together."

Wyatt put out his arm, and his mom stepped into the hug, letting her fancy blouse get wet against him. Her right arm clenched Wyatt's ribs so fiercely it hurt, but there was no way he was going to complain.

"I love you, sweetie," his mom said, her voice hoarse in his ear. "You're my son, and I love you."

Wyatt managed to squeak the words out. "I love you guys, too." He told himself to not cry. That this was a good thing. But his face was wet all the same.

Standing by the door, Rhonda found Martin's hand and squeezed it tight. He squeezed back as they watched.

After a long moment of the ice thawing inside Wyatt, his dad held him out at arm's length. "Now, you go take a hot shower. You're shivering." Wyatt hadn't even known he was.

But it didn't matter. He had told them. And it was okay.

Wyatt was all warm again and toweling dry when he heard the knock on the outside of the bathroom door. "Wyatt?"

Martin. His voice was tender. Wyatt double-knotted the towel around his waist.

"I'm really happy for you. It took me three days to get to the hug." He was just on the other side of the door.

But they didn't need a door, or anything, between them anymore. Wyatt just had to be brave enough to act on what he'd finally said. His heart jackhammered in his chest.

There was a long pause, and then Martin said, "Congratulations, man."

Do it! Wyatt held his towel tight with his left hand and with his right whipped open the bathroom door. Martin was right there, his deep brown eyes meeting Wyatt's. Wyatt leaned forward, lips together, to get a *real* first kiss . . .

"Whoa! Not so fast, astronaut." Martin blocked him with a hand on Wyatt's chest, pushing him back.

What about spooning in the not-Lincoln bed? Their hands touching in Martin's room? The almost kiss by the school rock? "But I thought, now . . . ?" Wyatt could feel his face getting hot.

"You're, like, traveling at supersonic speed. You just came out to other people for the first time. To me, my mom, your parents! Give that half a minute to sink in."

"But I want to kiss you!" Wyatt did. He'd never been able to say it out loud before, and it sounded good. He wanted to know what it was like. He tried to lean over Martin's hand, get his face next to his. Martin felt it, too, didn't he, this thing between them?

Martin's hand, warm against Wyatt's chest, held him away.

"Don't you like me?" Wyatt was so confused.

"Yeah, but right now you'd kiss a frog if it was Gay."

Wyatt tried to make a joke of it. "I hear some frogs turn into princes!"

But Martin was all serious. "I don't want to be wanted just because I'm the only other Gay guy you know. That you've ever met. I want to be wanted for *me*."

"I do!"

"Wyatt." Martin stepped back, hand leaving Wyatt's skin. The place over Wyatt's heart where it had been was suddenly cold. Empty. "For now, let's just be friends."

Wyatt's face must have betrayed him, because Martin said right away, like he didn't want to hurt Wyatt's feelings too much, "*Good* friends. And . . . let's see where it goes."

So Wyatt didn't get his first real kiss.

All he got was his first Gay "let's be friends" kiss-off.

Chapter 26
Monday, January 26

THE SCHOOL ROCK read:

No Fags in History!

Wyatt had a great view of it from his window-aisle desk in detention.

He'd tried to get through the day zombie-style, with a plan to let nothing bother him—because really, what bothers the undead?—but it wasn't working at all. Every time he'd been within earshot, Jonathon had started selling John Wilkes Booth Appreciation Society T-shirts out of his locker and backpack. Mr. Clifton had trapped him after History, instructing Wyatt to tell his dad that their bowling team had decided Wyatt's dad would be "better off on another team—I'm sure he'll understand why." And Mackenzie had been a no-show the whole day. She still hadn't answered any of Wyatt's texts. Was she okay? She hadn't done anything stupid, had she? The guilt seeped through him, filling every pore.

As soon as Ms. Valens released them, Wyatt ran directly to Mackenzie's place.

He took the stairs two at a time and rang the condo doorbell.

Mr. Miller answered, holding a bunch of dresses on hangers.

"I need to talk to Mackenzie," Wyatt said.

"Leave her alone, Wyatt."

"I have something really important—"

"I'm sure you think it is. But we're dealing with hard stuff here." Mackenzie's dad stared at the dresses in his hands. Behind him, half-filled cardboard boxes were lined up by the kitchen counter. The one closest to the door had purses in it. "Moving on is hard."

"But that's what—"

"Stop!" Mr. Miller's voice broke with pain. "Just go, okay? This is important healing time for us. Mackenzie will see you at school tomorrow."

Wyatt's eyes went wide when he saw the bottle of alcohol on the entry bench. It was only two-thirds full. Had Mr. Miller started drinking again? Because of *him*?

Mr. Miller followed his gaze. "Schnapps. For some reason, she liked this peppermint schnapps stuff, and I just couldn't . . ." He picked up the bottle and thrust it into Wyatt's hands. "Here. Take it to your parents. Better we don't have any of this stuff in the house, after all."

And then he shut the door in Wyatt's face.

Wyatt stared at the bottle of alcohol. If he gave it to his parents, he'd have to explain this whole thing. . . .

The building's Dumpster was around the side. Its top was open, and when Wyatt was ten feet away, he spun the bottle through the air. It sailed in and smashed against the metal bottom.

Wyatt winced, hoping no one had heard that. He walked over and peered in. The smell of peppermint slapped him in the face as he saw the broken glass at the bottom of the otherwise empty Dumpster. He wondered how long it would smell like that. *There's no fixing any of this, is there?*

Heading home, he glanced down Fourth Street to Union Square, one block away. Where were all the banners? They hadn't changed any of the ones on Fourth, so there should be all these banners announcing the parade. . . .

Wyatt walked up the block to see the whole square. Every light pole was empty. Their town wasn't advertising Abe and Mary's "great love" anymore, but it also wasn't even saying there was going to be a parade in nineteen days!

He raced home and got on the Reception computer. It wasn't on the Lincolnville Chamber of Commerce calendar anymore, either. No parade ad and no listing.

But the parade had to happen! Without it, his mom was out of a job and they were going to be forced out of here. Wyatt looked about at their wacky Queen Anne Victorian.

The history and dust.

Wax Lincoln and the military mannequin.

His soldier.

The fake bed upstairs, and so many memories.

It was a weird place to live, but . . . it was home.

When Wyatt got to his room, there were two thin envelopes that had come in the mail sitting on his chair, since his desk was kind of a mess. They were both hand-addressed to him, one in a scrawl, the other in fancy script.

The scrawled one had a sheet of yellow notebook paper folded inside. Wyatt opened it, and a five-dollar bill fluttered out. The note read:

> WYATT—
> LOVED LEARNING LINCOLN WAS GAY!
> CAN'T COME TO STAY AT YOUR B&B
> BUT HOPE THIS HELPS. STAY STRONG
>   MARK

Wyatt held the five in his hand and took in the good feeling. He didn't know who Mark was, but there was someone out there who believed in what he was doing!

Kind of excited, he opened the second envelope. On cream-colored paper, the fancy script read:

FROM THE DESK OF
MRS. DAISY LOCKE

My Dear Wyatt, and of course,
Mr. & Mrs. Yarrow as well,

Please do not allow small-minded people to hold you back. After all,

"The Truth Shall Set You Free."
- John 8:32

However, in my life I have learned that sometimes, the truth can be expensive.

Wishing you blessings of peace,
Mrs. Daisy Locke

There was a check inside. For $500.

Wyatt started shouting as he ran for the stairs. "Dad!"

He raced along the downstairs corridor to the kitchen, check and Lincoln five-dollar bill in his hand, but stopped short at a pottery *smash!*

"No parade!" His mom's voice was high and scary.

When he got to the doorway Wyatt saw his mom let go of a plate—*smash!* It shattered on the tile by her feet. His dad's eyes were wet with tears as he watched her. And Rhonda and Martin were by the dining room door, silently taking in the whole thing.

Wyatt's mom picked up another plate from the stack on the counter. "No parade!"

Smash!

"No!"

Smash!

She cursed, freaking Wyatt out even more.

Smash!

"Parade!"

Smash!

"Mom! Stop!" Wyatt entered the room cautiously, pushing shards away with his sneakers.

"Hi, Wyatt," she said like normal, grabbing another plate. "Did you hear the news?"

He tried to speak fast, before she dropped it. "Yeah—about the parade."

"It's official. You can't have a parade with two entries. Even Tykes on Bikes canceled." His mom put the plate back on the stack, like she'd changed her mind. Then she shoved all five remaining plates off the counter. They *crumped* into large pieces on the floor. She let out a long breath. "I always hated that pattern."

It seemed safer, since she'd run out of plates. "Mom, there's something I need to show you." Wyatt stretched out his arm over the jagged debris.

"What's this?"

She took the check and money, and he explained to them all about the letters.

"Five hundred and five dollars is nice, but it's not going to get us out of the financial hole we're in." His mom handed the check and bill back to him. "I have to clean this up. Gregory," she said to his dad. "I think it's time to sell the Lincoln bed and all the things in the museum."

The bed. Wyatt avoided looking at his dad. It was his dad's secret to tell, and he didn't want to give anything away.

His mom leaned heavily against the counter. "I'm sorry. I know . . . it's not what any of us wanted. But when they foreclose, we're not going to have anywhere to store—"

"Stop! No!" Wyatt cut her off. "You don't have to!" He swiveled between his parents. "We're not going to lose this place."

His mom raised a weary hand. "Wyatt, I know you want to help, but you have to let us adults deal with this."

"We need a parade, right?" Wyatt said. "If there's a parade, and it's a big success, the mayor said you can keep your job. Well, we've been trying for the wrong kind of parade!"

Blank stares. None of them knew what Wyatt meant.

"Mom, you've been calling, trying to get people to be in the Lincoln-and-Mary parade, right?"

"I must have made two hundred calls," his mom said.

"We need people to come to the Lincoln-and-*Joshua* parade!" Wyatt looked at them all.

Martin's eyes went wide. "You want to do a parade about Lincoln being Gay?"

Martin was right. Who would come to that? They needed a crowd. Like that March on Washington. Like going back in time to add Gays to Dr. Martin Luther King Jr.'s list. . . .

Wyatt felt goose bumps prickle his skin, traveling up his back and neck, as the idea took shape.

"Black men and White men. Jews and Gentiles. Protestants and Catholics."

And Gays, and Women, and the Disabled, and . . . everyone. That was it!

Everyone!

"All men are created equal—Lincoln believed that, right?"

The goose bumps crested the top of Wyatt's head like a wave as he tried to get them to see it, too.

"And Martin Luther King Jr.! What if it's more about *that?* About how we're all created equal. Men, Women. Black, White. Gay, Straight. No exceptions." He repeated it, feeling it sink in. "No exceptions! That's our new parade theme. *All people are created equal—no exceptions!*"

Wyatt held up the check in one hand and the five-dollar bill in the other. "And people will come to that!"

His mom looked to Rhonda. "What about our permit? Could they pull it?"

"Parade permits aren't theme-dependent. . . ." Rhonda shook her head as she thought it through. "Even if they don't like the new theme, they can't stop it."

"Which means they can't stop *us!*" Wyatt said.

Martin did a quick search on his cell phone for a number, then dialed. They all watched as he pressed the speakerphone button.

A man's voice answered, "University of Oregon switchboard."

"Hi!" Martin said, giving Wyatt a wink. "Can I speak with the person who books your marching band?"

WYATT WALKED RIGHT by Mackenzie in the school hallway and almost didn't recognize her. She was in all new clothes—a belted cardigan sweater over a funky dress, and bright pink shoes that weren't his mom's. And she'd cut her hair—it was now a short black bob. She looked like a completely different person. Because of him.

He was drowning in guilt—he had to tell her. But she was never alone. All week, he couldn't find the right moment. He knew the instant he told her, Mackenzie would hate him. Again. Which made it . . . impossible. What made things even weirder was that Martin had made Wyatt promise to not tell Mackenzie about their new parade plan, so he felt like he was keeping three secrets from her.

Rhonda had agreed she and Martin would stay on until the parade. Wyatt didn't want to think about Martin leaving, so he just tried to focus on making the parade a success. By Friday, he, Martin, and Wyatt's dad and mom had made fifty-eight calls—his dad on the reconnected B and B line and everyone else on their cell phone—and they'd already gotten three yeses! It still wasn't enough to be a parade, and nothing was for sure. But there was a chance. There was hope.

Enough to keep going.

Saturday, January 31

Wyatt   9:48 a.m.

> I tried 2 talk 2 u all week. hate 2 do this as text, but got 2 tell u. martin kind of helped move the thingy in the seance. it wasn't spirits.

> sorry.

> really sorry.

It was early afternoon when Mackenzie just showed up at the B and B, all flushed, still in her karate *gi*. Wyatt stood awkwardly opposite her in the entry hall.

"I'm really sorry!" They said it at the same time.

That got them both to smile.

Wyatt was so glad she was there. He felt guilty, but still angry, too. He wanted her to go first and tried to keep his voice neutral. "What are you sorry about?"

"I haven't been a very good friend." Mackenzie stared at the Persian carpet's pattern of reds and blues as she spoke. "I didn't realize what you were going through, and it just sort of hit me . . . or, I hit it."

Wyatt scanned her for injuries. "What do you mean?" She didn't look like she'd gotten hit.

"I was at Albany Junior High, for the tournament, and I got your text—"

Wyatt started, "I feel terrible about—"

"Please." Mackenzie put up a hand. "Just let me finish. I needed to clear my head, so I went out to the hallway to get a drink, and these two high school guys were making fun of Becca. You know, the cheer-leading thing, and how the only letter she could make was a *Y*, because she only has the one leg . . ."

"Cretins," Wyatt said.

"Yeah," Mackenzie agreed. "Anyway, I wanted to tell them off, but before I could, they were calling me a Lesbian, and I told them I wasn't"—Mackenzie swallowed—"and then they said the only way I could prove it was if I kissed the bigger jerk."

"Holy crap," Wyatt breathed.

"So then the joker grabbed my arms from behind"—Mackenzie's breaths came faster and faster as she relived it—"and I wasn't even thinking. It was like all those years of karate just sort of took over— muscle memory or something, you know? And I shouted my *kiai* and heel-struck his foot, and he let go, howling, and then I elbow-struck him in the gut. He fell back, and the big guy came at me. I front-kicked him as hard as I could, and he went down, screaming and grabbing his ribs. But the first guy was back up, hopping on one leg, swinging his fists at me, and I blocked and back-kicked him in his good leg. Hard. Knocked him down. Then I had my hand on the fire alarm and told them if they even *thought* about touching me again, I would pull it."

She breathed out a laugh that was almost a sob. "And then my dad came looking for me. I've never been so happy to see anyone. We filed a police report and everything."

"Are you . . ." Wyatt hesitated. It was a stupid question, but he had to ask. "Okay?"

Mackenzie shook her head. "Not really." She sniffed, and another laugh came out in a burst. "I did break the jerk's foot, which was sort of justice, after he made fun of Becca." She reached for a ponytail that wasn't there, and instead twisted a lock of short black hair. "But what I wanted to tell you was, on the ride back home, I realized how it wasn't safe for Lincoln. And it hasn't been for you, either. And I'm so sorry about that. And even more, I'm so sorry it took this for me to realize it."

They looked at each other for a long moment, eyes trying to express what words couldn't.

Wyatt set his face in his fiercest expression. "I wish I could have been there."

Mackenzie's mouth twisted wryly. "Then I would have had to defend you, too."

"I could have done something!" Wyatt protested.

She gave him a *like what?* look.

"I could have pulled the fire alarm."

That got them both smiling again.

"Can I apologize now?" Wyatt asked.

Mackenzie nodded.

"I'm sorry about the séance." Wyatt made a guilty face. "And your hair. I feel terrible about it."

Mackenzie dropped her hand. "I like my hair. And, well, it was a lousy thing to do, but maybe . . . I still want her to come home, but, even if I don't know for sure, I can't stop my life and just wait. Not anymore."

"So I guess"—Mackenzie shrugged—"it's not like it was right, but it's okay?"

But it couldn't be. Not until she knew everything. Wyatt could feel his Adam's apple shoot up and then down again. He was so tense, and afraid of what she'd say, but he couldn't wait even another second.

It was like jumping into Jenson's Stream. He had to tell her.

Now.

Right now.

Stop stalling and say it! "Mackenzie?" His voice shook. "I'm Gay."

"I know."

He staggered back like she had hit him. "You know?"

"I had a hunch, the way things went with us. And then when I saw you with Martin, it all started to make sense. . . ."

Wyatt headed over to the store area and started tweaking things that didn't really need to be adjusted. "He's just a friend."

She walked over to join him. "You don't sound too happy about that."

He poured out the rifle pens from the Lincoln coffee mug, checking for Confederate rifles that had ended up in the Union cup by mistake. Keeping his eyes down, he asked, "Is it okay to tell you I'm not?"

The only sound for a bit came from pens sliding across the top of the glass display case. She leaned over and moved a few Richmond carbines to the correct pile. "It's okay. He *is* cute."

They were quiet, but Wyatt could tell that the space between them felt different now. Like it actually could be okay. And maybe soon.

Mackenzie walked over and balanced the two bears that had fallen behind the Reception computer screen back up on their small speakers. "There you go, little Blue, and Gray."

When Mackenzie turned back, Wyatt was staring at her. "I miss my best friend," he said.

"I miss you, too."

They hugged, and Wyatt felt the warmth of it. The relief of getting to this place—friends, again.

He pulled back. "You know what the worst moment was?"

"What?"

"When you went out with Jonathon, just to get back at me. Man, I felt so stabbed in the back. I'm glad you told off that homophobic loser."

Mackenzie closed her eyes, like it was just as painful for her, and then said, "Me, too."

Chapter 28
Sunday, February 1

MARTIN'S LAPTOP WAS open on the bed when Wyatt stuck his head through the doorway. Martin wasn't there, but Wyatt could hear the shower running in the second-floor bathroom. He wondered if he should wait for Martin or if that was too weird. But he didn't want to leave. Martin would be gone after the parade. . . .

It had been a crazy week. It seemed like Wyatt had kept coming out, again and again. But the whole straight-at-school, himself-at-home back-and-forth, five times, had been rough. This weekend had been a lot easier. Come to think of it, maybe that was what his soldier was smiling about in the photo downstairs. Maybe just being yourself *was* the secret . . .

The screen saver of naked guys hanging out and swimming by the river's edge glowed. One more coming-out, and he could be done.

Wyatt could feel the chill of the water in his bones. That was where the sharks lived. But he could outswim them and stand tall on the far shore.

I can let freedom ring.

Queer as a Five-Dollar Bill Blog

QUEER AS A FIVE-DOLLAR BILL

Blog Post: Sunday, February 1, 10:19 p.m.

I am Gay!

I know people are going to think I'm only saying Lincoln was Gay because I am. But that's not it. Someone really smart once asked me, since I've got all the same evidence about Abraham Lincoln that everyone else does, how come *I'm* the only one who can see that Lincoln was Gay? Well, maybe all those historians couldn't see it because they weren't looking for it.

I could see Abe was in love with Joshua because I was open to seeing it. The proof is there—on this blog, and in *Joshua Fry Speed: Lincoln's Most Intimate Friend*, and in all those other books with the Lincoln letters.

If you look for it—with an open mind—you can see it, too.

Monday, February 2

Wyatt woke up at 4:23 a.m., sheets drenched in regret and sweat.

What the hell had he done?

He had to delete it. No, that would look even worse, like he was hiding again. *Shit!*

Mr. Guzman had told them about how getting something back once it was online was as hard as getting pee out of a swimming pool.

This was more like shit in a swimming pool. You might as well try to drain the whole Internet.

He kicked at the knot of sheets. There was no way to take it back. They were all going to know.

Maybe he could get homeschooled like Martin.

Or run away to somewhere where they didn't have Internet.

He got up, peeled off his clammy T-shirt, and put on dry stuff. There was no way he was going to fall back to sleep. He sat on the edge of his bed for five minutes, staring at the beads of misty rain on his windows, trying not to panic.

It didn't really work.

He snuck down the flight of stairs and quietly knocked on Martin's door. No answer.

He's asleep. This is stupid.

Wyatt was on the first step to go back up and suffer on his own, when the door to Room 2 opened an inch.

"Wyatt?" Martin was rumpled and adorable, and, weirdly enough, just seeing him made the tightness across Wyatt's chest loosen up a little. "You okay?"

Wyatt answered truthfully, "No."

Martin pulled the door wide. "Come in."

"So they say, 'Dude, don't turn your back on him—he could jump your bones.' And then you can say, 'I'm Gay. I'm not desperate.'" It was an hour later, and Martin was sitting on his bed, wrapped in his comforter, running through all these different scenarios. Telling Wyatt how he could get the upper hand for each one.

"Or they go, 'Hey, read about your being a fag!' And you can act all happy and surprised for them: 'You learned to read!'"

Wyatt picked at an embroidered flower on the armchair he'd pulled over by the bed. "I wish I didn't have to go to school."

Martin made this *I wish I had better news to tell you face*. "Mom says you have to go, or they'll get you for truancy. Even with a doctor's note, it wouldn't be credible."

Credible. Martin was sounding like a lawyer again. Wyatt wondered if, after he got creamed and was in the hospital, that would be a good enough excuse not to go to school.

"For what it's worth," Martin said, "I wish I could go back in time to my school, knowing what I know now."

Wyatt gave him a skeptical look. "Really?"

Martin thought for a second and shrugged. "Maybe not. But if I did, at least now I'd know what I could say back!"

Wyatt crossed his arms.

Martin kept the advice rolling. "Here's another one. If Jonathon says, 'You like my ass, faggot?' you can say, 'It's amazing how it can talk!'"

That one got Wyatt to crack up.

"You can do this." Martin seemed so confident Wyatt could.

But Wyatt wasn't.

Martin put his hand on top of Wyatt's, but Wyatt was too freaked out to feel anything. And then Martin said something Wyatt didn't expect. "Call Mackenzie. Maybe she can help."

LINCOLN WAS GREAT—LINCOLN WAS STRAIGHT!

THE YARD SIGN on the way to pick up Mackenzie felt like a slap in the face the first time, but by the third one, Wyatt was feeling numb. By the tenth one on the way to school, he told himself he had to stop counting. He was on number thirteen when his mom made the turn onto Polk Street.

His mom was so happy Wyatt and Mackenzie had made up that she hadn't stopped talking since the moment Mackenzie had gotten in their truck, wearing a new sweater and dress outfit. "Two more weeks of these detentions? I don't see why Rhonda couldn't get you out of them. Something about respecting the principal's authority on the little things to help him save face, but really, it's so unfair!"

"Mackenzie, did you know your profile's been offline?"

"Yeah," Mackenzie said. "I needed a break."

"Hmm. I hear you. I wish it wasn't part of my job." Wyatt's mom snorted. "But then, I don't know how much longer I'll have that, so I shouldn't complain!"

Busy merging into the drop-off line while talking, Wyatt's mom didn't see it. But Wyatt spotted it through the drizzle and elbowed Mackenzie to check out the latest graffiti: blue spray paint had added a line to their school sign, so it read:

LINCOLNVILLE HIGH SCHOOL
HOME OF THE FIGHTING SOLDIERS
NO QUEERS ALLOWED!

"I bet no one gets in trouble for that," Wyatt muttered. Mackenzie didn't disagree.

"All right, have a great day, you two!" Wyatt's mom pulled to a stop in the drop-off zone, and her voice was so cheery, Wyatt knew for sure she had no clue what he had done.

His eyes slid to the school rock:

NO FAGS IN HISTORY!

was still there. Nine days and counting. But they'd erased the truth in just a few hours.

He got out and shut the truck door behind them, waving as his mom pulled away.

"Thanks, Liz!" Mackenzie called.

Wyatt pivoted to face the school and said low to Mackenzie, "Here goes nothing."

"I'm going to be like Yoda on Luke Skywalker's back," Mackenzie assured him, as they started for the entrance.

Star Wars? He gave her a *What's up with that?* look.

She shrugged it off. "No one's going to do anything to you. I promise."

At lunch, Wyatt sat with Mackenzie, Jennie, and some of the other girls Mackenzie had rallied to be Wyatt's personal bodyguards. There was at least one of them in each of his classes, and Mackenzie had even promised to sit in on every detention with him so Wyatt wouldn't be alone at school at all. She'd even figured out a way to be there in his PE class that morning with a camera, ostensibly for the yearbook. It had been enough to keep Coach Rails and Jonathon and everyone else in line.

Wyatt was grateful, but kind of embarrassed, too.

As long as he didn't have to pee, he'd be fine. He pushed away his chocolate milk and took another bite of his dry, leftover-chicken sandwich. He could drink when he got home.

Jonathon passed their table.

Mackenzie had just taken a big bite of pasta and looked like she wanted to say something to Jonathon, but before she could, he sneered at Wyatt, "Fag."

Wyatt pretended to stare at his milk, but he was ready to run for it.

Mackenzie finished chewing and stood up, dabbing her lips with a napkin. "Jonathon, we need to talk." She took him by the arm and led him to the side of the cafeteria.

Wyatt watched them, wishing they weren't out of earshot. There was a lot of arm movement as they talked back and forth. Mackenzie crossed her arms. Jonathon got mad, and then calm. And then he reached out to touch her, but she stepped back and turned and saw Wyatt watching them. She gave him a confident nod, then swiveled back to Jonathon. A minute later, she was striding back across the cafeteria to Wyatt and the girls.

When she sat down, she said, "That's taken care of."

"What did the jerk say?" Wyatt asked.

"He's not a jerk. He's just . . . acting out because he's afraid of what he doesn't understand."

"Well, I don't understand *him*, but you don't see me making *his* life miserable."

"Remember . . . ," Mackenzie began, but checked first to see if anyone was listening. Jennie was busy talking with the other girls about starting up a math club that could visit elementary schools and change the whole "girls are bad at math" myth. "Promise you won't tell?"

"What?"

"Remember how much Jonathon loved *Star Wars* stuff? Back in third grade? Remember how we all got along?"

"He wasn't mean back then."

"Wyatt." She lowered her voice. "You have to imagine that he's still the same kid—he still loves Luke Skywalker, and C-3PO, and R2-D2, and pretending to save the universe."

Wyatt snorted, not buying it.

"Really," Mackenzie insisted. "I was in his room—his bathroom—and he has all these action figures hidden there, in the toilet tank. Like a diorama. Luke saving Princess Leia."

"So what?"

"He's hiding it! They have a nine-thousand-square-foot house, and the only place he can be himself—the only place he can like what he really likes—is inside this shoebox-size toilet tank!"

"So that's what the Yoda reference was about?" Wyatt asked.

"It's been on my mind." She looked back across the cafeteria at Jonathon, just as Charlie gave him a punch to the arm. "Maybe we need to think of him as a sci-fi nerd trapped in a cool kid's life."

Wyatt made a face. "Are you saying I'm supposed to feel sorry for him?"

Mackenzie shook her head. "I just want you to know that, on the inside, he's still this good little kid who just needs to find his way to the outside. So, you see? I talked to him, and it's going to be fine."

Wyatt looked over at Jonathon, who was laughing with his sharks at something—or someone. "And you believe him?"

Mackenzie unconsciously touched her fingertips to her lips. "I do."

With a start, she moved her hand away, fast. When Wyatt turned back around a second later, she was busy twirling spaghetti around her fork.

After detention, which Mackenzie announced was "a lot like study hall," she and Wyatt walked to the B and B. When they got there, Wyatt told Martin how Mackenzie saved the day at school. Maybe saved every day, going forward.

Martin sang Mackenzie this corny "I'm Sorry" song to some tango melody on his guitar. It was the first time he'd seen her since the séance.

When he finished, Mackenzie said, "Let's just . . . move on."

Martin stared at the guitar in his hands. "Thanks."

Wyatt couldn't help grinning as the two biggest people in his life made up. He leaned close to Martin and whispered, "Can we tell her about the parade? Please?"

"Sure," Martin said. "She's earned it."

Once they had explained, Mackenzie jumped in feetfirst, getting them organized with a chart of printed-out pages taped above the B and B's living room fireplace. The final list was 262 organizations, and by 5:00 p.m., the three of them and Wyatt's dad had made eighty-two calls in all. They were up to seven yeses, one maybe, and a "we're not sure, but we'll get back to you." They had to get through the list this week—the parade was only twelve days away, and no one would be able to come at the last minute.

His dad left the room to call Wyatt's mom with an update, and Wyatt and Martin hung out while Mackenzie worked out the math. She ran down the numbers for them: "If we make forty-five calls a day for the next four days, we'll do it. And if we can get four yeses a day, it will give us twenty-three entries total, three more than the bare minimum. . . ."

Wyatt put his arm, friend-like, around Martin's shoulders as he finished the thought for her: "And we'll have a parade."

His arm stayed there as Martin said, "Forty-five calls a day? That's fifteen each. Less if your dad helps."

Mackenzie put out her fist for them to stack their hands. "We can totally do it."

"Go, Team Us!" Martin put his hand on hers.

Wyatt added his hand on top. He swallowed hard. "We have to."

Wednesday, February 4

"You can? Great! That's great!" Martin hooted as he hung up, wrote *YES!* on the phone-bank spreadsheet, and bent down to the dry-erase board Mackenzie had brought over. He erased the big *12* and wrote *13*. "Lucky thirteen!" Wyatt put up his hand, and they high-fived.

On a call herself, Mackenzie shivered, jotted down, "Let's get to 14 fast!" and held the pad up for Wyatt, his dad, and Martin to see. She spoke into her cell phone. "Yes, *this* February fourteenth . . . It's not a lot of notice, no."

Rhonda was on another case up in Seattle, and Wyatt's mom had just left the living room to grab today's mail. The mayor had made her wash down all the folding plastic Rails Realty signs yesterday, insisting she do it while she was all dressed up, and Wyatt's mom was still angry about her ruined clothes. She'd emailed Mayor Rails to say she was working from home today, and she'd told Wyatt's dad that she wasn't going to check for a response until late tonight. Wyatt thought it was a lot like what he'd done to avoid school but didn't say it. Why kick her when she was down?

Martin's was their second yes today: Northwest Disability Rights. And Wyatt's dad had gotten this Gay-family-and-friends group from Philomath, PFLAG, to come, too.

"Nicely done," Wyatt's dad said to Martin, and they high-fived, too.

Wyatt watched them, thinking it was kind of wonderful.

Wyatt's mom came in with a stack of mail, five envelopes on top. "More donations!"

"We're on a roll, Liz." Wyatt's dad gave her the news.

"So, that means we need only two more yeses today?" Wyatt's mom asked, checking the board.

"Yeah," Wyatt said.

"We thought it would be an opportunity . . ." Mackenzie twisted a lock of short hair as she talked on her cell. "But this is for a really good—" She stopped. "I understand. Thank you for your time." She hung up and put an *X* next to *Albany College Marching Band*.

It turned out they'd told her what the St. Mark's Episcopal Church of Bend, Oregon, had just told Wyatt: that if they'd known months ago, they might have been able to make it work. But at least they had wished them well.

Wyatt checked the sheet for the next number and dialed. When they answered, he said, "Yeah, hi! I was wondering if Fight Anti-Semitism Now! has a group that can march in local parades?"

At 4:58 p.m., Mackenzie got the Asian Pacific Islander Women's Color Guard confirmed, which got them up to sixteen entries—one ahead of schedule. They even had three rooms booked for the parade weekend.

As Mackenzie circled *16* on the board, Wyatt's mom asked, "Do we have any floats yet?"

Wyatt shook his head. "None of our yeses has the money to build one."

"Or the time," Mackenzie added.

Wyatt's dad thought for a moment. "Maybe we can turn our pickup into a float. After all . . ."

Wyatt and Martin looked at each other, and then all five of them said, at the same time, "We have Lincoln!"

That was the moment Wyatt felt a glimmer of real hope. They were going to pull this off.

Queer as a Five-Dollar Bill Blog

QUEER AS A FIVE-DOLLAR BILL

Blog Post: Saturday, February 7, 10:19 a.m.

Two-Nights-for-One Special!

Coming to Lincolnville, Oregon, for the
Lincoln's Birthday/Valentine's Day

All People* Are Created Equal

*No Exceptions

Parade February 14?

Stay at the

Lincoln Slept Here Bed & Breakfast

Experience our

Cozy rooms with period furnishings

Old-time hospitality

And let your taste buds travel back in time as they enjoy our

Civil War–Era Supper!

Book your room now and get our special
two-nights-for-one rate!

WYATT HEADED DOWNSTAIRS for breakfast, and Martin was already in the kitchen, fiddling by the coffee machine. Probably making himself a warm coffee ice cream.

"Morning," Wyatt told his back, and grabbed the generic Cheerios and some milk from the fridge. He smell-checked it, then poured a bowl. He'd just crunched the first bite and sat at the table, when Martin came over, hiding something behind his laptop.

With a flourish, Martin pulled out a rainbow-sprinkle chocolate cupcake and set it in front of Wyatt. A single candle was lit on top. "Happy Lincoln's birthday!" He winked at Wyatt, then sat and checked something on his computer.

The cupcake smelled awesome. Way better than Wyatt's cereal. "Thanks!"

"Sure," Martin said, but he kept reading. Was he working on some new lyric?

Wyatt waited for him to stop whatever he was doing, but Martin didn't. "You wanna watch me blow it out?" Wyatt asked.

"I'm just trying to see if I can make something work." Martin sounded frustrated. And then he was quiet, clacking his keyboard. For a long, long moment. The candle wax dripped onto the frosting like the first big drops of a rainstorm.

"Martin?"

"Sorry, I'm just . . . distracted. Go ahead." He didn't look up from his stupid computer. "There's lot to do before Saturday."

Maybe Martin didn't like Wyatt that much after all. Maybe he didn't care that he and his mom were leaving after the parade. Maybe the "friends" thing was because that was all Martin wanted them to be. But the cupcake meant . . . What? Maybe he was supposed to be more worried about the parade. Did Martin think some of their yeses wouldn't show? That none of them would?

The candle flame sputtered in the frosting, and Wyatt blew it out, to put it out of its misery. Acrid and waxy, the smoke bit at his nose.

The cupcake didn't taste as good as he'd thought it would.

Wednesday, February 13

Mackenzie couldn't stay to hang out for detention number twenty with Wyatt—too much to do for tomorrow. But it didn't matter, since Wyatt was the only student in detention, just like he'd been the day before. Anyway, Jonathon and his sharks seemed focused on other things, whispering and planning and laughing among themselves. Wyatt didn't know what they were up to, but they were leaving him alone, which worked for him just fine.

When the fifty-ninth minute clicked over and it was 3:15 p.m., Ms. Valens told Wyatt that he'd "paid his dues to society" and was free to go.

Wyatt's mom was there to pick him up, and the whole five minutes home, they added to the punch list of things left to do for the parade. His mom dictated, "Check that the portable sinks will arrive with the toilets, and we need to test the sound system." Wyatt knew he already had those on the list in his notebook but checked anyway. It helped him not count all the new LINCOLN WAS GREAT—LINCOLN WAS STRAIGHT! plastic yard signs.

His mom pulled tight to the curb on the opposite side of the street from their B and B and told Wyatt, voice all relieved, "Some guests have already arrived."

"That's awesome!" Wyatt was thinking that would help them make the bank payment. The plan was working!

"Wyatt, there is one more thing . . . ," his mom started, but Wyatt was already out of the truck and crossing the street.

"I've gotta talk to Martin! Tell me later, okay?" He had an idea for a sign on the truck grill and wanted to see what Martin thought they could make it out of. He took the front porch steps two at a time and raced up the stairs to Martin's room.

"Martin!" Wyatt swung open the door to Room 2, but some woman was in there with short gray hair. Putting clothes in the drawer.

"Hi!" she said, all bright and cheerful. "You must be the owners' son. I'm Betty. Do you think I could get some extra towels?"

Wyatt's eyes searched the room. All of Martin's stuff, and his guitar, had disappeared. He rushed to the bed and ripped up the blanket and all the sheets from their tight corner, exposing the blue-and-ivory ticking of the mattress. The dust mite–proof cover was gone.

Maybe Martin had doubled up with his mom so they could book the extra room. . . .

Wyatt ran down the hall to Room 1. It was empty. Rhonda and the computers, the printer, and satellite hookup modems—all their things— were gone.

Wyatt almost tumbled down the stairs. His mom was standing in the entry, like she had known he'd come down.

"Where'd they go?" It was hard for him to breathe.

His mom shrugged sympathetically. "All they said was that there was something they had to do."

"So they're just . . . gone?" Wyatt's voice cracked. *They said they'd stay until the parade!*

His mom came over and put her hand on his arm. "With all the people coming, and things set for tomorrow, they knew we'd be okay. Maybe they just went to help someone else."

But . . . they'd worked so hard to make this happen. To do this together! Maybe Martin had texted him. Wyatt checked his cell. Nothing.

He must have left a note!

Wyatt tore up the stairs to his room, scanning the floor for an envelope. Some explanation. Another "Yours Forever."

Nothing.

He scoured the room, went through the laundry piles, turned things over on his desk, even pulled out the window seat cushions.

No.

The top comforter on his bed was all smoothed out, though. Weird. He never bothered to do that.

Wyatt walked over, and there on the pillow, folded into a square, was the Super *G* T-shirt. Blue and tie-dyed and proud. The one that looked so great on Martin.

But that was it.

Wyatt picked it up and held it to his face. He breathed it in deeply, but it didn't smell like Martin, just faintly of detergent and fabric softener. Like fingerprints wiped clean.

He was gone.

Martin was gone.

The parade was tomorrow at 9:00 a.m. In sixteen and a half hours, either Wyatt would be eaten alive by sharks, or he'd have to fight them off with his bare hands. Alone.

I guess it's easy to drop a "friend."

Wyatt felt hollowed out inside, like a guitar robbed of its strings. Mute.

He dialed Mackenzie, speaking past the lump in his throat.

"Hey, we've still got a lot of work to do to finish the float. Come over to help?"

"Hi . . ." Mackenzie sounded preoccupied. "I'm actually really swamped with homework. Three thousand words is a challenge." Wyatt would have bet money she meant keeping it that short. Their papers were due Monday, but Wyatt wasn't even going to bother. There was no way Mr. Clifton was going to pass him, even if he had the world's most perfect paper.

"Oh. Okay." He hated that he sounded like a little kid, all disappointed.

"But I can be over as soon as I finish this draft," Mackenzie said.

"When's that?"

"How about I'll come over for an hour or two around nine?"

Wyatt checked the time on his phone. Four and a half hours from now. He sighed. "I guess. I'll see you then."

Around 6:00 p.m., Wyatt helped his dad carry out Wax Lincoln, being careful with the right arm. They had filled every room of the B and B. A few of their guests were couples—one of them two guys in their thirties with matching wedding rings—and nearly all of them had offered to pitch in with decorating the pickup. They set up Wax Lincoln, standing in the back of the truck. There was no way to anchor him, so Wyatt would ride along to make sure Lincoln didn't tip over.

An hour later, Betty splurged and ordered pizza for everyone so they could "keep at it." They still had to make thousands of little waxed-paper flowers to stuff in the chicken wire that, along with the painted two-by-fours, created an arbor that arced high over Lincoln's stovepipe hat. More chicken wire draped the moving blankets they'd placed around the sides of the truck, and that needed more six-inch squares of waxy colored paper stuffed through every beehive-like gap in the wire. Wyatt's dad and mom seemed grateful that they didn't have to figure out feeding everyone, and Wyatt was sent along to help their guest pick up the pizzas. She didn't "believe" in delivery: "It always gets soggy."

"Just over here on the right," Wyatt directed. As Betty pulled her BMW into the Pies and Pool lot, Wyatt saw the plastic LINCOLN WAS GREAT—LINCOLN WAS STRAIGHT! ad on the small patch of grass in front. They were all over town now, a spreading plague of yard signs.

They parked and headed to the entrance. Betty pressed her key remote, and her trunk popped open. In one swift move, she yanked out the lawn sign, crossed the asphalt, and tossed it in the back of her car, shutting the trunk with a quiet click. The whole maneuver took five seconds. The sign was gone, and no one was the wiser. She winked at Wyatt as she walked back.

Wyatt opened the front door for her with a bow. She'd earned it.

The place was packed, pool balls clacking, air filled with the smell of beer hops and melted cheese. The first person Wyatt saw was Charlie, who was suddenly blocking his way. Charlie's sneer was a mirror image of Jonathon. "Hey, it's the big fag!"

Wyatt felt braver with Betty there beside him. "I'm not just bigger. I'm better at it than you."

Betty's snort emboldened Wyatt, and he walked around a speechless Charlie and led them toward the takeout counter in back.

"Nicely done, yourself," Betty praised him, and Wyatt wished Martin had seen that. He shook his head, trying to push away thoughts of Martin, when he heard Coach Rails laugh. He was talking with Mr. Asgur, who hosted the summer Civil War reenactments on his farm. Mayor Rails was with her husband at one of the wooden booths. Becca sat with her parents, fiddling with her phone. Wyatt didn't see Jonathon, but if Charlie and Jonathon's family were here, chances were, he was *somewhere*.

Wyatt kept going, wary. . . .

From the pool table on the other side of the mayor's booth, Mr. Anderson from the bank called out, "So, Kelly, is there going to be a parade after all?" He was the guy putting the squeeze on Wyatt's dad and mom.

Mayor Rails shook her head. "Nothing but a few stragglers."

"Parade brought in a lot of business," Mr. Anderson said.

Mayor Rails bristled. "The main thing is to get our town's reputation back."

Mr. Anderson's tone got sharper. "Do you know what this whole thing is costing us?"

Coach Rails snorted. "If he knew how much you spent on that Mary Lincoln dress you're not wearing tomorrow, he'd know for sure."

They didn't spot Wyatt, and he walked by them fast.

Jonah, a college dropout who worked the counter as he pursued his dream of being a painter, waved as Wyatt and Betty approached. "Good timing, Wyatt! It just came out of the oven." He started to ring up the order.

Betty pulled out her wallet and asked Wyatt, "Shouldn't we say something about the parade?"

"No," Wyatt whispered back. "Let's just get the pizzas and get out of here."

She made a frustrated face. Jonah set the five pizza boxes on the counter, and Betty handed over her credit card.

"So maybe we need a different strategy." Mr. Anderson was still arguing with Jonathon's mom.

"What's your pride cost, Benny?" The mayor stood up, soda in hand. "Listen up, everyone!" People quieted down. "We're a tourist economy, and look around: no tourists! The only important thing going on this weekend is getting us back on our feet. Save Lincoln's reputation and our town. Nothing else matters!"

Betty smacked her palm against the counter. "That's it!"

"I'll wait for you outside." Wyatt grabbed the pizzas.

He'd passed Jonah's canvas of a dog playing online poker and was halfway out the side door, when Betty said, loudly enough for the whole place to hear, "Actually, there *is* something else important going on this weekend. An amazing parade, celebrating the *real* Abraham Lincoln!"

Oh, man.

The sound of people shouting stopped when the door closed behind him. Wyatt was trying to figure out if he should go back inside to rescue this crazy woman, when he noticed there were two people in the mayor's Hummer, parked right in front of him. They were kissing.

He stepped closer. Who was in there?

It was Jonathon. . . . but that chin-length black hair . . .

Mackenzie!

They didn't see him, and Wyatt backed away slowly, like it was another basket of snakes he didn't want to tip over.

He'd wait for Betty by her car.

Betty came out five minutes later, face flushed. "Idiots!" She shook her head at Wyatt.

"Yeah," Wyatt managed, keeping the pizza boxes between him and the mayor's Hummer. They were *still* kissing!

He got them back to the B and B, and while Betty told everyone what had happened and they all dove into the pizzas, Wyatt wandered upstairs. He passed Room 2.

Where was Martin? He could call, but, dammit, shouldn't Martin be the one calling him? He knew the parade was tomorrow. Wyatt was so pissed at him! He grabbed his cell.

Wyatt   7:24 p.m.

> dude! where the hell are u?

Of course, no response.

Wyatt's mind careened. And Mackenzie and Jonathon! She'd lied to him. How long had they been . . . ?

He'd had this whole plan with Mackenzie and Martin to sell the cardboard Lincoln hats during the parade to help Wyatt's family raise the money to stay in business, and now neither of them . . .

Wyatt's heart pounded, and he felt like he might throw up. He texted Mackenzie.

Wyatt   7:26 p.m.

i saw u and Jonathon. don't show up 2night. or 2morrow. or ever.

He hit SEND and then shut off his phone. He was done. He didn't want to hear from either of them.

Martin was gone, and Mackenzie was making out with the enemy.

Heading downstairs, he could hear all the guests in the parking lot just behind the kitchen, where they were decorating the pickup. It sounded like a party.

Wyatt walked over to his soldier. Still cute. Unchanged. "It all finishes tomorrow, I guess. Wish me luck?" His soldier just smiled out at him from 150 years ago. Frozen in time.

He was just a photo.

Wyatt turned away. He had to do this himself. He could sell the hats right after the parade. That was, if anyone was going to be there to buy them.

There were five boxes of the souvenir Lincoln hats stacked in the corner behind Reception. They needed to get to the truck. He tried to lift the first one, but it was way too heavy for cardboard and glue. Wyatt opened it, and it wasn't hats—instead, it was all these old books. He'd been supposed to check out how much they were worth online but hadn't gotten around to it.

Wait . . .

Wyatt hauled out the over-one-thousand-page book on top, *Photographic History of the Civil War: Fort Sumter to Gettysburg.*

There on the cover was the photo. Flipped, or something. And cropped differently—all the guys in the background, behind the group of eleven, were missing. But there was *his* soldier. His Gay fantasy soldier on the cover. Who was he?

Wyatt scoured the jacket flaps, but there was no info about the cover image. It had to be in there somewhere. He flipped through the pages one by one, from the beginning. Battlefields, tents, portraits of generals, injured soldiers in makeshift hospitals. He found the photo just like the one in their display case on page 47. The caption read:

The first Virginia Militia, the "Richmond Grays," answered the call. They did not take part in the final capture of Brown, but they did arrive in Charles Town, Virginia, in time to form a hollow square around a gallows where old John Brown was hanged after his trial. . . .

One of their number present was John Wilkes Booth, an actor.

My soldier was a Confederate? On his way to the hanging of a guy who'd tried to free the slaves? And in the same regiment as John Wilkes Booth?

It was hard to process that he'd been crushing on a *Confederate* soldier all these years. He'd been so sure the soldiers in the photo were Union. . . . Wyatt looked past the rest of them at his soldier. Knowing all that, Wyatt didn't think he was so hot anymore.

Maybe he was a Gay Confederate. There had to have been some.

But I'm fighting for the right side. Fighting to redeem Lincoln. Fighting to reclaim our Gay history.

Determination flooded through him. *I guess . . . I really am a fighting soldier.* The thought made Wyatt crack a smile.

He checked the other four boxes—they all had the Lincoln hats inside them. He grabbed a carton and hefted it easily. He'd stack them in the back of the pickup for tomorrow and then help everyone finish transforming their truck into one amazing parade float.

At 11:10 p.m., the adults called it a night. Wax Lincoln looked good under his arbor, waxed-paper flowers hid all the chicken wire, and the homemade float was ready. The conversation and hot drinks moved inside, to the kitchen.

Wyatt let ten minutes pass and slipped out the front door, walking around the house to the pickup. Careful not to let anyone see him from the kitchen, he loaded his backpack with the brushes he'd washed out earlier and six pints of paint from the supplies. He gave Wax Lincoln under his plastic tarp a salute and headed out.

The moon wasn't up yet, and Wyatt kept his flashlight's circle of light close to the ground. He remembered sneaking out with Martin the last time. How they had been a team. But he guessed when the going got really tough, Martin just left. Like when he'd bailed on his old school and started homeschooling. Anyway, Wyatt was just a *friend*. Easy to discard. Pushing the thought down, he crossed the ford stones.

Wyatt stayed on Jenson's Stream Road to cut across the soccer field. Easier this way, with the heavy bag and flashlight.

He got to the school rock, still shouting out its message of hate:

NO FAGS IN HISTORY!

One by one, in the light from the gym, Wyatt pulled out his containers of paint and set them in a line on the grass: red, orange, yellow, green, blue, and purple.

What this rock needed was a big Gay Pride Rainbow.

Chapter 31

National Survey Results for the Week Ending
Friday, February 13
Von Lawson Productions

SAMPLE: 1,000 US citizens, statistically randomized

RESULTS:
Do you think Abraham Lincoln was romantically
involved with Joshua Speed?

No: 58%   (down 15% from last week)

Yes: 29%   (up 7% from last week)

Undecided: 13%   (up 8% from last week)

Queer as a Five-Dollar Bill Blog

QUEER AS A FIVE-DOLLAR BILL

Blog Post: Saturday, February 14, 2:17 a.m.

President Abraham Lincoln Was Gay:
The Elysium Letter

FACT: Abraham Lincoln wrote to his love, Joshua Fry Speed:

Springfield, February 25, 1842

Again you say, you much fear that that Elysium of which you have dreamed is never to be realized. Well, if it shall not, I dare swear it will not be the fault of her who is now your wife. I have no doubt that it is the peculiar misfortune of both you and me to dream dreams of Elysium far exceeding all that anything earthly can realize. Far short of your dreams as you may be, no woman could do more to realize them than that same black-eyed Fanny.

The Elysium—or Paradise—Abe wrote about was the dream that he and Joshua could end up together in their own happily ever after. And that didn't happen for them.

Joshua married Fanny.

And Abe married Mary. And then Abe changed our world forever. Because of him, our country was reunited and all the slaves were freed.

Like Martin Luther King Jr., Abraham Lincoln had a dream: that all of us would someday be free and equal. They both died on the way to making that dream come true.

Today, it's up to us—each one of us—to make our world the world they dreamed about.

Wyatt wasn't sure what woke him, but moonlight silvered streaks of fog outside, so he knew it was pretty early.

The parade.

Martin.

Mackenzie and Jonathon.

Would anyone come watch the parade? Would the people who'd promised to be in it even show up? And he still needed to iron those letters onto something for the truck grille banner!

Wyatt's mind raced. There was no falling back to sleep now.

He turned on his cell, and the light from the screen made his eyes feel raw. It was 5:29 a.m. No word from Martin and five texts from Mackenzie. He pressed DELETE ALL without reading any of them. What could she say? What could either of them say?

As Wyatt headed to the stairs, he tried to push them out of his mind. Instead, he thought about the whole B and B thing. How they had every room full and his dad was so excited about having thirty-four people prepaid for tonight's Civil War–Era Supper. How it was his dad's passion, and he'd set up his life so that Wyatt's mom, and even Wyatt, supported him in pursuing it with his whole heart. Maybe you didn't need millions of dollars to be a success. Maybe, you just needed to do what you really cared about.

The thought slowed Wyatt to a stop just as he reached the first-floor landing. He cared about the world knowing about Lincoln. About being Gay being okay. About people understanding that everyone is—*should be*—equal. No exceptions. Wyatt cared about this. With his whole being, he cared. Maybe he had more in common with his dad than he'd thought.

He turned around and went back up to his room to change clothes.

When Wyatt got to the kitchen, he snagged a yogurt and dipped a granola bar into it. He took a bite and glanced out the window. Wisps of fog rolled on the air. He could see the pickup through them.

Wait a minute.

Where was Wax Lincoln?

He headed outside to make sure it wasn't a trick of the moonlight.

The arbor was there, covered with waxed-paper flowers, but it was empty. Wyatt walked around the truck with its rainbow bunting, searching. He stepped on the plastic drop cloth they'd used to protect Wax Lincoln and the boxes of cardboard hats from getting wet overnight. It was twisted up by the left rear tire. Wyatt bent down to check under the truck, and the imitation-beaver-fur stovepipe hat was there, lying on its side in the gravel. Wyatt picked it up and placed it carefully on the passenger seat, scanning the parking lot.

He wasn't anywhere.

Someone had stolen Lincoln!

Wyatt searched the exhibit rooms and everywhere else, and even double-checked the parking lot. No Lincoln anywhere.

It was 6:14 a.m., and he was trying to figure out if he should call the police, or wake up his dad and mom, or what he should do. He came back inside from the kitchen porch, blowing on his hands to warm up, when the B and B line rang.

Wyatt stared at the phone on the counter. The nasty calls had been tapering off, and some calls were even people saying nice things. Before it could ring again and wake up the whole place, he grabbed it. "Hello?"

"Wyatt!" It was Mackenzie, whispering fiercely.

"I'm not talking to you." If she'd called his cell, he wouldn't have picked up. Which she probably knew . . .

"They have Lincoln!"

"What? Who?"

"Dress as a Confederate soldier, and get to Union Square."

"A soldier?"

"It's like a reenactment. Just do it. Bring a rifle and a belt set. You have to look real. And hurry!"

Chapter 32

Saturday, February 14

ORANGE-AND-WHITE road barriers and groups of high school guys in yellow John Wilkes Booth Appreciation Society T-shirts blocked the way to Union Square on Grant and Johnson Streets. The moon was more than half full, and Wyatt used the light to backtrack to Sixth Street and head to the park above the stream, figuring he could sneak in that way. He passed four empty buses, and everything was eerily quiet as he came around the corner of the Log Cabin. It was foggier here.

A soldier with two weapons over his shoulder stood in front of Wyatt, silhouetted against the yellow-white light coming from Union Square, just around the corner. Another guy, dressed like a grunt soldier, banged his way out of one of the five blue porta-potties on the park grass, saying, "For two hundred dollars, I'll make a four a.m. call. But damn, I'm tired."

The first soldier handed Porta-Potty Guy his rifle. "At least we don't have to shave." He took a sip from a takeout cup as they headed to the square.

"You never get the close-ups if you do," Porta-Potty Guy agreed.

Wyatt hurried to follow them, trying to look like he belonged in the butternut-gray uniform he'd borrowed from their military mannequin. The wool coat itched, and he pulled at the yellow bandanna on his neck. He'd tied it too tight.

"Gentlemen, you're late! We're racing the sun, and it's one take, no redos," someone with a clipboard and a walkie-talkie shouted at them. She stood by an old-fashioned lantern hanging from an iron rod. "Starbucks in the trash can, tattoos covered, and make sure those cell phones are off. They didn't have those in 1865! Everyone's lined up, and we're shooting in *three minutes!* Hustle up!" She spoke into her walkie-talkie: "I've got three stragglers."

The two other guys broke into a run and disappeared into the bank of fog ahead. Wyatt heard a different woman's voice from the clipboard lady's walkie-talkie behind him: "Roger that. Ease up on the fog. Cue sound."

A snare drum rolled, echoing through Wyatt. He walked into the mist, and as it swirled away from his legs, what he saw was unreal, like stepping back in time. Two hundred Civil War soldiers stood in silent formation, everyone staring up at a waist-high stage ringed by bright oil lanterns. It was where the metal arch spelling out LINCOLNVILLE had been, but that was gone.

Three men stood on the stage, one with a canvas sack over his head and his arm in a sling. The other two wore officer uniforms. Wyatt wove his way forward, trying to make sense of it. The soldiers all around him looked so real. Like his soldier in the photo come to life.

No one glanced Wyatt's way, but he was glad it wasn't daylight yet.

Suddenly, the drumming stopped, and everyone slapped their rifles to their sides, at attention.

Wyatt got his Springfield rifle from their display case in position and tried to look like a soldier. He reminded himself that some real Civil War soldiers had been younger than he was. He was five rows from a heap of scrap wood piled between the soldiers and the stage. His bandanna was too high, and the jacket collar continued to be super itchy, making him wish it wasn't buttoned up all the way. When was the last time they'd cleaned this?

He thought about Martin and his dust mites, and how those microscopic insects really did look like aliens. His neck itched worse, like the mites or alien lice or whatever they were had realized that instead of plastic, they finally had human flesh to eat. But Wyatt didn't dare move. Everyone but the officer walking the row was completely still.

Wyatt kept the forage cap low on his face as the officer approached, hoping the mix of oil lamp and predawn fog would camouflage him. The officer's brown and shiny brass scabbard with a sword in it came to a stop right in front of Wyatt. A fringed gold sash covered the officer's belt and was knotted at his right hip. Slate-blue wool pants tucked into high leather boots turned directly toward him. Hesitantly, Wyatt looked up at the officer's face. . . . *Mackenzie's dad!*

Mr. Miller stared at him, and Wyatt tensed up, expecting Mackenzie's dad to shout, blow Wyatt's cover, and kick him out of there. But Mr. Miller didn't say anything. He just gave Wyatt a *you be careful* look and started walking again.

"Soldiers of the Confederacy!" the shortest of the three men onstage shouted out. He had an odd, high voice. "I give you the president of the Confederate States of America, Jefferson Davis!"

The guy with the goatee walked forward, arms raised in a rockstar way that set off alarms in Wyatt's head. The goatee was new, and he was in period uniform, but Wyatt would have known those cowboy boots anywhere.

Ernest Von Lawson.

"Men. You are all witness to a moment that will change the course of our country's history. For we have here, as a prisoner of war, captured this very morning by our brave patriot John Wilkes Booth"—he gestured to the side, but Wyatt couldn't see who was playing the famous assassin—"none other than the Devil himself, false president of our brothers, our enemy to the north, Mr. Abraham Lincoln!"

The soldiers around Wyatt jeered and booed. They *did* have Wax Lincoln! Was that him under the bag? And where was Mackenzie? He'd been so mad at her . . . Wyatt's eyes searched, but he didn't see her.

Von Lawson continued, "This war, which has rent country and families in two, must end. And it *will* end, right here. As I have long said, we desire peace at any sacrifice, save that of honor and independence. Honor. Honor is the reason we gather here today, in this tribunal, to try Abraham Lincoln for conspiracy to subjugate us by arms, for indecency and lies, for offenses against our humanity, and for crimes against nature!"

With that, the shorter guy pulled the canvas bag off the third guy's head, revealing Wax Lincoln. His right arm, which was usually out to shake, was tight against his chest in a makeshift sling. He was gagged, and his hair stood up on one side, which made him look scared, even though Wyatt knew it wasn't real. Despite everything, it was good to see him.

Von Lawson pointed at Lincoln. "We have seen evidence of his unholy and heinous crime, lying with a man as one lies with a woman, if one is so blessed."

I gave them the evidence. This is all happening because of me. . . .

"A crime from the time of Sodom and Gomorrah to today. How do we find Lincoln?"

The men around Wyatt roared the word: "Guilty!"

Von Lawson dipped his head. "The sentence is death."

What?

Before Wyatt knew what was happening, three soldiers rushed onstage, carried Wax Lincoln down, and pushed him, standing up, into the middle of the stack of scrap wood. They piled the pieces higher on his legs.

Von Lawson jumped down. "We end this war now, with a new dawn. A new day."

They had timed it perfectly, shafts of sunlight just cresting the Cascade Mountains behind Wyatt.

Von Lawson picked up a brightly glowing lantern. "In flames of righteousness, their disgraced and discredited commander in chief will be gone. The North will be left in chaos. And the South will rise . . . to victory!"

Wyatt's feet felt frozen in place.

Von Lawson whipped the oil lantern through the air, and it smashed at Lincoln's feet, an exploding ball of glass shards and fire. The wood, which must have been soaked with lighter fluid, erupted into flames.

"*Nooo!*" Wyatt screamed, but it was drowned out by the cheers of two hundred soldiers around him shouting, at the top of their lungs, "*Huwwwaaaaaaaah!*"

Wyatt watched, horrified, as Lincoln's face sagged in the heat. His suit was on fire now, and the wax figure kept melting, sloping down like a pyramid in the flames.

The fire consuming Lincoln lit up Von Lawson's satisfied expression, as the soldiers in their rows cheered.

In minutes, only the metal armature of the statue was left, and even that toppled and fell into the flames. The soldiers stopped their shouting, and for a long moment, everything was silent.

A woman dressed in jeans and a sweater walked forward with a megaphone and addressed the crowd. "And . . . that's a wrap! Thank you, and our PA, Jessica, will have your cash for you on the buses." The soldiers broke formation, and she put the megaphone on the edge of the stage. Von Lawson high-fived her.

"I can't wait to get this footage to the edit bay," she told him.

Wyatt walked closer, spotting Jonathon in a yellow John Wilkes Booth Appreciation Society T-shirt. He was standing with his parents and sister by some of the crew, who were taking down the large film-shoot cameras.

Von Lawson peeled off the fake goatee and rubbed his chin as they walked back to the crew area. "Civilization, here I come!"

Someone spoke into a walkie-talkie. "Let's clear this area and take down the barricades. We have to be out of here before their parade starts, and that's at nine."

Wyatt saw his chance and cut past the burned-down fire to grab the megaphone. He pressed a button to talk, and a siren blared. *Ow,* that hurt his ears.

Everyone stopped moving. Wyatt tried again, pressing the other button. "What about slavery?" His voice, amplified, carried across the square.

Wyatt watched Von Lawson push back through the crowd to face him from twenty yards away. The TV host stood there like a gunfighter out of some cowboy movie, about to draw and fire. Wyatt forced his voice not to shake as he pressed the megaphone's TALK button again. "What about slavery, Mr. Von Lawson? If the South wins?" Everyone was listening. Watching him. Wyatt felt his face heat up but told himself it didn't matter.

"Wyatt . . . Did you enjoy the show?" Von Lawson didn't need a microphone.

"No." Wyatt's voice got stronger. "What about slavery?"

Von Lawson was casual. "Slavery would have ended on its own, eventually."

Anger pushed everything else aside. "That's supposed to be good enough? Eventually?" Wyatt snorted his disgust. "And what about all the soldiers like me? One in ten is Queer, like Lincoln was. Even back then." *Like my soldier probably was.*

Von Lawson inclined his head toward the fire's smoking embers.

Maybe Wyatt could get him to say it, with all these witnesses. "Is that your *Real America?* Just kill the people you don't like?"

"Phineas didn't kill people he didn't like. Phineas acted to mend the displeasure of the Lord. Anyway, we haven't killed anyone. It was just an effigy. Just a short film project we thought could maybe turn this thing around. Let people think it through to its obvious conclusion. If they want to believe Lincoln was this immoral practicing sodomite you think he was, America might have turned out to be a very different country. One they might not be so keen on. Though, for some us, it could have worked out." Von Lawson smiled, the biggest shark of all. "And, as an added benefit, without your Lincoln, you can't have your parade celebrating queerness now. You ruined that word for us, you know? *Queer* used to be a perfectly good word, meaning *disgustingly different.*"

There was a honk, and soldiers moved out of the way as a green pickup with paper flowers all over it slowly pushed through to the stage and stopped ten feet from them. A three-person camera crew jumped down from the back and started filming Wyatt, Von Lawson, everything. Iron-on letters on a white pillowcase attached to the truck grille read:

ALL PEOPLE* ARE CREATED EQUAL
*NO EXCEPTIONS

Wyatt looked to see who was behind the wheel.

Martin!

Martin put up a hand and smiled at him.

Inside Wyatt, hope soared. He ran over to the passenger door and wrenched it open. "Hey! You're like the cavalry."

"Not exactly a Bond-car entrance, but we made it!" He beamed. "It's good to see you."

Wyatt tossed in his rifle and grabbed Lincoln's hat from the passenger seat, where he'd put it earlier. He spoke into the megaphone. "We're still going to have our parade."

"How?" Von Lawson mocked him. "You don't have a Lincoln!"

In that instant, Wyatt realized he wasn't scared anymore. The weight of holding the secret was gone. Everyone there knew he was

Gay. Some people weren't okay with it, but that wasn't Wyatt's problem—it was theirs. And a lot of people were okay with him being him. Some of the people who had been to his blog. And probably all of the ones coming for the parade later this morning—fingers crossed some people would show up! But it wasn't about what strangers thought.

There were his dad and mom. Mackenzie and Jennie and all their friends who had been watching his back at school. And Rhonda. Martin. Most of all, Wyatt himself. He was okay with it. Okay with being 100 percent Wyatt.

He felt the camera lights on him as he said two words under his breath, for courage. "Soul force."

Wyatt leaped into the back of the pickup, took off the bandanna and belt set with his bayonet, and, Superman-style, pulled off his wool jacket. The leather suspenders holding up his butternut-gray soldier pants framed the Super *G* on his chest. It was time to be his own superhero.

The boxes of Lincoln hats were by his feet. But he had the one from Wax Lincoln, which, even though he knew it was imitation beaver fur, felt more real now than ever. He picked up the hat in one hand and the megaphone in the other.

Von Lawson had said they didn't have a Lincoln, but he was wrong.

Wyatt put the stovepipe hat on his head and spoke into the megaphone. "I'll be Lincoln. All men are created equal. Women, too. Everybody! That's the world I want to live in."

Von Lawson scoffed. "Nobody who wrote the Declaration of Independence was thinking about Gay people being equal."

"Right!" Wyatt got sarcastic. "Equality should only be for rich, White, straight men who are the descendants of other rich, White, straight men from Europe."

"Raahhhhh!" "Get him!" "Shut him up!" Twenty shouting guys from school and the freshman basketball team, all of them in yellow John Wilkes Booth Appreciation Society T-shirts, rushed the truck. They started pushing it sideways, rocking the whole pickup back and forth.

"Wyatt!" Mackenzie screamed, and he saw her running toward the truck from the other side of the stage. More people were coming behind her.

Martin shouted, "Hold on!" A grinding sound told Wyatt that he was trying to start the engine. Wyatt clung to the cab roof as the arbor snapped and its top crashed to the truck bed, missing him by inches. He was sure they were going to flip the truck over.

"Stop!" Someone in a yellow shirt was waving his arms. Wyatt looked at him, wide-eyed.

It was Jonathon.

"*Stop!*" Jonathon yelled it again, pulling Charlie's arm off the pickup. The guys stood down. "It's gone far enough."

Mackenzie came to Jonathon's side, out of breath. "Let them be equal! Everyone equal."

"Whose side are you on?" Charlie snarled at his best friend.

Jonathon paused. He looked at Wyatt. At Mackenzie next to him.

"Your choice, big brother," Becca called to Jonathon, as she strode over from where she'd been standing with the film crew, alternating steps on her pink zebra-print prosthetic leg. "You can be Luke or Darth Vader. But Von Lawson, he's pretty much Emperor Palpatine."

Wyatt wasn't sure what Jonathon was going to do. The crowd pressed in thick around them, soldier-actors and townspeople drawn to the commotion.

Suddenly, Jonathon stripped off his John Wilkes Booth Appreciation Society T-shirt and threw it to the ground. Camera lights on him, he vaulted into the back of the truck.

Was that so he wouldn't get his shirt dirty when they fought?

Wyatt resisted the urge to take a step back. He met Jonathon's eyes, determined. He was not going down without a fight. Not this time. Not ever again. He spoke into the megaphone, his voice mocking. "What, no lightsaber for the big *Star Wars* duel?"

Jonathon flinched and then put up his palm. "I don't want to fight you."

A hard laugh burst from Wyatt's mouth.

One of the boxes of souvenir Lincoln hats had broken open, and Jonathon bent to pick up a stovepipe hat made out of heavy paper. Looking right at Wyatt, he stood tall and put the hat on his own head.

Wyatt was stunned.

"What the hell?" Von Lawson shouted. The guys from Jonathon's team, in a cluster around the truck, looked lost.

"You're right. We're all equal, or should be," Jonathon told Wyatt. He took a deep breath, like he was about to reveal something big. He turned to the crowd and cameras and his sister and watching parents. "If the Galactic Republic can include everyone, freaky-weird aliens like Wookiees and Twi'leks and humans, too, then shouldn't there be an equal place in our world for humans who are different than us?" He looked at his teammates. "Come on, Cohen: Asians and Jews. Anderson, what about girls like your mom and sister?" His eyes swept Miguel from the basketball team and up to Martin, who was standing on the truck step bar, staring at him. "And Latin people. And Black people . . ." Jonathon looked back at Becca, who was standing there with one eyebrow raised, watching him. He smiled at her in apology. "And disabled people!"

He turned back to Wyatt. "Even Gays. And if celebrating all that needs a Lincoln, okay. I'm Lincoln."

Mackenzie came closer to the truck and reached up a hand. Jonathon lifted her to join them. She grabbed a hat and put it on. "And I'm Lincoln, too!"

"Count me in," Becca said, and with a leap hoisted herself up into the truck bed as well. She put a hat on her head and crowed, "I'm Lincoln!" She hugged her brother and put her hand out to Mackenzie, who clasped it.

"I'm Lincoln!" Martin beamed at Wyatt and pulled on a hat.

A hand shot up from among the soldier actors, a guy with a beard. "I'm Lincoln!"

"And I'm Lincoln!" That was Jennie.

"I'm Lincoln!" Another soldier.

"I'm Lincoln!" Sandee, from the candy store.

And more soldiers, and townspeople, like a wave.

"I'm Lincoln!" "I'm Lincoln!" "I am Lincoln!"

Mackenzie glanced at Wyatt. "I'm sorry I didn't tell you about Jonathon, but I didn't think you'd understand. But now maybe you can see what I knew all along. . . ." She smiled at Jonathon with a mix of admiration and pride. She turned back to Wyatt. "Are we okay?"

Slowly, Wyatt nodded. "Yeah." He turned to Jonathon. "Hey, why did you help get word out about Lincoln, like with the radio program?"

"I needed you to be a big deal," Jonathon said.

Wyatt gave him a *What does that mean?* pop of his hands.

Jonathon shrugged. "Luke wouldn't be anyone without Darth Vader. I mean, he wouldn't be a hero."

"So I was your Darth Vader?" Wyatt asked. Not much of a compliment.

"Well, yeah," Jonathon admitted. "It didn't really work out that way, but . . ."

That explains the Death Star.

"Guys, it's quarter to eight!" Martin looked up from his phone.

Wyatt tilted his head to where the parade groups were supposed to line up on Hayes Street. "We should probably go help them get ready." He looked over at Mackenzie. "You staying for the parade?"

"Wyatt!" Then she shook her head. "It was going to be a surprise, but . . . I'm *in* it. Sensei Jodi got our whole dojo to march!"

She was about to hug Wyatt, when a voice cut the air. "I am your commander in chief!" Wyatt whipped around to see it was Von Lawson, on another megaphone. "Soldiers of the Confederate States of America—I order you to block that street and stop this parade!"

No one moved.

Von Lawson pointed to the northwest corner of the square. "If you want your two hundred dollars, you will form a human barrier at that intersection and prevent anyone from marching in this so-called 'parade' honoring perversion, immorality, and the radical homosexual agenda."

The reenactment actors grumbled.

"I thought we were done. Didn't the director call wrap?"

"I didn't wake up at two a.m. for nothing."

Von Lawson spoke again. "In fact, I'll double your pay for every man who stands his ground until their parade permit expires at noon."

Wyatt heard a reenactment soldier by the truck. "Four hundred dollars? Okay!"

What looked like half of the soldiers started to move in a group to block Route 37 at Johnson Street.

Wyatt looked at Mackenzie, Martin, Jonathon, and Becca but didn't know what any of them could do to stop it.

"Enough playacting!" Mr. Miller pushed through the crowd to get in front of the men heading into Johnson Street.

His costume outranked them, but would they listen to him?

"I am a duly sworn officer of the law, and the permit allowing this reenactment filming has expired!"

Mackenzie seemed to hold her breath.

"First of all," Von Lawson spoke through his megaphone, "you're working for me right now, Security. And second, you're not even a real cop." Von Lawson sneered at him. "You're a meter maid! You write tickets."

Wyatt noticed Mackenzie's hands ball into fists.

"That's right." Mackenzie's dad pulled his parking-ticket pad out of his uniform's jacket pocket. He flipped the book open and with a raised pen faced the reenactment actors who had started for the intersection. "You all need to go back to your buses, or I will be forced to issue you citations for obstructing a public thoroughfare. And jaywalking."

Wyatt saw Mackenzie's proud look as she watched her dad.

Mr. Miller continued, "Trust me, it'll cost you a lot more than four hundred dollars. *And* you'll have to show up in court."

The mass of men hesitated.

Von Lawson threatened them. "Leave now, and you don't get paid!"

Martin stood on the top of the truck bed side, his Lincoln hat making him even taller. He shouted, "My mom's a lawyer! She'll help you sue Von Lawson for wages, but you can't stop this parade from happening!"

Wyatt put his arm out to Martin, and they grasped hands. "But you can stay and be in the parade!" Wyatt spoke into his megaphone. "Come on! What kind of world is it going to be? Shouldn't everyone be equal?"

"Please." Mackenzie said it quietly. Almost like a prayer.

They waited to see what the crowd would do. Jonathon put his arm around Mackenzie.

"How about one of them hats, if we're staying?" one of the soldiers called up to them.

Mackenzie turned to Wyatt. "I have some birthday money saved up, and I can't think of anything better to spend it on!"

He nodded at her, grateful.

Mackenzie handed the soldier a hat. "Here you go . . ."

"I want a hat!"

"Absolutely!" Mackenzie said.

"Me, too!"

Mackenzie, Wyatt, Martin, Jonathon, and Becca passed out Lincoln hats to the crowd that surged forward. No one went to block the street. The tide had turned, in their favor.

Wyatt watched Von Lawson slink off into his limo and drive away. *Good riddance.*

Mackenzie moved closer to Jonathon, and Wyatt heard her ask, "You stole the wax figure, didn't you?"

"I wish I hadn't," Jonathon said, like he really meant it.

She touched his cheek. "But when it counted, you came through."

He gave a shrug. "What can I say? I'm a Jedi."

"I think you really are." And with that, Mackenzie kissed him.

Wyatt looked away, but this time not out of anger, or betrayal, or hurt. He wanted to give them a moment of privacy. After all, Mackenzie was his best friend. And, he realized, he was happy for her.

ROOOAARRR! ROAAAR! RAAARRRRRRRR! The motorcycles got everyone's attention. It was a great way to start a parade.

Dykes on Bikes blasted into Union Square ahead of their pickup. Wyatt's dad drove, and, with Lincoln hats tall on their heads, Wyatt, Martin, Becca, Mackenzie, and Jonathon rode in the back. Mackenzie had changed into a white *gi*, and Jonathon into a red polo shirt.

Wyatt and Martin handed over Lincoln hats to a cluster of three older women who waved and asked for them.

When they'd pulled out the broken arbor, Betty had overheard Wyatt ask his dad if, without making Mackenzie pay for it, they could just keep giving out the hats for free—everyone was so excited to get them. She'd called it "very clever promotional marketing." Turned out she worked in PR. Wyatt's dad gave his okay.

"You're welcome!" Wyatt waved at the women, who thanked them and giggled at how they looked in the stovepipe hats.

At least one hundred soldiers from earlier were marching behind them in Lincoln hats. As they passed Sandee's Liquor and Candy Mart, the square opened up before them. It was less than an hour and a half later, but now it was packed, and more people were crossing down from where traffic had been diverted onto Second Street. Usually they said two thousand people attended Lincolnville's annual parade, but Wyatt thought this seemed double last year's crowd.

Amid all the craziness, he had his first chance to talk to Martin. "I thought you left."

Martin shook his head. "We didn't know about Von Lawson's plan. But the mayor told everyone the parade wasn't happening, and John Stevens's producer wouldn't listen to my emails or get on the phone. But I knew we had to document this with the right people. So we drove down to San Francisco. Mom and I talked to John himself, convinced him, and got his crew to drive back with us."

"But, you didn't even call. Or answer my text!"

"Mom doesn't let me have my phone on when I'm driving. And . . . I didn't want to tell you, in case it didn't work out. Even when they agreed to come, we weren't sure we'd make it in time." Martin lowered his head. "I got my first speeding ticket."

He didn't leave. He did all of it—even drove over the speed limit— for me.

Behind them, drums and cowbells started up. *Ba ba ba Bap—Bap Bap Bap—Ba ba BOP! Ba ba ba Bap—Bap Bap Bap—Ba ba BAHH!*

The rhythm got people cheering.

"I'm really glad you're here," Wyatt shouted over the noise.

"Me, too," Martin said, then winked at Wyatt. "Nice shirt, by the way."

Wyatt felt this crazy rush, and he couldn't even try to return the wink. He just shouted, "You're not getting it back."

Martin laughed, and Wyatt joined in.

Wyatt's dad made the turn onto Lincoln Boulevard. They'd moved a section of the stage next to the road, and Wyatt's mom stood on it with her clipboard and microphone. As they rolled past, she ad-libbed the new parade addition: "Civil War–reenactment soldiers who support equality!"

Wyatt's eye caught a movement by the library door. It was Mr. Clifton, closing the big entry door, shutting himself inside.

Wyatt just felt sad for him as they rolled forward.

His mom's voice bounced off the library, amplified on speakers they'd set up all around Union Square.

"The Asian Pacific Islander Women's Color Guard!"

"The Eugene County African American Equality and Justice Society!"

Wyatt spotted Mr. Guzman and his girlfriend with the pink hair in the crowd. Mr. Guzman gave Wyatt a thumbs-up. Wyatt waved back. He was so glad his old teacher got to see this. All of this.

Wyatt's mom and the parade behind them kept going as they handed out Lincoln hats.

"The Corvallis Valley High School Gay-Straight Alliance!"

"The Society for Progressive Islam, Salem Chapter!"

In the front row of spectators, Rhonda looked out from behind her video camera and blew them a kiss. Martin grinned at his mom and Frisbeed her a hat. She snagged it midair.

"The Lake Medford Fire Department!"

"Northwest Disability Rights!"

Jonah from Pies and Pool and his girlfriend ran up to get two hats from Wyatt. Jonah insisted on shaking Wyatt's hand. "Great job, man. Great job!" he shouted over the cheers.

Dykes on Bikes and their pickup led the parade past the Log Cabin. The buses were gone, and they kept passing out hats to the people five and seven deep on the sidewalks and parkway. The stores were open along Fifth and Johnson streets, busy with customers. Mr. Woo even waved to them, all friendly, as people browsed the costumes on his outdoor racks and talked about which photo packages they should get.

The parade finished just a block from their B and B. Wyatt's dad stopped the truck and leaned out the window as they all jumped down. "You kids go catch the rest of the parade."

"I've got to find the dojo." Mackenzie waved bye as she headed up Sixth Street to where the parade groups were lined up on Hayes.

Wyatt checked with his dad. "You sure?"

"Go!" His dad chuckled. "I have a lot of cooking to do. Have fun!"

"Thanks!" Wyatt ran up Grant Street, Martin at his side. In three blocks, they made a right, and there were even more people in Union Square now. Wyatt's mom kept announcing the entries:

"The Albany Art Museum's Jewish Film Festival!"

"The Multnomah County Women's Rights Project!"

Wyatt took Martin's hand, partly to not lose him, and partly because he just wanted to. And he could!

It looked like everyone had shown. Forty-one parade entries in all. Forty-three, with Mackenzie's dojo and the soldiers. It was a record, and twelve more than had signed up to march in the old version of the parade.

"The Pacific School for the Deaf!"

"Gresham's Sci-Fi, Anime, and Comic Con!"

Making their way through to the stage where Wyatt's mom was, they passed a young guy with curled fingers walking with crutches on his arms. He was all happy, chatting with a Latina girl with a Mohawk. For the first time, Wyatt really looked at the crowd. Under the Lincoln hats sprinkled everywhere, they were a mix of farmers and city folk, students from Oregon State and the University of Oregon, old people and kids, disabled and abled, straight and Gay, and probably Bi and Trans, too. They were Black and White and Asian and every color— and everyone was in great spirits, celebrating equality.

Lincoln's idea. King's idea. And, for this parade, Wyatt's idea, too!

"From Ashland, the Oregon Theater Festival Players!"

"Parents, Friends, and Families of Lesbians and Gays, PFLAG Philomath!"

They'd just broken through to Lincoln Boulevard when Wyatt's mom announced, "The Corvallis Yoshukai Karate and Martial Arts Center!"

Wyatt cheered for Mackenzie, Martin at his side. Mackenzie and twenty-five other teens and kids whipped their nunchucks through the air in perfect unison with a black belt counting out in Japanese, *"Ich, ni, sahn!"* Mackenzie grinned at Wyatt and Martin as she marched past, nunchucks flying.

The parade kept coming. "Western Oregon Atheists!"

"The Gay Veterans Association, Pacific Northwest Chapter!"

Then Wyatt's mom announced, "And a last-minute addition: please welcome our very own mayor, Kelly Rails, and her husband, high school coach and country music star Bryan Rails!"

Wyatt dropped Martin's hand. The people around them applauded Jonathon's parents sitting on the trunk of Coach Rails's open convertible. Principal Jackson was driving, and Mayor Rails, dressed in jeans and a USA flag T-shirt, waved to everyone like she was the Queen of America.

Martin snorted and leaned into Wyatt's ear. "Just watch. She'll be all over the news as a 'champion of equality.'"

Wyatt scowled. "She's just doing it because it's popular, and she's probably figured out a way to make money, or get reelected, because of it."

"It's a good thing, Wyatt. Doesn't matter why she's doing it." Martin's hand swept the parade and crowd around them. "You've already changed this part of the world."

Martin was right. Wyatt wasn't going to let anyone ruin this.

Wyatt's mom announced the final parade entry, now number forty-four. "The First Metropolitan Church of Portland's gospel choir!"

All fifty choir members, in their gold-and-red robes, tambourines shaking and arms raised, started singing, "Free at last. Free at last. Thank God Almighty, I'm free at last. . . ."

Their voices rose up and filled the square, and Wyatt's chest swelled with the words.

Martin was smiling at him. "We did it, didn't we?"

His lips were beautiful.

He was beautiful.

"Hey, it's Valentine's Day!" Wyatt said.

"Is it?" The light sparkled in Martin's eyes. He knew, all right.

"And . . . I'm going to kiss you for *you*, you know?" Wyatt told him.

"Yeah. I know," Martin said, moving in toward him. "Me, too."

And with thousands of people around them, and the singing lifting them all, Wyatt leaned in to touch his lips to Martin's. Wyatt could feel Martin's biceps graze the sides of his Super *G* T-shirt as they pulled each other close. Wyatt kissed him, and Martin kissed him back. He tasted like spice . . . and cinnamon.

Free at last.

How long can I make this kiss last?

A sigh escaped Wyatt, and it was the big finale. No birds, or chipmunks, or little people. But music, inside as well as out.

And goose bumps.

And this feeling in Wyatt's chest. His throat. His lips.

Glowing. He was glowing.

He was standing there, in front of the whole world, and he was kissing Martin.

His first *real* kiss.

And Wyatt was, finally, himself.

Everyone around them was singing, and Wyatt pulled back to look at Martin. *Friends, and more. Much more.*

And in that instant, Wyatt knew. He didn't have to go anywhere else to be himself. He'd found it right there. *Elysium.*

Ninth grade had been a war. And he'd won.

From his heart, Wyatt started singing along. Martin joined in, and their fingers and voices wove together and rose with the others to the sky. "Free at last! Free at last! Thank God Almighty, I am free. At. Last!"

National Survey Results for the Week Ending Saturday, June 27
Von Lawson Productions

SAMPLE: 1,000 US citizens, statistically randomized

RESULTS:
Do you think Abraham Lincoln was romantically involved with Joshua Speed?

No:	47%	(unchanged for the last 5 weeks)
Yes:	47%	(unchanged for the last 5 weeks)
Undecided:	6%	(unchanged for the last 5 weeks)

"TWO LOVERS"
MUSIC BY IRVING GORDON
NEW LYRICS BY MARTIN SYKES

For Wyatt

Two lovers on their way,
One wore blue and one wore gray
No one knew that they were Gay
All on a beautiful morning

War was hell, they had their share
One felt hope and one, despair
Cannonballs tore through the air
All on a beautiful morning

War was hell, they made it through
Didn't care if the whole world knew
A kiss between gray and blue
All on a beautiful mo-r-ning!

QUEER AS A FIVE-DOLLAR BILL

Blog Post: Sunday, June 6, 10:32 a.m.

Lincoln's Rainbow

Bed & Breakfast

Invites you to celebrate LGBTQ Pride with us

in beautiful Lincolnville, Oregon!

with

Civil War–Era Suppers with Gregory

Tours with Mackenzie

Music with Martin

Hikes with Wyatt

*Book early—we have only a handful of room nights
still available!*

And if you fall in love with our town like we have,
Elizabeth Yarrow Real Estate can help you find
a place to call home.

If you're in town the weekend of June 28, the Lincolnville
Chamber of Commerce and the Straight for Equality:
Rails for Governor campaign will be sponsoring a block
party for local businesses, the community, and visiting
friends opposite the Log Cabin on Johnson and Fifth.

The chamber has distributed Gay Pride Rainbow Flag stickers, which you'll see in nearly all of the storefronts in town.

And that Sunday, the anniversary of the Stonewall Riots, Nora Roberts (our new town librarian) is hosting a party installing *Joshua Fry Speed: Lincoln's Most Intimate Friend* on permanent display in the Lincolnville Public Library. You'll have to ask first, and put on white gloves to touch it, since it's now a Reference: Special Collections book, but anybody who wants to can read it.

ABRAHAM LINCOLN AS A YOUNG MAN

Abe lithograph created by Leopold Grozelier, printed by J.H. Bufford in 1860

JOSHUA FRY SPEED,
"About The Time He First Met Abraham Lincoln in 1837."

Joshua image is from the Filson Historical Society, and is on page 4 of
Joshua Fry Speed, Lincoln's Most Intimate Friend

THE CIVIL WAR PHOTO SHOWING WYATT'S SOLDIER

(Cook Collection, the Valentine Museum, Richmond, VA.)

Author's Note

Dear Reader,

Wyatt, Martin, Mackenzie, and Jonathon are fictional characters, but the evidence that convinces Wyatt that Abraham Lincoln loved Joshua Fry Speed is part of American history, and every historical quote used in this story is true. (And every direct quote by Abraham Lincoln is in **bold**. Check out the Endnotes section that follows.)

While historians will continue to argue over whether Lincoln was Gay, or Bi, or straight, each one of us can read the letters, look at the evidence, and make our own decision.

To me, it's very clear that Abraham and Joshua were in love. Had I known, when I was growing up, that Abraham Lincoln loved another guy, it would have completely changed how I felt about myself—and maybe made my coming out as a Gay young man easier.

I hope my fictional story of Wyatt and his friends, and the true story of Abraham Lincoln and Joshua Fry Speed, will inspire you to be authentic, too!

This is my debut book, and I'd love to hear what you think. You can write me at authorleewind@gmail.com, or reach out on Twitter, Facebook, or Instagram. You'll find all the links at my website: www.leewind.org.

And now you have the power—to share this secret from history, and to help make this book a success. If you're willing, I'd love a review of *Queer as a Five-Dollar Bill* wherever you read reviews. Reviews, and word of mouth, can make all the difference. So thank you. And please know that, for me, your having read this book means the world.

The light in me recognizes and acknowledges the light in you,

Lee
Los Angeles, California

Acknowledgments

I'm grateful for . . .

Randy Harrison, whose talk about Lincoln's letters to Speed changed my life.

M. T. Anderson, for the editorial guidance, and the Highlights Foundation, for the space, to do revision number eight—the one that took this story to a whole new level!

Godeane Eagle, who helped me find (and stop losing) my voice.

My writer/Society of Children's Book Writers and Illustrators friends, who encouraged me, gave me feedback, and shared the journey so far: Rita Crayon Huang, Claudia Harrington, Maya Creedman Ho, Sara Wilson Etienne, Karol Silverstein, Ruta Sepetys, Jane Yolen, Ellen Hopkins, Bruce Coville, Laurent Linn, Emma Dryden, Esther Herschenhorn, Lin Oliver, Stephen Mooser, Sara Rutenberg, Alice Pope, Martha Brockenbrough, Paula Yoo, Lori Snyder, everyone in the SCBWI main office, and all the regional team members and board members and team bloggers who are my tribe . . . and so many more, I'd need a whole other book to shout out to you all!

Yapha Mason, for the friendship, encouragement, and amazing blurb.

Elizabeth Abarbanel, Ellen Wittlinger, Brent Hartinger, Alex Sanchez, and Cindy Maloney, for the early reads and blurbs.

Librarian Mary McCoy and the entire reference librarian team at the Los Angeles Public Library.

Diana Gleason, reference librarian at the Oregon State Law Library.

The UCLA Young Research Library, Special Collections, team.

Jennifer Pitts and Bahar Soomekh, for the cultural-competency reads.

Sandra Martin and Martha Heredia, for the Spanish advice.

Bill at Ursula's Costumes in Santa Monica, California, for the Civil War reenactment wardrobe education.

Angela Bole, Terry Nathan, Caitlin Walker, Francie Droll, and everyone at the Independent Book Publishers Association for the independent-publishing education and encouragement.

Greg Pincus, for being my book marketing and brainstorming friend.

Jessica and Kayla Weissbuch, for believing in this project and putting up Camp Brave Trails as a nonprofit partner so we could use this book to empower LGBTQ and Allied teens.

Margot Atwell, for the encouraging and sage Kickstarter advice.

Matthew Winner, for amplifying the Kickstarter campaign and cheering on this project.

David Pisarra, for the advice (even when I didn't take it).

Brooke Warner, for the guidance.

Laurie Young, for the design expertise and friendship.

Karen Maneely and the BookBaby team, for helping put it all together.

WATCH THIS!, the winning designer of the 99designs cover contest, for a cover that showed this book is all about a modern teen—while still including an irreverent image of Lincoln.

Mom, who isn't here to enjoy bragging about this.

John and Dad, who have been so supportive.

My husband, Mark, and our daughter, for loving me, which makes all things possible. Like writing and publishing this book!

And when traditional publishing wouldn't rise to the challenge of sharing this story with the world, a whole community stepped up. In a successful Kickstarter campaign, 182 backers joined me to fund both professionally publishing this book and donating 810 copies to empower LGBTQ and Allied teens.

THANK YOU

Kathleen Ahrens
Sean Akers
Aino Anto
Kathi Appelt
Pádraig Conor Winifred Archer-Morris
Li Ashfield
Jim Averbeck
Brian Bogdan
The Brooks Family
Angela Cerrito
Charlie Cohen
David Jay Collins
Constance Cone
Dana Herman Covey
Mike Curato
Zaza D
Francesca Droll
Emma D. Dryden
Rebecca Dudley
Amber Elizabeth
Sarah Joy Erskine
Stephen Fischman
Eric G
Cate Gallivan & Julia Lanigan
Petey J. Gibson
Sherry N. Gick
Glenn Hargett & Everett Vaughn
Alli Harper
Claudia Harrington & Ken Kallmeyer
Jeffrey Holder

Jason Jenn
Nora Jung
Melissa Killian
Steve Krantz
Fran & Finn Lampert
Kristin Bartley Lenz
Sylvia Liu
Kimberly M. Lowe
Jacqueline Lozano
Deb Lund
Cheryl Manning
Joanna Marple
Nora Lester Murad
Edie Pagliasotti
Jerry Pang
Linda Sue Park
Katherine Quimby
Cheryl Rainfield
Portia Reddy
ShadowCub
Erica Silverman
Karol Silverstein
Peter Strömberg
Tracy Tai
Laurie Ann Thompson
Jan-Henrik Wilhelm
Matthew C. Winner
Ellen Wittlinger
Laurie L. Young

And many thanks to the 123 others who contributed anonymously!

IN CHAPTER 1, the Lincoln quote Wyatt uses in his video is from a letter Abe wrote Joshua Fry Speed on August 24, 1855. That's more than thirteen years after their flurry of correspondence surrounding Joshua's marriage to Fanny in February 1842. You can find the letter on pages 64–67 of *Joshua Fry Speed: Lincoln's Most Intimate Friend*, by Robert L. Kincaid (Harrogate, TN: Department of Lincolniana, Lincoln Memorial University, 1943). (Yes, that's the book Wyatt gets for his book report later. . . . Hey, I'm an author, and I liked how it foreshadowed Wyatt's discovery!) The full quote is:

I am not a Know-Nothing. That is certain. How could I be? How can any one who abhors the oppression of negroes, be in favor of degrading classes of white people? Our progress in degeneracy appears to me to be pretty rapid. As a nation, we began by declaring that *"all men are created equal."* We now practically read it "all men are created equal, *except negroes."* When the Know-Nothings get control, it will read "all men are created equal, except negroes, *and foreigners, and Catholics."* When it comes to this I shall prefer emigrating to some country where they make no pretence of loving liberty—to Russia, for instance, where despotism can be taken pure, and without the base alloy of hypocrisy.

That same letter is also online at http://www.abrahamlincolnonline.org/lincoln/speeches/speed.htm and on page 323 of *Collected Works of Abraham Lincoln, Volume 2* (Springfield, IL: Abraham Lincoln Association, 1953), which is where I imagine Wyatt found it.

Lincoln's most famous use of **"all men are created equal"** may be from his 1863 Gettysburg Address, which opens with these words: **"Four score and seven years ago our fathers brought forth, upon this continent, a new nation, conceived in liberty, and dedicated to the proposition that 'all men are created equal.'"** You can see the actual handwritten speech at the National Archives website, here: http://www.ourdocuments.gov/doc.php?flash=true&doc=36#.

In that Gettysburg Address, Lincoln quotes, "All men are created equal" from the founding document of the United States of America, our Declaration of Independence. The second paragraph of the Declaration of Independence begins, "We hold these truths to be self-evident, that all men are created equal. . . ." You can read a transcript of the Declaration of Independence online here: http://www.archives.gov/exhibits/charters/declaration_transcript.html.

In Chapter 3, Wyatt tells the visiting students about the Civil War child soldier Edward Black. You can find out more in this "The Boys of War" opinion piece in the October 4, 2011, New York Times: http://opinionator.blogs.nytimes.com/2011/10/04/the-boys-of-war/?_php=true&_type=blogs&_r=0. There's additional info on (and a painting of) Edward Black, "who was 8 years old when he became a drummer for the 21st Indiana Volunteer Regiment," in this online slide show: http://www.nytimes.com/slideshow/2011/10/05/opinion/disunion-children/s/disunion-child-soldiers-slide-HM3H.html

In Chapter 4, the books I imagine Mr. Clifton gives our three main characters are: for Mackenzie, *Lincoln at Home: Two Glimpses of Abraham Lincoln's Family Life*, by David Herbert Donald (New York: Simon & Schuster, 1999); for Jonathon, *The Lincoln-Douglas Debates*, edited by Rodney O. Davis and Douglas L. Wilson, Knox College Lincoln Studies Center (Champaign, IL: University of Illinois Press, 2008); and for Wyatt, of course, *Joshua Fry Speed: Lincoln's Most Intimate Friend*.

In Chapter 5, Mackenzie discusses the séances held in the White House while Lincoln was President. The séances are discussed on pages 40–41 of *Lincoln at Home: Two Glimpses of Abraham Lincoln's Family Life*.

Wyatt reads the whole 70 pages of *Joshua Fry Speed: Lincoln's Most Intimate Friend*. The October 5, 1842, letter where Abe asks Joshua, **"Are you now in *feeling* as well as *judgment* glad that you are married as you are?"** is on pages 54–55, and is also found on pages 161–62 of *Abraham Lincoln: His Speeches And Writings*, edited by Roy P. Basler, preface by Carl Sandburg, Da Capo Press paperback edition (Cleveland, OH: Perseus Books Group, 2001). The excerpt explaining how Abe met Joshua, wanting to buy stuff for a bed from Joshua's store, is taken from pages 9–10 of *Joshua Fry Speed: Lincoln's Most Intimate Friend*. That same book includes the five letters Wyatt noticed Abe wrote Joshua that ended with the sign-offs **"Ever Yours," "As Ever," "Yours Forever," "As Ever, Your Friend,"** and **"Yours Forever"**— on pages 53, 52, 50, 49, and 48, respectively.

Wyatt also refers to their B and B's President Abraham Lincoln Timeline, and the timeline dates and quotes I used are from the Abraham Lincoln Chronology (Historical Documents Co., 1993). I purchased my copy at the Lincoln Memorial Shrine, Redlands, California, in April 2011. Their timeline was "reproduced on antiqued parchment that looks and feels old," which inspired Wyatt's antiquing chore.

Martin's video song about Friedrich Wilhelm von Steuben, the Gay man who helped the United States win the Revolutionary War and who "single-handedly turned a militia, consisting mostly of farmers, into a well-trained, disciplined and professional army that was able to stand musket-to-musket combat with the British," is also based on real history. You can read more about von Steuben, his being Gay, and his role in US history here: http://www.huffingtonpost.com/nicholas-ferroni/american-military-history_b_1606530.html.

In Chapter 7, on his blog, Jonathon quotes Lincoln's joke about how "calling a tail a leg doesn't make it so." Abe did say this, but it wasn't included in the Lincoln-Douglas Debates book I imagined Jonathon had for his book report (not on page 4 or elsewhere). I actually found this Lincoln quote on page 194 of *The Wit and Wisdom of*

Abraham Lincoln: A Treasury of Quotations, Anecdotes, and Observations, edited by James C. Humes (Bexley, OH: Gramercy Books, 1996).

In Chapter 9, Jonathon quotes Lincoln again for his blog: **"With public sentiment, nothing can fail. Without it, nothing can succeed."** This *is* from the Lincoln-Douglas Debates and was said by Lincoln at his first debate with Judge Douglas, in Ottawa, Illinois, on August 21, 1858. A transcript of that debate is online at the National Park Service's website, at http://www.nps.gov/liho/historyculture/debate1. htm, and the quote is also found on page 32 of *The Lincoln-Douglas Debates.*

In Chapter 11, Mr. Clifton sends Wyatt the letter stating that the *Joshua Fry Speed: Lincoln's Most Intimate Friend* book is very rare. While the estimated value is my invention, it is true that the book is quite rare. As it says on the page facing page 70:

> "Two hundred fifty copies of this book have been printed by the Standard Printing Company, Inc., Louisville, Kentucky. . . . Bound and completed during the month of August, 1943. Only two hundred twenty-five copies for sale."

The copy I found and read numerous times throughout the writing of this book was from the Los Angeles Public Library's collection in Los Angeles, California.

In Chapter 12, Wyatt annotates the letter Abe sent Joshua on February 13, 1842. It is indeed found on pages 47–48 of *Joshua Fry Speed: Lincoln's Most Intimate Friend.* Contrasting the **"Yours forever"** sign-off to Joshua, Wyatt references a letter Lincoln wrote his wife, Mary, where the sign-off was **"Affectionately."** That June 12, 1848, letter to Mary is on pages 21–22 of *The Words of Abraham Lincoln,* selected and with an introduction by Larry Shapiro (New York: Newmarket Press, 2009). That same letter to Mary is also found on pages 70–71 of *Lincoln at Home: Two Glimpses of Abraham Lincoln's Family Life. Lincoln at Home* also includes four additional letters from Abe to Mary that are all signed in the same way, found on pages 69, 71–73, 74–76, and 88–89. One letter, on pages 61–65, is signed, **"Most Affectionately."** There are also thirty letters Abe wrote to Mary in that same book with no sign-off, just the **"A. Lincoln"** signature, and you can find them on pages 83–112.

In Chapter 15, just as my fictional character Mr. Guzman reveals to Wyatt, that exact February 13, 1842, letter from Abe to Joshua (the one Wyatt annotates on his blog) is found in numerous other historical sources, including pages 79–80 of *A. Lincoln, Speeches and Writings: 1832–1858,* compilation and notes by Don E. Fehrenbacher (New York: Literary Classics of the United States, Inc., 1989) and pages 56–57 of *Abraham Lincoln, Complete Works: Comprising his Speeches, Letters, State Papers, and Miscellaneous Writings, Volume One,* edited by John G. Nicolay and John Hay (New York: The Century Company, 1894). The letter is excerpted on page 175 of *Herndon's Life of Lincoln: The History and Personal Recollections of Abraham Lincoln,* as originally written by William H. Herndon and Jesse W. Weik (New York: Albert & Charles Boni, 1930). The old slang definition of lavender is from page 607 of *The*

Routledge Dictionary of Modern American Slang, edited by Tom Dalzell (New York: Routledge, 2008). And the quote about Abe and Joshua having "streaks of lavender, spots soft as May violets" is from page 266 of *Abraham Lincoln: The Prairie Years, Volume I,* by Carl Sandburg (New York: Charles Scribner's Sons, 1945).

IN CHAPTER 16, Wyatt comes across the poem Abe wrote in his twenties about two guys marrying each other. As cited, it is from page 48 of *Herndon's Life of Lincoln.*

IN CHAPTER 19, Rhonda reads and Martin finishes the Martin Luther King Jr. quote from his famous "I Have a Dream" speech. You can read the entire speech transcript and listen to the audio here: http://www.americanrhetoric.com/speeches/mlkihaveadream.htm. The speech video, which Wyatt and Martin watch in Chapter 21, is available from www.thekingcenter.org.

IN CHAPTER 20, Wyatt gives Martin a tour of their B and B's exhibits. The DVD they watch, *The Civil War in Four Minutes,* really exists, and the Civil War casualty numbers I used are from that. The video is available from the Abraham Lincoln Presidential Library and Museum here: http://www.lincolnlibraryandmuseum.com/m5.htm.

IN CHAPTER 22, Wyatt quotes Lincoln as saying, **"Whenever I hear anyone arguing over slavery, I feel a strong impulse to see it tried on him personally."** That's from Lincoln's speech to the 14th Indiana regiment on March 17, 1865. You can find it cited at the National Park Service's "Lincoln Boyhood: Thoughts on Slavery" web page here: http://www.nps.gov/libo/historyculture/thoughts-on-slavery.htm. In their dinnertime discussion, Martin tells Wyatt that Lincoln had a plan to deport Black people from the United States, and that's true as well.

"The colonization of freed slaves, to either Africa or the tropics of Central America and the Caribbean, featured prominently in Abraham Lincoln's formative beliefs on race and slavery. Enabled by a $600,000 appropriation from Congress, Lincoln aggressively pursued the policy in the early part of his presidency."

That's from page 1 of *Colonization After Emancipation: Lincoln and the Movement for Black Resettlement,* by Phillip W. Magness and Sebastian N. Page (Columbia, MO: University of Missouri Press, 2011), where you can read more about it. As far as the seeming contradiction of Lincoln saying, on the one hand, that Black and White people are not equal, and on the other hand that Black people have the right to equality, here are his own words—spoken on more than one occasion (this is from his Quincy debate with Judge Douglas on October 13, 1858, as found both online, at http://www.nps.gov/liho/historyculture/debate6.htm, and on page 217 of *The Lincoln-Douglas Debates*):

Now gentlemen, I don't want to read at any greater length, but this is the true complexion of all I have ever said in regard to the institution of slavery and the black race. This is the whole of it, and anything that argues me into his idea of

perfect social and political equality with the negro, is but a specious and fantastic arrangement of words, by which a man can prove a horse chestnut to be a chestnut horse. I will say here, while upon this subject, that I have no purpose directly or indirectly to interfere with the institution of slavery in the states where it exists. I believe I have no lawful right to do so, and I have no inclination to do so. I have no purpose to introduce political and social equality between the white and the black races. There is a physical difference between the two, which in my judgment will probably forever forbid their living together upon the footing of perfect equality, and inasmuch as it becomes a necessity that there must be a difference, I, as well as Judge Douglas, am in favor of the race to which I belong, having the superior position. [*Cheers.*] I have never said anything to the contrary, but I hold that notwithstanding all this, there is no reason in the world why the negro is not entitled to all the natural rights enumerated in the Declaration of Independence, the right to life, liberty and the pursuit of happiness. I hold that he is as much entitled to these as the white man. I agree with Judge Douglas he is not my equal in many respects—certainly not in color, perhaps not in moral or intellectual endowment. But in the right to eat the bread, without leave of anybody else, which his own hand earns, *he is my equal and the equal of Judge Douglas, and the equal of every living man.*" [*Cheers.*]

Rhonda references how Frederick Douglass spoke kindly of the way Abraham Lincoln treated him, and you can read, starting on page 350, about the meeting between these two men in Douglass's autobiography, *The Life and Times of Frederick Douglass in His Own Words: A Complete History of an American Freedom Fighter* (New York: Citadel Press, 2002). The song Martin sings the chorus of after he and Wyatt watch the Martin Luther King Jr. "I Have a Dream" speech is "Man in the Mirror," by Glen Ballard and Siedah Garrett.

In Chapter 25, Wyatt considers how Abe and Mary had separate bedrooms in their home, in contrast with Abe and Joshua sharing Joshua's bed for four years. You can see the online photos of the Lincoln Home National Historic Site in Springfield, Illinois (showing Abe and Mary's different bedrooms), here: http://www.nps.gov/museum/exhibits/liho/houseTour.html.

In Chapter 30, Wyatt discovers that his soldier was actually a Confederate. The photo that inspired this element of my story was indeed from *Photographic History of the Civil War: Fort Sumter to Gettysburg,* edited by William C. David and Bell I. Wiley (New York: Black Dog & Leventhal Publishers, 1994). The photo and caption are on page 47, as cited, and a version of the photo including Wyatt's soldier is on the cover. You can see a reproduction of the photo just before this Endnotes section.

In Chapter 31, Wyatt's blog post includes the paragraph from Abe's February 25, 1842, letter to Joshua where Abe speaks of their dreams of Elysium. That's from pages 48–49 of *Joshua Fry Speed: Lincoln's Most Intimate Friend*. The same letter is also online at http://www.classicreader.com/book/3237/45/, and on pages 143–44 of *Abraham Lincoln: His Speeches and Writings,* and the Elysium section of the letter is included on page 176 of *Herdon's Life of Lincoln.*

In the epilogue, the "Two Brothers" Civil War song that Martin wrote new lyrics for is credited to Irving Gordon. A version with the original lyrics is included in Smithsonian Folkways' *Songs of the Civil War* album here: http://www.folkways.si.edu/songs-of-the-civil-war/american-folk-historical-song/music/album/smithsonian.

You can find out lots more at my website, *I'm Here. I'm Queer. What The Hell Do I Read?*, at www.leewind.org, and at your local public library.

LEE WIND is the founding blogger and publisher of *I'm Here. I'm Queer. What The Hell Do I Read?*, an award-winning website about books, culture, and empowerment for Lesbian, Gay, Bi, Trans, Questioning, and Queer youth, and their Allies. For over 10 years, readers from 100-plus countries have racked up 2.5 million page views—and counting!

In his "Clark Kent" jobs, Lee is the director of marketing and programming at the Independent Book Publishers Association and the official blogger for the Society of Children's Book Writers and Illustrators. His Superhero job is writing, inspired by our world's amazing—and untold—LGBTQ history.

Lee lives in Los Angeles with his husband and their teenage daughter. *Queer as a Five-Dollar Bill* is his debut novel. Visit him online at www.leewind.org

BOOK CLUB DISCUSSION QUESTIONS

1. Do the challenges Wyatt faces in the story seem realistic?

2. How do you feel about Mackenzie?

3. Can you forgive Wyatt for using Mackenzie as his cover?

4. Did Jonathon redeem himself?

5. What if there were out and proud role models in Lincolnville when the story started? Would other LGBTQ students or adults have changed anything for Wyatt?

6. If you were a student (or teacher) at Lincolnville High School, how could you have been a better ally to everyone facing discrimination?

7. What do you think happens after the story ends? With Wyatt and Martin? With Mackenzie and Jonathon? With Von Lawson? With public opinion?

8. Do you think Abraham Lincoln and Joshua Fry Speed were in love?

9. If Lincoln and Speed were in love, could that secret from history really change the world?

10. The author and publisher chose to capitalize "Gay" in all its uses. The idea was to honor LGBTQ people and show them the same respect shown to Asian Americans, African Americans, Christians, Jews, etc. What's your take on this?

11. If you were making a movie of *Queer as a Five-Dollar Bill,* whom would you cast?

12. If you were able to talk to Wyatt at any point in the story, when would you do so, and what would you say to him?